JONETTA'S DEATH
PART 2 OF THE MILLER FAMILY DRAMA

JONETTA'S DEATH

PART 2 OF THE MILLER FAMILY DRAMA

A NOVEL BY
REBEKAH S. COLE

Graphic Design by Mario Patterson

Sequel to: Women's Voices

Published and Printed in the United States of America.

First Edition
ISBN-13: 978-0692677148
ISBN-10: 0692677143

CreateSpace Independent Publishing Platform
North Charleston, SC

The publisher is not responsible for websites (or their content) that are not owned by the publisher.

DEDICATION

To those who understand that you can pick your nose, but not your family...

TABLE OF CONTENTS

JONETTA'S DEATH

PROLOGUE

Soul Ties

JOHNSTOWN, PENNSYLVANIA
SEPTEMBER 1968

Her mother insisted that she just come work for the Hamilton family alongside her in the kitchen. Jonetta scoffed at that suggestion. She just needed some new clothes for crying out loud. The last thing she was going to do was become a maid for white people. She respected her mother, but her mother's life was not the one she wanted for herself. Jonetta wanted more out of life, and it involved a rich man and definitely a new town. Besides she liked having soft hands, thanks to her homemade remedy of lard and mint leaves that she "found" in the neighbor's yard and lavender oil that she had stolen from Georgia. She liked being feminine and carefree, and wearing an old maid's uniform was simply not in the cards for her.

"We need the extra help in the kitchen now that Bessie's daughter don' married herself a teacher," her mother reasoned. Jonetta had a plan. In her fine clothes she would go into town to the department stores to "shop" around. Sunday was the best day to go because she knew fine gentleman would be out with their families looking their best. She could care less if they were available men or not. Jonetta knew she could have her way because of her good looks. If these men wanted to look at her then they would have to pay for her time and company.

Although her mother was away most of the time she was no fool. She knew that Jonetta had something up her sleeve because most stores were not hiring anyone on a Sunday. But she was willing to turn a blind eye for her favorite daughter.

Sunday was her mother's only day off from work. When she came home it was to a bunch of strife and headache with all the children running around. Most of the time, she played referee between the three youngest siblings. Georgia was still around trying to help their mother, but she was growing tired and bitter. She had dreams of her own of traveling east to the Big Apple near the ocean. She wanted to be on the bay catching crab and lobster right out of her own backyard. She read about people living like this in a magazine at the library she cleaned at night. Georgia was twenty years old, and in those days, she was getting old, too old not to be married and bearing children of her own. She was fairly attractive, "but nothing like Jonetta", she heard all the time.

Her suitors would always somehow inquire about her younger sister, Jonetta, which made Georgia hate her even more. "These men are small minded anyway. I'm gonna head east to a big city! I'll find me a good, hardworking man there. I just know it!" Georgia hid the money she earned in her bra with a safety pin. If Jonetta would steal her clothes, she knew that she was capable of stealing her money too. She had been working since she was fourteen and managed to save almost two-hundred dollars over the years. There was no way that she would allow all of her hard earned money to be stolen from her. Georgia also never offered her mother a dime.

"These ain't my children. I've got to save for my own!" Georgia confided in Jonetta once and Jonetta could only agree with her sister. They often resented their mother for having so many children. Next in line was Jonetta to look after the younger ones, but she always had her head in the clouds and could not be trusted to be responsible. She would sneak to watch the picture show that gave her big ideas about life. Jonetta had become a little actress in her own right over the years. She knew how to make the tears flow and flail her body about in order to get her way. Her mother saw straight through her, but in order to keep some peace, she let Jonetta get away with that behavior.

Jonetta was allowed to borrow Georgia's finest dress and fancy shoes. The moment Georgia brought the peach frock home Jonetta fell in love with it. "It's only a matter of time before I wear it." Jonetta snickered to herself. The time came for her "job search" this Sunday afternoon, but as expected Georgia put up a huge protest.

"You ain't foolin' nobody, girl! You tryna catch yourself a man in that dress. That's my favorite party dress!" Georgia whined and looked to her mother pleading for her to open her eyes to what Jonetta was up to this time.

"You're just jealous, Georgia," Jonetta sneered. "I look much better in it than you do. Besides, when is the last time you've been to a party?"

"Netta! Mind your mouth 'fore I make you take it off," her mother said finally.

"Mama, make her take it off!" Georgia fumed. Jonetta did look stunning in the dress and Georgia seethed. If her younger sister snagged a man before she did then she would be labeled as a spinster. Georgia would rather rip the dress off of Jonetta right then and there than have her find a man before she did!

"I'm gonna let her go in the city, Georgia. She need to find work to help out 'round here. I know you'll be leaving soon." Their mother placed a hand on Georgia's shoulder to calm her.

Georgia quickly glanced at the floor. She suddenly felt guilty that her mother knew her desires to leave that raggedy shack and poor town.

"It's time you leave anyway. You gettin' older. It's time to find you a man. You waited long enough and I 'preciate it."

Now that Georgia's inner most desires were out in the open, thanks to her mother, she felt better about her departure that she planned to make in a few months. "Fine! Jonetta can wear the dress, but I'll be moving on to bigger and better things. She can have these poor men around here. You're only going to find a life of trouble and poverty if you stay here, Netta!"

Jonetta smiled to herself as she walked the long road to the city. After a while though, she cursed those fine, lace-up shoes. Her feet ached something awful. The women in the picture shows make it look so easy walking in those shoes and now she was finding out different. She was about to curse God when she heard a car horn blow. Startled, she stepped aside to let the car pass, but it slowed alongside her. Jonetta kept her eyes straight forward and walking when she heard someone call out her name.

"How do, Netta!" It was Paul King. Jonetta had not seen him in almost two years now since… Jonetta rolled her eyes, sucked her teeth and slowed her stroll. Her feet were hurting, and maybe he could give her a ride to the city. She decided to be nice and hoped he still wasn't mad at her for the incident a few summers ago.

"Why, Paul King! Been quite a long time since I seen you," she acknowledged. "How are you this fine day?"

"Better now that I seen you out here! You looking miiighty fine, Netta," he cooed licking his lips. "Where you headed?"

"To the city," she smiled a big smile showing all of her perfectly even teeth. "Wanna give me a ride, Paul?"

"I sure do," he grinned. But he had another ride in mind. He opened the door for her. "I'm headed that way. Slide on in, get comfy."

Time had a way of healing old wounds. Jonetta was grateful that her feet were resting now, but she dreaded the small talk that she had to engage in for the duration of the ride. Paul was bragging about his new job in the coal mine and how good the money was. He was even thinking of buying some land to build a house on for his future family. Jonetta was not impressed, and he knew it. But since their last encounter he had learned a little more about women and how to handle them in a special way.

They drove through a beautiful pasture along the way. The plush greenery scattered with purple prairie clovers had Jonetta daydreaming about running through those beautiful fields with her bare feet and her hair blowing with the wind. The Mama's and the Papa's came blaring through the radio speaker, disrupting her thoughts. Jonetta smiled at the irony of the lyrics, but hummed anyway as "California Dreamin'" played. Paul's laughter broke her fluid melody.

"What's so funny?"

"You," he grinned shaking his head.

"How's that?" Jonetta demanded, wrinkling her brows.

"You always in your own world, Netta." Paul chuckled and shook his head. "Didn't you hear a word I said?"

"Yes," Jonetta sighed. "I heard all about the coal mine and building a house…"

"No, not that. I asked you if you wanted to take a trip down memory lane." He thought better of it. "Never mind." This time he would make the decision about making love to her. He drove off the path and cut through the grass.

"Paul King! Where are you going?" Jonetta demanded. "You're probably on private property. That's all we need is the white folks calling the sheriff! I have to get to the city." Jonetta was beside herself. Paul King was ruining her plans of snagging a rich man! On such a beautiful Sunday, she knew the finest men would be strolling about the town. She was fuming.

"Netta," Paul said softly, for he knew first hand of her fury. "Can I show you something? It will only take a minute. I promise."

"Fine!" Jonetta folded her arms across her chest and sat back in her seat. Paul pulled close to the riverbank and parked the car. He got out the car and went around letting Jonetta out. She sighed impatiently, but got out anyway.

"What is this all about?" She demanded.

He grabbed her hand and led her down to the water. "This is where I would like to build a house."

"You drove over here to show me that?" Jonetta scoffed. "Can we leave now?" She turned to walk back to the car but he grabbed her wrist and pulled her close to him.

"Alright," Paul said chuckling a bit. "It may seem a little silly to you, but it's a special place to me." He held her so tight around the waist that he could smell of freshly pressed hair and see where the pomade was lathered in her scalp. "Jonetta Mae Henderson, let me love on you, girl. Let me show you what I've learned since… since the last time…"

"Let me go you fool!" she tried to wrestle away, but he held onto her tighter. "You're hurting me!"

Paul laughed at her feisty behavior, it actually excited him. "I'll let you go when I'm done." He smashed his lips against hers and tried to stick his tongue in her mouth.

She leaned back and slapped him hard. "Get your filthy hands off of me!"

"Dammit! That hurt, Netta." Paul hugged her tighter and wicked grin came across his face.

"Good!"

"When I saw you walking in this beautiful, peach colored dress, I just had to have you. The very sight of you does something to me deep on the inside, girl." He took her hand and forced her to feel his hardened manhood.

"Feel that? It's all yours."

"I don't want it! I don't want nothing you got! I hate you, Paul King!"

"No, you don't. You know you never forget your first time with your first love," he whispered in her ear. "Who you think you foolin'?"

"Forget?" she scoffed. "There was nothing to remember!"

Just then, his eyes narrowed with fury. "You're not gonna make a fool out of me twice!" Paul shouted pointing his finger in her face.

Jonetta became frightened because he was not the same shy Paul King that she had known some years ago. That last bout of rejection made his temper flare. He balled up his fist and struck her against the side of her head. Jonetta wailed as she lost her balance, holding her face. This time Paul slapped her before she could even gather her composure from the first blow. Jonetta stumbled and fell flat on her back. Paul mounted her before she could scramble to her feet while he pushed her shoulders back toward the ground.

"I'm gonna show you once and for all what I got to offer, you little bitch!" Paul sneered.

Jonetta screamed, pleading for him to stop, pushing his shoulders away from her as hard as she could, but he was putting his full weight on her. Paul laughed at her and it infuriated Jonetta. She began scratching at his eyes and neck. Paul winced when she got a deep swipe in at his neck. He caught her flailing hands, placing them above her head. Jonetta screamed a blood-curdling scream, straining her throat. Paul glanced around to see if anybody was approaching, but nobody heard her cries deep in the woods. He grinned watching her squirm. Kicking her legs wildly only made it easier for Paul to lift her dress. It was ruined indeed.

"Get off of me Paul King!" Jonetta screamed. Her face was on fire where he struck her and she could taste blood in her mouth.

Paul grunted, continued to hold her wrists together, and stared into her eyes. He was sweating and out of breath from wrestling her. Jonetta looked up to the heavens with tear-filled eyes as the clouds began to roll and darken.

"Calm down, Netta. Why you acting so scared?"

Jonetta cried, "Just let me go!"

Paul loosened his grip from her wrists and lifted his weight just enough for her squirm from underneath him. Realizing that Paul was going to set her free she shoved him with full force.

"I hate you!" Jonetta yelled as she rushed to her feet. Her beautifully planned Sunday was being ruined by the very man who ruined her very first time at love-making. Just when Jonetta thought she was free, Paul caught her right ankle and she fell onto her face in the dirt, hitting her nose. She gasped inhaling a cloud of dirt and immediately began choking. She felt his arm across her back, his hot breath on her cheek made her clench her eyes shut. His other hand fumbled to get underneath her dress as his elbow dug deeper in her back, which caused her to arch her back and moan in pain.

"You like it like this, don't you?" Paul growled, misunderstanding her painful moan. His breath quickened like a dog in heat, he was excited.

Her coughs mixed with cries made it difficult for Jonetta to even speak.

"I knew you were the type that liked it rough!" Paul chuckled as his breath quickened. He was finally successful getting himself positioned. Once she felt Paul King tear inside of her flesh, the fight inside of her ceased. Her eyes were wide, mouth gaped open void of sound, body limp and soul escaping into thin air. Paul King had won.

It began raining when Paul was finally finished. Jonetta lied stiff in the grass, leaves stuck to her face while Paul rushed back to his car to roll up the windows. He was about to tell her to come in the car, until he remembered how she robbed him of his happiness a few summers ago, with broken ribs after insulting his manhood. He started the engine and drove away.

Jonetta walked home in pain, thighs wet and sticky from Paul's venom, spirit crushed and soulless. She finally arrived home after dark to see her mother, who was supposed to be back at the Hamilton's at this time, waiting for her on the porch with a switch.

"Where the hell you been, Jonetta Mae?"

Jonetta slowly approached the front steps and stopped with her head bowed. Her mother gasped at her appearance. The beautiful peach frock dress that Georgia was forced to let her wear was drenched, muddy like she had been rolling around in the mud on purpose. She carried the shoes in her hands and clutched them close to her chest. Her stockings soiled, toes poking through as if they needed to escape what just transpired.

Her mother flew off the porch, switch in hand, yelling. "You little heifer! You been out with some boy messing yourself up, haven't you? And you ruined Georgia's dress! I'm gonna kill you!" The hits across her arms and legs stung but she did not flinch. There was no point in trying to explain what had just occurred. The worst had already been done. Jonetta felt like dying somewhere, anywhere.

CHAPTER 1

Fresh Start

PRESENT DAY
CHICAGO, IL

It was a familiar fragrance. As it lingered in the room, tickling her nose, she remembered it well. The delicious lunch she had just eaten at Hidden Mannah Café was trying to work its way up the same way it went down. Clutching the strap of her purse tighter as if it would somehow provide relief from the bittersweet memories, she cleared her throat and shut her eyes. Tiny beads of sweat began forming on her forehead and down her spine. Jonetta repositioned herself in the hard, black chair as she felt her blouse cling to her skin. Frantically, she searched through her purse for a peppermint, cough drop, or anything to combat the nausea causing turmoil inside of her stomach. She let out a sigh of relief the moment she found a piece of butterscotch hard candy. It would have to do. She opened the cellophane yellow wrapper, popped the candy into her mouth and exhaled.

Jonetta shook her head in amazement that a smell could trigger such a reaction from her especially at such a late stage in life. But there she was, officially a senior citizen as of two months ago, waiting for a job interview when a flood of memories entered her mind due to a fragrance. A man's cologne, but not just any cologne, it was Mr. Lucky's brand. *These days only an elderly man could be still wearing that cologne*, she reasoned. Mr. Lucky used to dowse himself in it. Everyone knew when he was in the room or had just left. It was his staple among other things, like being a pimp.

The fragrance was torturing her nose. She glanced around the waiting area to identify the culprit, but there wasn't a man in sight. Whoever was responsible was still in the vicinity that was for certain. Jonetta hoped the hiring manager wasn't the one responsible for the reaction she was experiencing. This appointment just might have to wait until another time or not at all if she couldn't get herself under control. She glanced down at her hands and quickly clenched them. The wrinkles and loose skin was a reminder of just how much she had aged. Now she really felt like a fool for coming to a job interview for a receptionist role at retirement age. Truth be told, Jonetta didn't need a job that damn bad. It was just an idea to feel useful again and for a little freedom. Becoming a babysitter in her old age was never part of her plans. Although she loved her grandchildren, it was becoming a cramped lifestyle. The last thing Jonetta was going to tolerate was being smothered; she needed her space and peace.

Norman had been in his feelings ever since he learned of her experience as a prostitute in *that* house. He extended Jonetta an invitation to move into his home for a fresh start. The thought of moving in with Norman made her uneasy, but it was the only way she could be at peace and free from haunted memories of being in *that* house. Living in the suburbs wasn't as bad as Jonetta thought initially. It surely prevented her daughters from popping up unannounced now due to the distance from the city. It was perfect actually. Besides, Colette needed to learn how to swim to shore with her babies on her back even if she had to sink a couple of times. All women have to do it at some point in their lives, and Colette was not the exception. She sometimes wished that Colette would reconcile her marriage with Owen just for the sake of peace and quiet around the house. But Jonetta would never admit that.

The other reason Jonetta was waiting to be interviewed was to get away from Norman's watchful eye and needy behavior. Since they were both retirees, scheduled or planned activities didn't exist in their new world together. Each day was lived on a whim, certainly not how Jonetta was accustomed to living because the demands of her grandchildren and their daily routines used to fill most of her time. There was a time when Jonetta loved living with Norman before the children were born. Once upon a time, Norman was her ticket to freedom. Now Jonetta had to occupy her time with something more meaningful than occupying space in silence with Norman. It was awkward. Their whole living situation was awkward. Jonetta, of course, had a separate bedroom because according to her, "This wasn't *that*!" She made that perfectly clear to Norman and her daughters. It seemed like a refreshing idea at the time, especially, since Colette and her children moved in as well as Dawn who permanently moved back home from New York.

Although the house was spacious enough, with all of them living under one roof peace of mind was hard to come by. Jonetta needed her peace of mind and took Norman up on his offer with outlined conditions. It was a living arrangement. That was it. That was all. Jonetta made it clear that no extra love or special attention was to be given or shown. Norman agreed, but remained hopeful that Jonetta would come around to being open to loving him again.

Since Fred passed away Georgia no longer wanted the responsibility of operating their clothing store so she sold it for a hefty sum and was just fine sitting at home knitting her life away. Georgia barely uttered a word or left the house, she just knitted all sorts of things that nobody wanted or would dare to wear outside the house. Jonetta chalked it up to being grief stricken and left her sister alone with her thoughts. Jonetta had never before seen someone die. Dead bodies at funerals in a casket, yes. But to actually witness the soul leave from its body right before her eyes, absolutely not. Jonetta shuddered at the memory of Fred taking his final breath. Georgia had just left the room to refill the Styrofoam cup with ice chips. She heard his staggered breathing, almost sounding like he wanted to say something. She inched towards his bed, bent over to place her ear right at his left cheek to listen closely. Fred mumbled almost choking on his last words. Jonetta was about to look for a nurse but when she heard Fred gasp sharply she froze. In those three short minutes that Georgia was gone, Fred decided to leave this Earth. Mr. Lucky's death was different - under special circumstances - that Jonetta didn't want to think about, but this fragrance in the air was a vivid reminder.

"Mrs. Miller," the young receptionist said. "Doctor Franklyn will see you now."

Jonetta opened her mouth to respond, but nothing came out. She flashed a smile and headed towards the doctor's office. As she got closer to the door it was no doubt that she had found the culprit wearing Mr. Lucky's cologne. She was surprised that such a young man would choose such an outdated brand of cologne.

"Come on in, Mrs. Miller and take a seat," he said, extending his hand while flashing a smile with perfect teeth, of course. "I'm Doctor Bishon Franklyn."

Odd choice of cologne, odd name, just an odd person altogether, Jonetta thought. But she cleared her throat, shook his hand and replied, "Thank you. I'm Jonetta Miller."

"Nice to finally meet you, I've heard nothing but good things about you."

Jonetta knew it could only be one person blabbing about her, Norman. His former coworker, Stanton, had a son who opened two dental offices and desperately needed assistance at the front desk for his growing business. Norman knew that Jonetta was itching to get out of the house so he referred her. Only time would tell if they all would live to regret it, but he wanted to make her happy.

"You have a unique name." Jonetta flashed a smile.

"Yes, you haven't heard the story?"

"No, only that you were a successful dentist."

"Well, my mother had always wanted a Bichon Frise," he explained. "You know the little white, fluffy dog?"

Jonetta nodded raising her eyebrows.

"Well, she could never afford a pure bred, but when she found…" Bishon cleared his throat and his composure stiffened. "She said that as a baby, I had a head full of wooly hair that reminded her of the dog's hair. So… she named me Bishon. But everybody calls me Shon."

Jonetta gave him a once over, he was young, had to be early forties and still had a head full of wooly hair that was a tad salt and pepper. Dr. Franklyn wasn't a very tall man, but he was handsome with a nice build. His eyes a lighter brown than most slanted down at the corners, giving the impression that he was sad. On the contrary, his mouth curled up at the corners like the Jack Nicholson Joker in "Batman". His features reminded her of someone she knew, but she couldn't recall at the moment. His hazelnut skin was smooth and laced with Vaseline. She chuckled to herself. *Someone raised him right.*

"So, your mother wanted a dog, had you instead, and named

4

you after a dog?"

Bishon shrugged and smirked. "Something like that."

"Well, I don't care too much for nicknames. I've always hated them," Jonetta replied, recalling how Mr. Lucky always called her "Johnnie".

"Understood, Mrs. Miller. Around here everyone calls me Doctor Franklyn, so no worries on the nickname, unless we become friends outside of these four walls."

Jonetta laughed, knowing full well they never would see each other outside of the office let alone become friends.

"I look forward to having you on my team," he said, standing to his feet and extending his hand.

Jonetta stood to shake his hand and replied, "That's it? I have the job?"

"Of course! Usually, I have the office manager interview new staff, but I wanted to meet you myself due to our connection."

"Well, things certainly have changed since I was last employed," Jonetta remarked.

Dr. Franklyn smiled warmly, walked from behind his desk and escorted Jonetta to the door. "I hate to cut our meeting short, but I do have patients to see. Can you begin on Monday?"

"Absolutely," Jonetta replied with confidence. She was actually anxious to begin leaving the house regularly. "May I ask what the name of the cologne is you're wearing?"

"Yes, it's Brut by Faberge."

Jonetta nodded in confirmation, not approval.

Back at home, she sat on the patio feeling accomplished. Jonetta firmly believed that an idle mind was the devil's workshop. She needed to get away from Norman and busy herself on a daily basis before Norman's presence began to rub her the *right* way. She didn't trust her own judgment on men since Mr. Lucky. Marrying Norman was her way of escaping a life she wanted erase from the fibers of her soul. How could she have fallen in love with a pimp? She asked herself that question so many times. Now that her family knew of her past, she wondered just how much should be revealed. At first, she wanted to divulge all of her experiences from being raped, to the lonely train ride to Chicago, to living in such a grand house compared to the shack where she grew up, to being forced into in-house prostitution by her mother's aunts, to finally using her brain to escape it all. She hoped that her daughters would see that their circumstances were frivolous, yet fixable compared to the horrors she had to experience. But…continuously keeping secrets to herself suited Jonetta just fine.

Norman had been more patient and understanding with her, but his affections were not welcomed. Jonetta just needed to get away from that house and she needed to get away from him. It was official; she had a job now as a receptionist at a dentist office, where she would be reminded of Mr. Lucky on a daily basis if Dr. Franklyn continued to wear that cologne. Jonetta seemed to have jumped out of the pot into the flames on this one. She chuckled and shook her head as she recalled how Mr. Lucky sprayed that cologne everywhere on his muscular body, inside of his fedoras, the arm pits of his stiffly pressed shirts and even the satin sheets. The image of the burgundy, satin sheets on his king sized bed where Jonetta succumbed to his incantation for the first time flashed across her thoughts.

CHICAGO, IL
1971

Jonetta rolled around in the sheets gliding her hands up and down the fabric. With her eyes closed Jonetta inhaled sharply as she had never felt nor seen anything in a bedroom so beautiful. When her eyes opened, she saw herself on the ceiling. The mirror on the ceiling was for the pleasure of his guests and his excitement when they discovered it. His eyes gleaned when he saw the expression of astonishment grow across her face. Jonetta was young and fascinated, perfect for grooming.

"These feel so good!" she squealed.

"They feel even better without clothes on," Mr. Lucky replied, grinning and biting his bottom lip. Jonetta understood exactly what he meant. She stood to undress herself while he took pleasure in watching. He motioned for her to do the same to him. After Jonetta took his clothes off Mr. Lucky loosened her hair clip, allowing her hair to fall on her shoulders. He gently pushed her onto the satin sheets and flexed all of his muscles so she could see exactly what she was getting herself into.

Jonetta was nervous. He was not like the other low class men that came to visit her at her aunt's house. Mr. Lucky was an educated businessman, wealthy and had style. His sex appeal was on another level with clothes on and now without clothes on Jonetta's appetite for him grew from hungry to starvation. Her heart pounded with anticipation. Jonetta wanted to impress him and hoped she wouldn't be a disappointment. As Mr. Lucky climbed on top of her and gently caressed every inch of her body with his large hands her body immediately relaxed. Tenderly, he kissed her stomach, nipples and nape of her neck and she giggled, covering her mouth. Finally, he kissed her lips with so much passion that Jonetta was sure this was love. He spread her legs and gently eased himself inside of her moist paradise. Mr. Lucky moaned and took his time as he eased himself in and out her. His rhythm was consistent until he lifted her legs near her ears and began thrusting faster. Jonetta finally experienced her first climax and the addiction was born. Afterwards, he held her close to his chest. She dozed off to sleep listening to the rhythm of his heartbeat go from rapid to regular.

"Don't forget we have guests coming." Mr. Lucky was fully dressed again as he gently woke Jonetta.

Jonetta slightly opened her eyes and nodded then closed her eyes again.

"Johnnie, we have to get ready," he announced with authority.

"Johnnie?" She frowned at the sound of that name.

"Yeah, I've decided that's gonna be my nickname for you."

"But that's a boy's name!" Jonetta protested. She propped herself up on one elbow.

"Now it's your name, Johnnie."

"Well, I don't like that nickname."

"It's *my* name for you," Mr. Lucky insisted getting louder, stepping closer to her. "When I say 'Johnnie', you'll answer."

"So what do I call you now?"

He laughed heartily and replied frankly, "Mr. Lucky."

Like she told Dr. Franklyn, she hated nicknames. The love-hate relationship she had with Mr. Lucky often led Jonetta to wonder how she could have been so easily manipulated. The woman she was today would have dominated and won that conversation. She searched her purse for a lighter, opened a fresh pack and lit a cigarette. A car door slammed with the alarm chirp to follow let her know that Norman was home. She heard him call for her, but didn't respond. He would figure out that she was outside on the patio eventually.

"Netta!" Norman called. A nickname that she learned to live with since her whole family called her by that name.

Jonetta turned to stare at him, blowing a cloud of smoke in his direction.

"There you are!" he rushed to kiss her forehead. "How did it go?"

"I got the job," Jonetta replied casually.

"Good! I'll let Stanton know," Norman replied. "Shon is a good cat. He'll treat you right, Netta."

"I'm sure Doctor Bishon Franklyn told his parents by now. What's his mother's name again?"

"Barbara," Norman replied. He studied Jonetta's face for a moment. She was still beautiful in spite of her distant behavior and he loved having her in his presence on a daily basis.

"He told me why she gave him that name." Jonetta raised her perfectly arched eyebrows and pulled another drag from her cigarette.

Norman laughed because he heard the story from Stanton about their son's name. "Yeah, well we all have our reasons for naming our children. Just like you did with our girls, insisting that none of their names could be formed into some sort of nickname."

"True and it worked," Jonetta replied, raising her eyebrows again. She blew out another cloud of smoke as she gazed into the yard as if she were expecting something to appear any moment.

"Did something happen today?" Norman asked, pulling a patio chair closer to her. "You don't seem to really be present. It's like you're in another time or place. What's going on?"

Jonetta sighed and rubbed her forehead. "I wasn't going to say anything but… Doctor Franklyn wears this cologne. I haven't smelled it in decades. I didn't even know the brand still existed. It's like I'm in the twilight zone."

"What?" Norman chuckled, nervously. "Run that by me again."

"It's the exact same cologne that Mister Lucky wore."

"Who is Mister …"

8

Jonetta raised her eyebrows for the third time during their short banter and pursed her lips. They had countless conversations about Mr. Lucky regarding her escape back when they were sneaking just to see one another. Norman was instrumental with putting her plan to action to be free of Mr. Lucky finally. At the time, Norman was not quite available. He was a happily married man until he met Jonetta. But as far as Jonetta was concerned it was not going to be an issue. At the right moment, she would just pack her bags and leave Mr. Lucky to be with Norman once he broke it off with his wife. She dared anyone to try to stop her from being free to make her own decisions.

CHICAGO, IL
1973

Jonetta wanted to be honest with Norman, but without revealing the worst part of being a prostitute living with her pimp. She didn't want to ruin her chance of him truly loving her. Instead, she had only told Norman that Mr. Lucky was abusive, which was true as well. Norman responded with love and understanding, "One day at a time Jonetta. That's how we both ended up in our situations and that's how we'll get out."

For almost a year Jonetta had been secretly meeting with Norman Miller, making passionate love in the back of his Ford, while maintaining her relationship with Mr. Lucky and other men who were regulars on her roster. But being the hustler that he was Mr. Lucky was nobody's fool. On several occasions, he caught her whispering on the telephone, or sneaking in the house at a late night hour. Instead of questioning Jonetta, he simply struck her in the face. "That's to keep you from lying to me. I don't want to hear any lies," he had told her. He threatened to kill her if he ever caught her with the son-of-a-bitch she was sneaking around with. Jonetta believed that he was capable of it especially after he kicked her in the ribs after she returned home later than expected one afternoon. She had run into an old friend, who worked for her aunts, but Mr. Lucky had not believed a word she said and so he punched her in the stomach repeatedly until she vomited, bruising her ribs.

When she showed Norman her bruising he demanded that she

leave Mr. Lucky once and for all. His plans to move out of his home into an apartment were already set in motion and his wife had accepted that their marriage was over. But Jonetta had to be more careful in her situation. Norman warned that Mr. Lucky wasn't going to let her go so easily and they had to devise a plan. Jonetta agreed and reassured Norman that she would come up with something soon. Jonetta knew that Norman would have that same concern and care now.

"Oh, right…" Norman replied, clearing his throat. "If it's bothering you that bad, I'll definitely let Stanton know to make mention of it to Shon."

"I appreciate it." Jonetta patted his knee softly.

"Consider it done!" Norman replied, rubbing her hand and kissing it softly. "We can't have you in misery when you're supposed to be happy in this new phase of your life."

Jonetta smiled. *Problem solved.*

CHAPTER 2
New Day

Dawn let herself in the Hummer when it pulled up to the curb. The Versace sunglasses she sported blocked out all the radiance of the sun exactly how she liked. Her soft pink tank top complimented her skin tone, and her skinny jeans were like a second skin. Her usual wild curls cascaded past her shoulders into a wavy pattern thanks to the four braids that she put in her hair overnight. The humidity was hijacking the summer breeze and it was ideal just to stay inside with central air on days like this in Chicagoland. Nevertheless, she agreed to leave her comfort zone today to meet with a friend. She felt awkward about it, but agreed anyway. *I sure hope that he's not on some bullshit today.*

"Hi, Raffi."

"Hey, there, Queen. Thanks for meeting with me." Raffi opened his arms wide to hug Dawn. She hesitated but leaned over to extend a hug. He embraced Dawn inhaling her scent, and clutched her hair in the palm of his hand not wanting to let go, but released her quickly before it became awkward.

Dawn gave him a once over and flashed a smile. He smelled delicious as usual. Raffi sported a button down with an Eddie Bauer vest, vintage YSL sunglasses, baggy jeans and Timberland boots. His locs were groomed nicely, as usual, braided neatly in cornrows on both sides. Raffi Wilson had really grown into his looks over the years since high school days. Dawn buckled her seatbelt, relaxed in the camel colored leather seat and adjusted the vents allowing the cool air to blow directly on her face.

He shifted gears and pulled off from the curb. "Where to, my Queen?"

"This was your idea to meet," Dawn reminded him. "You tell me."

"Are you hungry?"

"Always."

They shared a laugh. Everyone always teased her about how thin she was yet she ate like there was no tomorrow in sight. But this time she really was hungry, having skipped breakfast thanks to the mayhem in the morning with the kids. Besides, Georgia decided to make porridge and toast for the kids. Dawn's palate for food had graduated since she was nine-years-old so she only drank a cup of coffee, like an adult.

"How about Frontera Grill?"

"All the way downtown?"

"You have a problem with that? Seems like we'll need the time to talk anyway."

"I'm just saying, Ja'Grill is right in Hyde Park and it's black-owned."

Oh, my God! Here he goes with that shit! Dawn took her sunglasses off so Raffi could see her expression better. She batted her eyes and pursed her glossy lips. "And?"

"Alright, alright. Frontera Grill it is."

Dawn smiled, placed her sunglasses back on and stared out of the tinted windows. Raffi took Lake Shore Drive and Dawn appreciated the view. Part of her missed New York City, but she was grateful to be home. Life seemed to be much slower in Chicago, but it was still urban enough to keep her satisfied and interested. Raffi turned up the volume to Chris Brown's latest album that he downloaded disrupting her thoughts.

"Have you heard this new joint?" Raffi increase the volume, blasting "Grass Ain't Greener".

"Raffi, I didn't agree to this ride-along to discuss Chris Brown!" Dawn hissed.

"Hey, what's going on with you? Why are you so snappy? Damn!" Raffi turned down the volume.

"Because you have me out here feeling like I'm sneaking around with my best friend's husband! What did you want to talk about in person that couldn't have been said in a text message?"

"Give a brother a chance to warm up to drop the bomb on you."

"What bomb?" Dawn jerked her neck and snatched off her sunglasses. She opened her Coach purse to get the Versace eyeglass case out, placed her sunglasses in there for good, and slammed it shut. "What's going on with my girl?"

"You know this cancer is eating her up, right?"

"Can you be a little bit more sensitive with your choice of words, Raffi?"

"What did I say wrong now?"

"Ovarian cancer is eating her up…literally! She is dying on the inside. Her womanhood is deteriorating by the minute. So just choose your words a little bit more wisely."

"Alright, my bad!" Raffi patted Dawn's knee. "You know that I love my wife. I'm not making light of this situation at all. I feel like I'm not doing enough for her pain. Dawn, I love Chena. This shit is killing me to see her like this, man." Raffi's voice cracked.

Chena was her best friend since the fifth grade. They attended the same high school and were also supposed to attend the same college until Dawn decided that she wanted to pursue modeling. It was the first time that they were ever separated. While she was trampling the streets of Chicago, Los Angeles and Atlanta pursuing her modeling career, Chena was getting closer to Raffi at Illinois State University where he was on a basketball scholarship. The next thing Dawn knew she was being asked to be a bridesmaid in their wedding. At the time Dawn didn't have time to process how all of this took place because she was busy doing fashion shows. But somewhere along the way apparently the line of communication was broken. When she looked to her mother for answers at the time, she had said, "Don't be too broken up about it. After all, she's only getting a husband, a headache. While you're having an amazing modeling career, traveling, and rubbing elbows with celebrities."

Not that it was any consolation, but her mother was right. Dawn couldn't be upset about her high school crush marrying her best friend because she was having an amazing career at the time. Over the years, the idea of them grew on her and she learned that she was not wife material anyway. So she harbored no ill feelings towards neither of them. Now that Dawn was back in Chicago, she tried her best to be available since Chena was diagnosed with ovarian cancer last year.

Dawn rubbed his shoulder and sighed. "Get off at Thirty-first Street Beach real quick. Let's talk without having an accident."

13

Raffi agreed and put his right blinker on, exiting Lake Shore Drive. "Shit! We gotta pay to park here. Where's the damn pay box?" Raffi scanned along the grassy area for the pay box.

"Don't worry about it. We'll be gone before the cops roll around. Just park right there," Dawn instructed pointing to an open parking space. The dashboard temperature read a whopping 89 degrees, but people were still taking advantage of the weather along the lakefront where it was cooler. The lakefront was packed with joggers, moms with strollers, bikers and dog walkers. It was a beautiful summer day in Chicago. The sun had made an appearance after three days full of rain.

Raffi continued as he slowly eased into the parking space, "Well, she's been doing a lot of planning these days. Thinking ahead for Shiloh's sake, you know?"

"What type of planning?"

"Long term planning, ya feel me?" Raffi unfastened his seat belt and turned to face Dawn. He exhaled and continued, "Dawn, she's been planning her own funeral, calculating how much Shiloh will need for therapy, sports and whatever else she can think of! She's even been suggesting that I start seeing other women. I think the medication is getting the best of her."

"She can't be serious!" Dawn frowned, shook her head and stared out of the window.

"That's what I said! But your girl is dead serious, Dawn."

Dawn grabbed her hair out of frustration. She unfastened her seatbelt and lowered the window to get some fresh air circulating. The thought of her best friend's mental and physical state deteriorating made her queasy.

Raffi placed his hand on her knee again and pleaded with her. "Please talk to Chena. She's being so extra right now acting like it's the end. It ain't all over yet."

"Sounds like she thinks so," Dawn replied biting her bottom lip. She placed her hand on top of Raffi's and squeezed it gently. Her thoughts raced about medical care, new treatments, holistic healing, anything to ease her friend's pain. Dawn swiftly turned towards Raffi to ask questions, but she stopped herself once she saw the look on his face. Worry was etched across his face and suddenly she regretted having mean thoughts about him. Raffi was always one of the good guys since they were kids, he was just lazy

14

sometimes. He came from a good home with both parents and three younger sisters to look after. Surely, he got a dose of womanly issues from his sisters growing up over the years. Especially his sister, Fatima, the feisty middle sister, who was in the same class as Dawn and Chena; she always had a quick tongue, but she was Dawn's favorite. Fatima always fantasized about being a real sister to Dawn once she married her brother, but that never manifested. Why things worked out the way they did between them doesn't even matter all these years later. They were still her friends whom she loved. Dawn removed his sunglasses and touched the side of his face. He was suffering through this ordeal too. She almost cried, but instead bit her bottom lip.

"Can you just come by to talk to her?" Raffi pleaded.

"Of course, but I don't think it'll do any good!" Dawn threw her hands up. "You know how Chena is once she has her mind made up."

"She's now trying holistic methods along with taking her meds."

"What are the doctors saying about that? I thought cancer patients chose one or the other."

Raffi shrugged his broad shoulders, exhaled and rested his head back on the headrest. "The doctors are trying this new medication on her. It's supposed to put her in remission soon, so they say." He shook his head gazing out the window.

"Well? Is it working?

Raffi shrugged. "They say signs of improvement should be seen in three to six months…but…"

"But…what?"

"But Chena has been taking the meds for five months now without improvement." Raffi rubbed his beard and exhaled. "Why her? Why *my* wife?"

"Don't start, please," Dawn replied, shaking her head. "I've asked God that question so many times."

Raffi put the truck in reverse when he saw a Chicago Police car in the distance.

"Buckle up." Raffi told Dawn as he did the same.

Dawn put her seat belt on and wiped a tear away that escaped. "Let's just go to Ja' Grill. It's closer and now I'm really hungry."

"Cool," Raffi replied and guided the truck south on Lake Shore Drive.

They rode the rest of the way to Ja'Grill in silence. Once inside Dawn gave the menu a glance, but she knew that she wanted the salmon fillet and a Ja'Rum Punch.

"Maybe we should place an order for Chena too." Dawn suggested viewing the menu again.

"She can't eat this stuff." Raffi frowned at the suggestion. "She'll only throw it up."

"Oh, sorry." Dawn placed the menu at the edge of the table. "What's her diet like these days?"

"She eats toast, lots of toast and rabbit food here and there. Chena barely eats or leaves the bedroom."

"When we talk on the phone she never lets on that it's that bad." Dawn flipped the menu over to search the back for kids' meals, but didn't find one. "Well, at least order something for Shiloh before we leave."

"No doubt." Raffi looked for the waiter and motioned for him to take their order. After the waiter exited Raffi stared at Dawn as she scrolled through her Instagram timeline on her iPhone. The same girl he crushed on back in high school was still so beautiful. Raffi cleared his throat to clear his lustful thoughts that was about to lead to an erection.

"I don't want our conversation to be all doom and gloom. Tell me what's going on with you lately."

Dawn shrugged, glancing up at Raffi. "Not much."

"Are you happy to be back in the Chi?"

"Definitely." Dawn turned her attention back to her iPhone.

Raffi jerked his head. "What's with the short answers?"

"You're just being nosey, Raffi." Dawn continued to scroll on her phone.

"Am I? Here I thought that I was chatting with my friend."

"Chena is my best friend since the fifth grade, not you." Dawn pointed her long, slender finger in his direction and placed her phone back in her purse. "You and I were friends back in high school, a long time ago. But if there's anything you want to know about me...I'm sure she's already told you."

"I wanna hear it from you!" Raffi insisted, folding his muscular arms across his chest.

Dawn smirked at his persistence. She had tried to maintain a neutral relationship with Raffi over the years since he decided to marry her best friend, but it was difficult at times. Like right now, with his cute-self wanting to know her business. Had he been another chick's husband, she would've spread her legs wide open for Raffi years ago. But since he was Chena's husband, she kept it cordial with him over the years. Being away from Chicago off and on also helped create the distance.

"So you're not denying that Chena tells you my business?" Dawn teased. The waiter placed the rum punch on the table along with two glasses of water and Coco bread. *Right on time*, Dawn thought as she slurped down the drink.

Raffi raised his thick eyebrows in anticipation for her to divulge her new life back home.

"Alright, already! Geesh! Since you're dying to know," Dawn replied, covering her mouth as she realized the expression she just used. "I gotta be more careful with my choice of words, too!"

"We're human. Don't sweat it." Raffi shrugged off the comment.

Dawn nodded in agreement. "Well, I have some gigs lined up. You'll see me soon. That's all I'm gonna say about it really. Other than that, I've been chillin' trying to find a solution to my living arrangement because it's for the birds."

"I just wanna let you know that I'm proud of you, if I've never actually said it," Raffi replied, patting her hand across the table. "When I saw you in that ad for Givenchy I was hella proud! I also tuned in to see the runway show... I can't remember who the designer was, but I saw it."

"I appreciate that." Dawn tried to sound appreciative, but she knew that lifestyle came with a price. Some of those experiences were all a blur because she was so doped up. There was a real ugly side to the business, but oddly enough, Dawn missed that lifestyle. *I gotta get back on my shit.*

"So where do you want to live? North side, south side, downtown, or suburbs?"

"Right now, anywhere but with my family!"

"That bad, huh?"

"How much time you got?"

"For you? I got all day!" Raffi leaned back in his seat, smiling seductively.

"Seriously, though, I cannot continue to live with Colette, the kids and my Aunt Georgia." Dawn dramatically shook her head in absolute certainty. "It's really messing up my head space and puff time."

Raffi laughed, amused by her choice of words. "Your 'puff time', huh? Just hit me up anytime you need to escape for that. You know I'm there for it."

"Maybe all three of us should…"

"Nah… that ain't Chena's thing."

"But it's supposed to help with the pain. Well, at least that's what I heard." Dawn shrugged.

"Even with all of her pain, Chena is not about to smoke nothing." Raffi leaned forward on the table, rested his fists underneath his chin and grinned. "Like I said, let me know when you need an escape. We can chief together."

The waiter came with their food. *Perfect timing.* The food smelled good and tasted even better. There was nothing like Chicago food, but Dawn had to be conscious about her weight with so much tempting food choices. She had been sticking to fish, veggies and whole grains. She scarfed down the salmon in no time at all, it didn't stand a chance. While they waited on the Jerk chicken to-go Dawn ordered another Rum Punch. She felt the alcohol work its magic as her muscles relaxed, her feet became lighter and she smiled. As they were walking back to his Hummer Dawn had to hold onto him to maintain her balance.

"Come on light-weight," Raffi said, shaking his head.

"I needed that!" Dawn replied clutching his arm tighter. "Thanks for scooping me up today."

"I got you. Now get your tipsy ass in this truck." Raffi pointed the remote at the truck to unlock it and helped Dawn into the passenger seat. He slowly eased out of the parking spot and another car swooped in right behind them. Parking was always hard to come by in Hyde Park that if you found a spot it felt like you hit the jackpot.

"Hyde Park is always poppin'. I heard the Silver Room has as an event tonight."

Don't you have a family waiting on you? She wanted to ask, but decided against it. "To the castle, sir!" Dawn pointed straight ahead. She couldn't hang out with him all day, especially not in her condition now. Raffi nodded and turned on the radio. As they rolled down 53rd Street she let the window down allowing the summer breeze to caress her face. Just as she adjusted her seat, leaning it back so she could relax she leaped forward.

"What's the matter with you?" Raffi looked back and forth between Dawn and bumper-to-bumper traffic.

"Is that..." Dawn stuck her head out the window as far as she could before the seat belt prevented her from leaning any further. "I know that's not who I think it is getting in the car with that bitch!"

"Who?"

"My brother-in-law, Damien and that bitch Shante!"

CHAPTER 3

It Could Be Different

Phyllis stood at the bathroom sink patting a damp towel on the back of her neck scolding herself for working up a sweat in the August heat. The thick haze and humidity wasn't unusual for Chicago this time of year, but the central air unit was broken in this old house and it was hot and sticky. She got angry just thinking about why they had to move to his house in the first place. But Damien seemed to be doing much better with their finances since Phyllis bought a home budget software. Thank God. There was certainly a surplus of almost eight hundred dollars per month consistently over the past few months. Since her Mama always taught her to save for a rainy day because there would be plenty of those in the forecast, Phyllis stashed half of it in another account every month. She finally had a "Oh-No-He-Didn't" bank account that she always wanted. It was just in case shit hit the fan and she had to pack the twins up to leave his ass. Her Mama always told her that a woman could never be too sure about her man, and always prepare for the worse. Her nest egg was increasing monthly and looking secure so far.

Damien was the first man she had ever depended on financially and it scared the shit out of her. He loved her, Serena and Sabrina, their six-year-old twins, that was something she never questioned. Based on his monthly income, Phyllis finally believed that her husband could handle the rent, car notes, utilities and extra expenses that popped up. Although Damien was keeping his word so far by working extra hours, he was also securing a home they could call their own, yet she still wanted more. Phyllis never seemed satisfied. However, Damien reassured her months ago that she didn't need to get a job after all to help with bills like her father advised because, unlike Phyllis, Damien kept his end of the bargain and finally stopped gambling.

Phyllis was never good at keeping her word. Like the time she promised Damien that she would cut back on spending, only to find a plastic bag stuffed in the attic crawl space with expensive shoes, clothes and purses. Since Damien worked for UPS Phyllis cleverly ordered everything via FedEx. She had an addiction to nice things, and…vodka. Phyllis wanted to stop drinking, really, she did, but she couldn't. Phyllis tried, but by day two, she had already baked four cakes, a batch of brownies, that Dawn begged her to sprinkle some weed in it so she could sell to college kids at University of Chicago, and prepared gourmet dinners. By the end of the week, Phyllis gained five pounds thanks to cooking gourmet meals for breakfast, lunch and dinner. It reminded her of when she on maternity leave with the twins. She cooked all the time and gained more weight on top of the baby weight. *I'll be damned if I ever get that fat again!*

Vodka, along with her reality shows, were the only vices she found comfort in to help her escape her boring, daily routine. Although Phyllis didn't deem herself an alcoholic, she did take the time to Google alcoholic websites outlining symptoms and signs of being an alcoholic just to be on the safe side. When Phyllis didn't meet all the criteria for being an alcoholic, she carried on with secretly drinking with pleasure. Since she was the Queen of keeping everyone's schedules, she was safe with her secrets. In the morning, a mimosa with vodka after the twins were on the school bus, vodka tonic with lime before Damien got home suited her just fine unless Damien pissed her off, then she would indulge a straight shot of vodka, maybe two. Nobody could ever tell the difference. She blamed her profuse sweating on the extreme heat and lack of central air, which was partly true. This time she decided to hide her vodka in plain sight. She poured bottles of vodka into empty water gallons and set them on the basement steps. To everyone else, Phyllis was on the wagon and doing just fine.

Phyllis preferred to drink her calories, keep her shape intact and watch her shows. Lately, she was obsessed with cooking shows, especially since Martha Stewart and Snoop Dog debuted. *I could do that myself and in less time it's taking them!* Inspired, Phyllis installed Periscope on her phone and began filming her cooking skills. Jonetta always said that she and Damien needed their own show, but since he was always busy working, Phyllis did it herself. Periscope was dead, not many of her friends followed, so she switched to Facebook Live. It was a hit! She had over 500 viewers each week. They tuned in every Friday evening to watch "Friday Food Fanatics with Phyllis". She was always cooking up something different. The food varied from vegan specialties, fancy feasts for a celebration, to grilled cheese sandwiches with a variety of cheeses. The number of viewers watching would easily hit up to 100 as soon as she hit the Go Live button and greeted her viewers with: "Hey Friday Food Fanatics! It's time to get cooking with Queen Phyllis!" They were anticipating her show each week, by the time she would hit the Finish button, she had numerous comments, likes, and shares.

If only their central air worked, Phyllis would be in the kitchen baking Damien's favorite spinach and bacon quiche right now to show her viewers today. But since their only source of relief from the thick, humid suffocating air that filled their house was an air conditioner jammed in the dining room window, she had to settle on making pan seared cod with a lemon butter sauce. She hung a bed sheet at the entry-way of the dining room to ensure the air would only circulate in there and towards the kitchen. A trick she learned from her mother because they grew up in a house that also lacked central air.

Phyllis sucked her teeth, wiped her sweaty brow as she sorted through the twins' laundry. Their other house was more modern and the central air worked, but the damage was done and the chores were waiting on her. She couldn't explain to Damien that the house looked a wreck because it was just too hot to clean up. Maybe in the past she would have tried that excuse when she was pregnant, but since that's not the case she continued picking up socks and dolls from the floor. Motherhood was 24/7, no days off. One thing she was certain of, she wasn't going to get pregnant again, ever. After having a vertical C-section just to get Serena and Sabrina out, leaving a horrible scar, she vowed that being pregnant again was *never* going to happen.

"You can just forget about having a son!" Phyllis had told

Damien after her first week home from the hospital. Damien said that he understood, but often hinted that he still wanted a son. She had to give credit to any woman juggling motherhood, a husband and managing a job at the same time. Her mother did it the "right way". She married her father then had three children with him. Rainbow colored as they were, they still had the same blood running rapid through their veins. Although they are divorced now, but living together again, Phyllis was convinced that her mother ran their father away on purpose because she didn't know how to love. She was convinced even more that her mother confessed to being an in-house prostitute. Every time Phyllis thought about everything that their mother confessed about her past life in that house, she shuddered with anger and resentment towards her mother began to rear its ugly head.

"She could've just kept all that shit to herself!" Phyllis fumed, discussing it with Damien one night.

"Why? Your mom was coming clean after four decades. I'm sure she felt relieved!"

"Yeah, but what about us? Did she ever consider how it would make us feel about her?"

"Well, Aunt Georgia did kinda bully her into confessing, but still… Babe, it's a good thing that your mom got it all out. Secrets can literally kill you!"

"I guess you would know." Phyllis remarked, rolling her eyes.

Damien glared at his wife and fell silent. Phyllis always had a smart mouth or a quick come back that he couldn't match. He let that comment slide that night because Phyllis was definitely in her feelings about her mom being an in-house prostitute. "Look babe, it really should not affect you at this age. Y'all are grown women who are not on drugs, nor prostitutes. It had nothing to do with you. All of that is in her past life. You should show more compassion for your mom than anything."

"It does too have everything to do with us! Kids don't want to know that their mother was a whore! It changes things! It changes our views about her, decisions she made, people she associated with, all of that matters! That sort of thing shapes your character, whether you want it to or not it does! I just want to view my mother like I always have, and now I just can't!"

"Babe, you're not kids…"

"We'll always be our parents' kids, Damien! Don't get petty and technical on me, okay?"

"But it was way before…"

"Oh, to hell with it! I'll just discuss it with Dawn since it's *our* mom who was a whore!"

"Feel how you wanna feel, but don't go being disrespectful!"

That was the last time Phyllis mentioned her feelings about the entire situation to him. *Why did I expect him to understand in the first place?* Still she had resentment towards her mother. Always being so critical of everyone. Always so judgmental, but she had these types of secrets? As far as Phyllis was concerned, their relationship needed a fresh start. Phyllis had more questions that Jonetta was unwilling to answer which put more strain on their relationship. Everyone kept telling her that it didn't matter, it was in the past, but she couldn't let it go.

For now, her focus was to get more followers on her cooking page. Currently, Phyllis only had 600 followers. She wanted to hit one million followers by the end of the year. It was a reach, but still it was a goal. Her last resort would be wearing skimpy clothes even if Damien opposed, and she knew he would. He wouldn't know until after she went live anyway because he was always working when she went live on Facebook. As Phyllis tossed the last pair of socks in the washer, she heard the buzzer go off on the oven letting her know it was hot and ready for whatever she was going to prepare.

The kitchen was much cooler now that she sectioned off the air circulation. *I can work in these conditions.* She pulled her hair up in a ponytail, grabbed her apron from the pantry and positioned her phone in the cabinet that got the perfect view of her workspace. Each Friday she would go live an hour before the twins came home. Most of her viewers were mothers and Phyllis found that people related well to women with children. Making mention of Sabrina and Serena always went over well with tons of comments from the viewers relating and sharing their stories about foods their children liked or disliked. Phyllis always encouraged the viewers to send their meal requests if they wanted her to cook something different. Only two people ever sent a suggestion. One was for banana pancakes, which she did try and hated, but the twins loved them. The other was lamb chop with minced glaze, which Phyllis knew was out of her league and refused to waste the time and money on that request.

For the most part, Phyllis was good at cooking and she enjoyed showing off her talents. But she was even better at making cocktails and frozen drinks. She thought about just displaying her special cocktail creations, but she knew Damien would find out. *One of these days I'm just gonna do it live and have fun with it.* Her phone rang interrupting her preparations. She looked at the time, having a 15-minute leeway she decided to answer.

"Hey girl!" Dawn screamed in the phone.

"Good grief! What are you on girl?" Phyllis cringed from her high pitch tone.

Dawn laughed at her sister's insinuations. "Nothing yet. It's still early in the day."

"Ha. Ha. What's up? You know I'm about to go live on Facebook in a few."

"Oh, right! Just checking on you and the fam. Everything good?

"We're good. Damien's working like a dog and the twins are being busy bodies as usual. What's up with you? Make it quick though." Phyllis laughed, but she was serious.

"Nothing much. I'm heading down to Atlanta soon for an audition on a new reality show."

"Oh yeah? Which one?" Phyllis asked, opening the utensil drawer. She paused, waited for Dawn to respond, but didn't hear anything. She removed the phone from her ear to look at the screen. The call was still connected. "Hello?"

"Promise you won't tell Mama?" Dawn finally responded.

"Okay, I promise!"

"It's called *The Real Mistresses of Atlanta.*"

"What type of stupid shit is that?" Phyllis shook her head. "Are you somebody's mistress heffa? You better spill your guts now! Don't wait until it airs to drop a bomb!"

"No!" Dawn laughed nervously. "Not really…"

"Well, which one is it? No, or not really?" Phyllis demanded to know, slamming the kitchen drawer.

"No, I'm not a mistress. It's just an audition. Anyway…" Dawn sighed. "I wanted to see what your schedule is like for next weekend."

"Not sure yet. Why?" Phyllis glanced at the clock on the kitchen wall. She had approximately nine minutes to get up and running on Facebook Live.

"I was thinking we should chat about throwing our parents an anniversary party."

"For what!?" Phyllis rejected that idea already. She had not shared with her sisters how she was feeling about their mother lately. Celebrating her was the last thing on her mind. "They aren't even married anymore. They're basically shackin' up like a bunch of silly twenty-somethings! You wanna celebrate our parents shackin' up, Dawn? Don't think so!"

"I think we should celebrate their new beginnings together in this phase of their lives."

"Again, for what?" Phyllis asked sharply.

"How about we discuss it with Colette next weekend at your place?"

"Girl, if you just want to get together as sisters just say so!" Phyllis rolled her eyes. "You don't have to go creating reasons to hang out."

"That's not what I was doing!" Dawn retorted on the defense. "I seriously want to celebrate our parents. They did get married in August, so maybe we can just celebrate them while we're all in the same city for once."

Phyllis grunted. "So, basically, this is about you?"

"What? No...kinda..." Dawn cleared her throat. "If I get this role, I'll be gone again soon. I just want to do something for our parents because honestly, I don't know when I'll be back."

"Look, I only have a few more minutes before I go on air. I gotta get my utensils prepped for my show. I need my bowls, and... Dammit! I forgot to leave the butter out at room temperature!" Phyllis snatched open the refrigerator only to find a tub of margarine. *Where the hell is my butter?* "Dawn, I gotta go!" Phyllis ended the call, sifted through the shelves in the refrigerator looking for a stick of butter. When she couldn't find one she slammed the refrigerator door, shaking the contents on the inside of the refrigerator as well as on top of the refrigerator. She positioned the phone back in the cabinet as she heard the front door open. Phyllis snatched back the sheet separating the dining room from the hallway. It was Damien.

"Did you use the last stick of butter?" Phyllis asked impatiently.

"Well, hello to you too!" Damien replied, closing the door behind him.

"Wait a minute, what are you doing home so early?" Phyllis asked as she disappeared behind the sheet. Damien followed her looking bewildered.

"Whew... sure feels good back here." Damien removed his UPS cap, wiped his brow with the back of his hand. "Babe, what's going on in here?" He placed the cap on backwards, eyeing the kitchen set up.

"I'm supposed to be going live in two minutes on Facebook, but not without a stick of butter!" Phyllis placed her hand on her hip and shifted her weight. "Since you're here, could you run up the street to the store real quick for me?" Phyllis clasped her hands together as if pleading.

Damien shot her an incredulous look. "In case you haven't noticed, I've been pulling a ton of overtime so I decided to finally take some time off." He explained slowly walking towards Phyllis. "I came home early to surprise you so we could spend time together before the girls came home."

Phyllis glanced at the clock on the wall again and sucked her teeth. Before she could respond Damien had her wrapped in his arms kissing the left side of her neck, leading down to her cleavage. *Terrible timing, babe.* Against her wishes, goosebumps raced all over her body betraying her thoughts of resistance. But even after all these years, she could not resist his touch. Seven months ago, when they brought the New Year in together they vowed to dedicate more time together, go on dates once a month or send the girls to a sleepover just to spend time with each other. Over the past five months they failed miserably at keeping that commitment. Whether it was bad timing, being exhausted from their daily routines, or being angry with one another, it was always something.

"Take this off," Damien instructed as he lifted her black tank top. Phyllis followed his instruction hesitantly. "The viewers can wait. It's my turn." Damien lifted her by the waist, placed her on the countertop, kissed her passionately and began to unhook her bra with one hand.

27

Phyllis broke their embrace and pushed Damien's chest away from her. "Wait! Let me at least tell the viewers why I'm running late and that I'll go live later."

"Are you serious?" Damien asked frustrated.

"Just hold on!" Phyllis hopped down from the counter, fastened her bra and dashed for the phone.

"Unbelievable!" Damien threw his hands in the air. He repeatedly adjusted his cap on top of his sandy brown locs as he watched his wife in action.

Phyllis smoothed her hair, pinched her cheeks and hit the Go Live button. The countdown ended and Phyllis announced, "Hey Friday Food Fanatics! I was hoping to get started because I know you're waiting to see what the Queen was cooking today… But I just realized that I don't have butter! I can't make a lemon butter sauce without the butter now can I? But you see my hubby is here to save the day! Say hey babe!" Phyllis put the camera on Damien.

"Hey, y'all…" Damien said dryly and waved to the camera.

"When I come back, y'all I'll have my hubby in here with an apron on too! You're gonna help me, right babe?" Phyllis turned the phone towards Damien and he put two thumbs up. Phyllis turned the phone towards her and continued, "Hey Miss Mel! I see you girl. We'll be back after this butter break!" She was pleased to see the viewers tune in to hit the Love button as she recorded live. She hit the Finish and Post button with a huge smile on her face.

"Okay, all done. Where were we, babe?"

Phyllis turned around to find herself in the kitchen alone.

CHAPTER 4
Purpose Found

"Amen," Colette said as she closed a prayer for the Women's Bible Study class. She squeezed one of the sister's hands tight, then released it. She felt more confident now that she was studying the Word of God. It gave her more power and affirmation with her thought process regarding Owen. When she felt stressed out, she would simply pray. Before she decided to turn her life over to Christ, she would consult Jonetta, Phyllis or anyone who would listen. But now God was her resource of strength.

"Ladies, don't forget that we will have a mandatory meeting for the upcoming Appreciation Day for our Pastor in two weeks. All ideas are welcomed and we need all hands on deck. We want to show him just how much we love him." Sister Kimball announced putting emphasis on "love" by squeezing her breasts together with her forearms.

"And how much she wants to be his wife." One of the women mumbled loud enough for the others around her to hear. Her comment was followed by giggles and gasps. Colette cringed at the comment because she had so much respect for him. It was true that the Pastor probably needed a wife, but more importantly he needed to stay focused on leading the congregation. Colette was extremely grateful when he hired her as his second assistant. She needed the change from her boring routine of being at home all day with Georgia while Cornell, Lydia and Ruthie were at day camp. This job gave her a sense of purpose. It was fulfilling knowing that she was being useful in the Lord's house taking care of minor, but necessary duties.

Colette revamped the Sunday bulletin and the church newsletter by adding more graphics and changing the fonts. She also wrote an inspiration column in the church newsletter that people began to look forward to regularly. The best part of her new job was she was allowed her to bring Delilah with her every day. She was a good baby, almost a year old and learning how to walk. The church daycare had a walker that Colette used for Delilah and she followed her all around the church, getting faster as she got the hang of it. The Pastor enjoyed having Delilah around as well since he never had children of his own. He often played with her and offered to feed her if Colette was busy typing or filing his financial papers.

They were becoming closer as Colette confided in him about her struggles with Owen, being torn on getting a divorce. "God hates divorce, Sister Colette." He reminded her. "But since your husband has neglected his duties and abandoned his whole family for another woman, your divorce would be justified." The very same week the Pastor had his attorney draw up the divorce papers on her behalf at no cost. Colette just needed to come up with a plan to present the divorce papers to Owen and then get him to sign it.

She often fantasized about becoming a Pastor's wife, but now she wanted to be *his* wife. The Pastor made it so easy to fall in love with him. He was a generous, compassionate and God-fearing man who knew how to deliver a powerful, thought-provoking sermon. But Colette kept her fantasies to herself as she watched the stiff competition of the other ladies in the church. *I hope he doesn't choose one of these loose women.*

"Sister Colette, I need you to make sure this scripture is in the bulletin on Sunday for the Scripture of the Day section." One of the elderly mothers of the church handed her a folded sheet of paper. Colette opened it, read it quickly and refolded the paper placing inside of her notebook.

There's no way the Pastor is going to allow this in the bulletin Sister Templeton, but you tried it though. "Everything must be approved by the Pastor before printing," Colette replied as nicely as she could.

"I know that!" Sister Templeton retorted. "It's scripture, ain't it? Have a good day." She waltzed away in a dignified manner as if she had not just dropped a bomb in Colette's lap.

"You, too, Sister Templeton." Colette shook her head, grimacing at Sister Templeton's feet that were stuffed into her shoes with meat rolls falling off of her ankles. *Lord, please don't ever let me get that fat!* She glanced down at Delilah who was fast asleep in her stroller and proceeded to the office. One thing for sure, she was good at her job. His executive assistant, Alyssa, had only done clerical work, but Colette implemented organization, design and beautification. Before Alyssa left on maternity leave she showed Colette where everything belonged, how the Pastor liked his paperwork filed, and how he liked special attention. Colette paid attention, followed instructions, but she knew there was much needed change around the Pastor's office and she saw fit to change it all.

Not only did Colette redesign the church newsletter and Sunday bulletin, she also color-coded all the files making it easier to find paperwork. Now that she had access to the funds, she took it upon herself to redecorate the hallway leading to the Pastor's office. She placed a mirror on the wall that she found in the basement at the house. It was an antique mirror with pelicans engraved in the wood. She stained it a darker color and used polyurethane to make it shine. She framed inspirational messages and hung them along the walls. And much like her mother, she believed that a living plant or flower should be in any living space so she brought in potted snake plants that lined the hallway leading to the Pastor's office. Inside his office she placed ferns in the windows and a ficus potted plant on the floor in the corner. The Pastor didn't object at all, he welcomed her creativity and complimented her efforts regularly. When Colette expressed the aesthetic changes that she wanted to implement, he instructed Alyssa to hand over the credit card that he had given her.

"Alyssa, I need the credit card that I gave you for expenses." The Pastor had said with authority. Alyssa was caught off guard and looked confused. "You won't be needing it anymore when you're on maternity leave." He held his hand out waiting for her to dig through her purse to retrieve the card.

"Pastor, I still had some items to take care of before…"

"That won't be necessary," he responded sharply. "Colette can handle everything from now on."

Alyssa nodded glumly as she handed over the credit card to the Pastor. As he passed the credit card to Colette, her expression grew dark, she placed her hand on her large belly, opened her mouth to say something but thought better of it. She shot a glance at Colette, cut her eyes at her and the left the office. From that moment on

Alyssa didn't have much to say to Colette before she left on maternity leave. The Pastor had expressed to Colette how sorely disappointed he was that Alyssa allowed herself to "become that way".

"Children are a blessing from God, Pastor," Colette reminded him just as her Aunt Georgia had to remind her mother while defending Colette. Even though Alyssa had become cold towards her before she left Colette still felt compelled to defend her. She knew what it was like to be ridiculed for being pregnant. Colette was married, but still ridiculed by her family for consistently getting pregnant.

"But Alyssa knew better than to let that happen! She should've been wise and taken precaution to prevent such ridicule. She's brought shame to herself and I cannot stand to look at her!" The Pastor admitted, slamming his fist on the desk. Colette thought his behavior was odd, he almost seemed jealous. Although she heard gossip that Alyssa might be pregnant by him or one of the deacons, she dismissed his behavior as being an over protective father figure to Alyssa. Naturally, he would be upset about her having a baby out of wedlock.

"We all sin, Pastor." Colette replied softly, trying to soothe his anger. She knew from being married to hot-head Owen all these years that a softer tone usually calmed the conversation before it escalated.

"Yes, but at least some of us are smart enough to hide it better!" He placed his hand on his forehead and sighed. "Well, she made her choices. Nothing I can do it about it now. I have you now…Sister Colette…" He flashed a grimy grin across his face.

Colette perked up hearing his tone change. "Yes?"

"You did things the right way, according to God's will." He clasped his hands together, still smiling at her. "You are smart and pure at heart. And your body is pure having only been with your husband. Yessss….You are a rare jewel, Sister Colette. Yes, God will bless you."

"Yes, but…" Colette shook her head, thinking of Owen. She pushed the stroller back and forth out of habit. Out of all of her children, Delilah looked just like Owen. It was hard not to think of him on a daily basis.

"Oh, I know things are not perfect with your marriage. Pretty soon that will be over. You just need to persuade your husband to sign those divorce papers." He rubbed his salt and pepper beard thoughtfully.

"But Pastor, you just preached last Sunday that God hates divorce and you keep reminding me that God hates divorce. So I've been thinking…"

"Oh, God hates a lot of things," he waved his hand dismissing her comments. "…but he's also forgiving, yes?" He walked from behind his large desk, approached Colette but stopped in his tracks as he continued. "My attorney did his part for you and I did my part for you. Now it is up to you to do get it handled, Sister Colette." He paced the floor again, finally he stood behind her, close enough for her to feel his breath on her neck. He placed his thick hands on her shoulders. He whispered in her ear, "You deserve to be happy, Sister Colette. You've made me happy. Now I want you happy."

Goosebumps raised on her arms as he spoke. His touch made her throb between her legs, her nipples were erect and her cheeks were flushed. It was an electrifying feeling that shot through her body. She had not felt this way in years. His voice and touch made her tingle between her thighs, her heart race, and her back arch. Her body responded to him in a way that it never did for Owen. *What have I been missing?* Maybe it was his Haitian accent, or maybe it was his cologne, or his touch that turned her on. Whatever it was she felt like she needed to go repent! He turned her around to face him with his hands still on her shoulders, his eyes met hers and his eyes glossed with lust. Colette blushed as he hungrily gazed his eyes all over her body. He stared long and hard at her breasts, unashamed. He bit his bottom lip, grunted, walked back to his desk and began working on his laptop as if that moment didn't just happen.

Colette felt light-headed as she stood in the middle of his office. Delilah squirmed in her stroller and whined. Colette dashed to her rescue, patting her on the legs. "Mommy is right here."

"Somebody is wide awake and hungry, yes?"

"I'll be back after I change and feed her."

"I'm hungry, too." He announced, raising his eyebrows. "Fetch my lunch from the refrigerator." He ordered Colette as he diverted his attention back to his laptop.

Delilah let out a wail of disapproval. Colette took her from the stroller, bounced her up and down trying to silence her cries. "Oh, baby cakes, you're all wet! Pastor, I need to change her and then I'll get your food."

"Sister Colette, your obedience is necessary in order for this to work." His tone changed drastically. He leaned back in his chair, placed his thick hands on his round belly and barked orders. "Give Delilah to one of the mothers of the church while you tend to my needs. Even Alyssa knew that all of my needs came first and she was never married. I shouldn't have to spell that out for you! I can see why your marriage has failed." He snarled.

Colette winced at his last comment. She swallowed hard on the lump growing in the pit of her throat to make room for the words he needed to hear. "Yes, Pastor. I'll get your lunch right away." She blinked back tears in her eyes as she left his office. She rushed to find one of the elderly sisters that lingered around the church all day for no reason. The last thing she wanted was him to be upset with her. She saw just how cold the Pastor treated Alyssa over the past several months as her belly grew larger. The more the baby grew inside of her, the less he wanted to see her let alone speak to her directly. Colette didn't want to be treated like that by him ever. She didn't want to disappoint or anger him in anyway. Funny how she didn't mind so much when Owen mistreated her, but with the Pastor it was different. She aimed to please him and wanted him to see her as a potential wife.

An hour later, his plate was clean of oxtails, rice, plantains and cabbage. He called for Colette to come to his office. Before she had the opportunity to fully enter the office he snapped at her.

"You forgot to bring my coconut water!" His eyes were cold and body language stiff.

"I'm sorry, Pastor. I'll go get it now." Colette offered.

"Never mind. It's too late now." He sucked his teeth clean of its contents, eyeing Colette. He pursed his lips and shook his head. "I want this to work, Sister Colette. Don't you?"

Colette nodded and closed the door behind her. She approached his desk with her hands clasped in front of her. "Yes, of course,

Pastor. You've been a savior to me. I knew there was something missing from my life and you've provided exactly what I need. I'm so grateful to you. I'll do better. I promise." She glanced down at her hands and bit her bottom lip.

"There's plenty of women in this church that would love to take your place, Sister Colette." He reminded her of all the women who were begging to become his next executive assistant when they learned about Alyssa taking maternity leave. The women were willing to do whatever it took to have that spot. He even tried a few women out for a few days, but he wasn't pleased with their services. He had already had an assistant with a toned shapely body, who wore sexy clothes, no underwear and lots of weave. Alyssa flaunted and advertised herself so much that the Pastor had no choice but to tame her into submission. At first it excited him because she was a challenge, but then it became a chore and it wore him out. He even offered her services to the deacons in the church because she was becoming a handful. This time around he wanted something different. Someone sweet, humble and modest. He chose Colette, the new member of the church to become his new assistant and all the women were disgusted by it.

"You chose the right woman, Pastor. I promise." Colette reassured him, smiling warmly.

He grunted, opened his arms widely, and smiled. "I hope so. Now come show me."

CHAPTER 5

No New Friends

"Dental Dynasty, how may I help you?" Jonetta answered the phone perky as she rolled her eyes. If anybody knew about faking "happy" it was Jonetta. She transferred the call to scheduling. The impressionable twenty-something girl, Kaiya, who sat directly beside her at the front desk cut her eyes at Jonetta, but it didn't bother her one way or the other. Jonetta glanced at the phone, there were three lights flashing, indicating there were people on hold. Instead of helping Kaiya schedule appointments, she opened the latest Essence magazine and casually flipped through the glossy pages. *That'll teach her about rolling her eyes at me!*

So far her job was easy and Dr. Bishon Franklyn made it a pleasant place to work. There was always a lunch being delivered for the staff. Smooth jazz always played over the intercom system, which suited Jonetta just fine. She was allowed to bring in pots of plants and flowers to spruce up the place a bit. The windows faced the east allowing plenty of sunshine to beam on the plants that Jonetta strategically placed along the floor. Working five days a week gave her something to do, but it was daunting on her to get up early each morning. She had become accustomed to getting out bed when she felt like it. But this is exactly what she needed to get some space from Norman. Jonetta was finally in a happier space. Only two things kept her from having the perfect set up: She was not allowed to smoke at her desk like back in her days of employment. And Kaiya's attitude needed an adjustment.

"Would it hurt if you picked up the phone to schedule an appointment?" Kaiya snapped, slamming the receiver in its cradle. "You know by now that Mondays are busy, Mrs. Miller."

"No, it wouldn't hurt at all." Jonetta replied matter-of-factly still flipping pages of the magazine. "However, little miss, that's *your* job so you should do it."

Jonetta did not take this job to be irritated, she could have stayed home for that. Nor was she willing to go above and beyond her call of duty. For what? There was no additional compensation, no awards, no recognition so she was just fine answering the incoming calls and transferring them to Kaiya. Bishon had hired Jonetta specifically for that reason only and so far, she was doing her job well at Dental Dynasty.

Kaiya sucked her teeth, turned her back on Jonetta and continued to punch the keyboard to update the doctor's schedule. Jonetta snickered to herself as she dog-eared a page advertising perfume. "I paid my dues working at the post office. Now I'm just enjoying the good life. Smooth sailing from here on out, yes indeed. You have a long way to go to be in my league, little miss." Jonetta laughed because she knew that Kaiya was listening even though her back was turned.

"Bitter Betty! That's your new name," Kaiya mumbled, nodding her head.

"What did you say?" Jonetta jerked her head, turned her chair to face Kaiya and waited for a response.

Kaiya continued scheduling appointments, ignoring Jonetta. The phone rang, Jonetta ignored it as she contemplated throwing something at the back of Miss-28-inch-Unbeweavable's head.

"You need to get that. It's *your* job." Kaiya remarked over her shoulder.

Jonetta rolled her eyes, turned her attention to the phone and answered as pleasantly as she could.

"Oh, hey baby. How are you?" Dawn was on the other end.

"I'm going to stop by in a few to drop off some books for Dad."

"Books? What books?"

"He was eyeing some books at the house and had me ask Aunt Georgia if he could have them. They are pretty old books by Agatha Christie, H.G. Wells, Walter Mosely and Richard Wright. You know how Dad loves his books."

"Yeah, and that's what libraries are for!" Jonetta barked into the phone. "Some of those books just might be mine. He's got some nerve taking things from the house. All he's going to do is junk up our house after I've reorganized it so nicely."

Dawn laughed at her mother because she was always stingy with her things. Even if she had no use for it, she didn't want anyone having her belongings. "Mama, I'll be on my way."

"Dawn, where am I supposed to put all of that? I'm at work."

"I have it in a box, nice and neat. Besides, doesn't Dad pick you up from work every day?"

"That's beside the point, Dawn."

"Well, I thought I'd kill two birds with one stone by seeing my Mama and doing what my Dad asked."

Jonetta grunted.

"Mama, while I have you on the phone. Is anything up with Phyllis and Damien lately?"

"Anything like…what?"

"You know… marital issues."

"Nothing out of the ordinary. Fussing about the twins' schedule, Phyllis hooked on her cooking show, the central air just gave out, Damien's been working a lot, which she shouldn't complain about at all. That's about it. Why?"

"Because last week I saw Damien getting in his car with a chick. But not just any chick, Mama… It was Shante!"

"Shante? I know you don't mean Owen's Shante!" Jonetta raised her voice, causing the patients in the lobby to look in her direction.

"Yep! I thought it was odd, too. It could be nothing though. I'll see you in a few."

Jonetta hung up the phone, shook her head and glanced over her shoulder at Kaiya. She made a mental note to revisit that conversation with Dawn, Phyllis and Colette for that matter. *No more secrecy in the family. Isn't that what they said?*

"Taking personal calls on the job phone, huh?"

"Little girl, mind your business!" Jonetta hissed.

Dr. Bishon Franklyn appeared at the desk, just in time, flashing a huge smile, sporting his white lab coat. Jonetta noticed that he had a new haircut, low fade on the sides with his curly hair on top. It suited him, made him look much younger, especially since his face was clean shaven.

"Ladies, it's almost quitting time!" Dr. Franklyn pumped his fist in the air, laughing.

"I cannot wait to start the weekend," Jonetta replied.

He directed his attention to the patients sitting in the waiting area. He counted four, but only recognized two faces as his regular patients. "How many more patients do I have this afternoon?"

Kaiya perked up, smiled seductively, rattled off his schedule and flipped her hair over her shoulder. Jonetta shook her head at her pathetic flirting efforts. *He doesn't want you little girl!*

"Cool beans," he replied tapping his knuckles on the desk. "Send the next one back."

As he turned to leave, he saw Dawn was struggling to pry the door open with a box of books she carried. Dr. Franklyn rushed to open the door. "Welcome to Dental Dynasty!" He greeted Dawn. "Can I take this for you?" He took the box from Dawn's hands before she could respond.

"Thank you so much!" Dawn responded, smiling. "Hey, Mama!"

Jonetta got up from the desk, walked around to give Dawn a hug. "Hi, baby."

"Mama?" Dr. Franklyn inquired still holding the box. He looked back and forth between Dawn and Jonetta.

"Let me take this Doctor Franklyn," Jonetta responded. She took the box, placed it underneath her desk as she introduced Dawn. "Yes, this is my youngest daughter, Dawn."

"Nice to meet you, Dawn." Dr. Franklyn shook her hand, held on to it for a minute, and stared at her. Dawn towered over him in heels, but without them on they were probably the same height. She had her hair wilder than usual, wearing ripped up Daisy Duke shorts, and a black T-shirt that read: Soul Child. That description fit Dawn perfectly. She was definitely a free-spirit, soul child who lived on a whim.

"Likewise, Doctor Franklyn," Dawn smiled warmly.

"Yes, this is my superstar, model and actress." Jonetta glared at Kaiya and rolled her eyes. She all but stuck her tongue out at her. *Take that you little twerp!*

"Impressive and stunning." Dr. Franklyn remarked, giving Dawn a once over.

"I don't know about a superstar, but yes, I've modeled and made appearances on TV shows," Dawn said, trying to be modest. "I just recently moved back to Chicago from New York. I'm anxious to get back in front of the camera, though."

"Welcome back home. I hope doors open for you soon."

"Thank youuuu," Dawn cooed and Jonetta frowned her face at her daughter's extra dramatic behavior. "I have a few things lined up. Something will come through soon."

Kaiya cleared her throat causing a distraction from all the drooling over Dawn. "Well, I have patients waiting. Kaiya send my next victim back."

"Will do, Doctor Franklyn," Kaiya cooed. She motioned for an elderly white man to come to the desk.

Dawn stepped aside, leaned in towards Jonetta and whispered, "Mama, you never mentioned that Doctor Franklyn was so handsome."

"Why would I, Dawn?"

"Ummm… Hellooooo…" Dawn glided her hands up and down her body. "Because you have an eligible daughter who hasn't been on a date in over six months!"

"He's not your type, Dawn." Jonetta dismissed her antics.

"Let you tell it, Mama, nobody is my type!" Dawn noticed a stack of Dr. Franklyn's business cards in a holder on the counter. She distracted her mother by pointing to the box of books on the floor. "Are any of those books yours like you thought?" As soon as Jonetta wasn't looking she swiped a card and put it in her back pocket. Kaiya noticed, but didn't say anything.

"They don't appear to be, but I'll dig through them in a minute. I collected so many things over the years it's no telling."

"Okay. I gotta go, Mama. I have some calls to make for an audition."

Jonetta perked up at that news. "What's the audition for?"

"A new reality show in Atlanta."

Jonetta cocked her head to the side, confused. *Why would she audition for something in Atlanta when she just got back to Chicago?* Jonetta had been enjoying Dawn being home the past few months. The family had a Christmas party at Phyllis and Damien's new house and surprisingly they all survived it without any harsh words being exchanged. For New Year's Eve Dawn stopped by to celebrate with Jonetta and Norman before she headed out to celebrate at Navy Pier. Dawn was the only daughter who consistently kept in daily contact with Jonetta and she appreciated it. Now she wanted to move *again*?

"Leaving again so soon?"

"Mama…"

Jonetta waved her hand dismissing any excuse that Dawn was about to offer. "It's mind boggling to me that you would have to audition to be a *real* person on a reality show anyway. But how are you going to drop two bombs on me like this then leave?"

"Two bombs?"

"Shante and Damien? Now you're leaving for Atlanta." Jonetta held up two fingers, blinking her thick eyelashes.

"Oh, that part."

"Never mind, we'll talk later." Jonetta knew Kaiya was all ears and didn't want her in their family business.

Before Jonetta left for the evening, she stopped by Dr. Franklyn's office to say good-night like she usually did. She began to embrace him over the past few weeks like a son. There was no sense in trying to be secretive when she knew that Norman probably told his parents everything that they needed to know about her anyway. Norman never was one for keeping secrets, he was worse than a leaky faucet. Once he opened his mouth a waterfall of information flowed out of it.

"Ah, my favorite receptionist! Come on in!"

"Careful, don't let Kaiya hear you say that. She might choke on her spit and die."

They laughed together.

"She'll be alright." Dr. Franklyn changed the subject. "It was nice meeting your daughter today. I hope to see her again."

"I'm sure you will since we're becoming a closer family."

"Speaking of family, my mother would like to meet you. I talk about you so much that she wants to meet you. What do you think about having a lunch with my parents and Norman, of course?"

Jonetta was caught off guard. She was just getting used to living with Norman again, being in his world. It didn't bother Jonetta that she was the topic of discussion, but making new friends was not her cup of tea. It was too late in life to have new friendships, especially with women. Jonetta did not have many friends in her youth, she didn't trust women. They always seemed to have a hidden agenda, like getting close to her man or being extra inquisitive about her life when it was unnecessary. The only person she developed a true friendship with was Lorraine.

CHICAGO, IL
1968

Lorraine did not reveal too much about herself, but Jonetta did know that Lorraine's parents dropped her off at a Catholic orphanage on the north side when she was twelve and she had been struggling to survive. "Your aunts are saints." Lorraine had often said when she got in one of her "gratitude" moods. Betty Lou and Adelle had been looking for a replacement to handle Jonetta's duties around the house ever since she had broken her leg. One of their girls knew that Lorraine needed a place to live, but didn't want to be forced to do anything more than clean. That suited the aunts just fine because they only needed a new girl to clean and keep their lingerie pretty. Lorraine was more of a blessing to the aunts than Jonetta.

She was a creamy cocoa complexion with chestnut eyes that she kept to the ground most of the time thanks to self-esteem issues. Her hair was a reddish-brown that she kept braided underneath a head scarf. She combed Jonetta's hair twice a week. It calmed Jonetta and lifted her spirits that a complete stranger would take interest in her well-being. Lorraine believed in saying her prayers at least three times a day. She would come read the Bible to Jonetta once a day, but that gradually changed to once a week when Jonetta began to challenge the good book. Besides Jonetta was still angry with God for allowing her rape to take place which turned into the loss of her son. She was learning that life could be cruel, and it was making her bitter. Jonetta had nothing to be grateful for… so far.

"You should take this time to get closer to God, Jonetta. Tell Him how you feel. Just talk to Him like you talk to me." Lorraine would advise, but Jonetta turned a deaf ear. She did not have anything to say to Him at this point in her life. But that didn't stop Lorraine from encouraging her regularly to talk to God.

Over the past two months, Lorraine assisted Jonetta with

walking again. She walked with a limp temporarily due to the fractures she endured, but she did not let that discourage her from recovering. She wiggled her toes every day to keep constant movement. Jonetta managed to bend her knee with slight discomfort, but the pain was manageable without the drugs Dr. Scott provided. The drugs made her feel woozy and out of touch with her surroundings. She had stopped taking them unbeknownst to her aunts. Jonetta noticed that her mood began to lighten when she stopped taking the medication. She was not always as sad as she had been in the past, although her thoughts of her son would sometimes cause her to cry, but that was only natural, she reasoned.

One afternoon, when she was in a good mood, Jonetta made it to the top of the basement stairs while the aunts were out shopping. Lorraine sat her in the living room by the window.

"There now, enjoy the view," Lorraine said pulling back the drapes. Jonetta watched a Robin fly by the window and wished she was just as free to move about without a care in the world. She really wished to leave the house and venture into this bad city her aunts kept warning about. What was the purpose of moving up here just to be trapped? She felt trapped inside a place that fronted as a house from the outside but on the inside told another story.

The "visitors" entered the back door, which led to the kitchen, and went upstairs where Jonetta's room had been. The special visitors were allowed in the aunts' boudoir, but that was on very rare occasion. It was bad enough she was crippled for the past few months, but the aunts decided to keep Jonetta in the basement, permanently, which led to her increased depression.

"We need the rooms in the attic for our visitors," Adelle reasoned. "You have the whole basement to yourself, you should be glad about having some privacy." But Jonetta was not glad to be alone in such an empty, dark place. It was a prison with concrete floors and walls as far as she was concerned. Now, sitting upstairs in fresh air gazing out the window was refreshing until it was interrupted by Betty Lou's wicked voice.

"Ahhh, look who has made it out of the dungeon… with Lorraine's help I suppose." Betty Lou remarked as she took off her lace gloves. Jonetta's thoughts had taken her to a far off place that she had not heard Betty Lou enter the house. Jonetta couldn't disagree with that description of the basement. It certainly was a cold, dark dungeon down there. Her aunt knew that her living conditions were less than comfortable. It was a step above living in the sewer, but still she didn't care about Jonetta's comfort.

Jonetta nodded and cleared her throat, "Yes, Lorraine has been helpful."

"She certainly has been helpful, more than you ever were before you were incapacitated for these past months now." Jonetta shooed away her aunt's snide remark and instead made a mental note to look up that word in the huge dictionary that was on a wooden podium in the dining room. "Which brings me to another point; we must find some work for you to do around here. Some work in which you will be sure to excel. Since you've been accustomed to lying down on your back all these months I figured you should have enough practice in that position…"

"Wait a minute. What are you saying?" Jonetta held her hands up in protest. If she could have stood on her own, she would have.

"Don't interrupt me while I'm talking, young lady. It's rude!" Betty Lou glared at her with those green piercing eyes. "Don't think for one minute that you'll be able to lie around here and not earn your keep, missy. You're a grown woman now. You have choices. You can either go out there to find work on your own," she said pointing out the window. "Or you can make money in the comfort of our home using what God gave you."

Jonetta's mind raced as she let Betty Lou's words sink in. Was she serious? She wanted her to become a prostitute? *My mother didn't send me up here to sell my soul*, she thought. Her stomach turned at the thought of strange men becoming familiar with her body. That was very reason she was in Chicago now because Paul King decided to take something that didn't belong to him. Her body. Now she had to endure more strange men, their rough hands groping her tender breasts and trying to force themselves inside of her because she was not going to do it willingly. Her aunts always spoke of God, even read out of the Bible regularly instead of going to church, but they must not have known the God that Jonetta was raised to believe in because if they had she wouldn't be having this very conversation about selling her body.

"Sounds like you leave me no choice," Jonetta finally said sinking back into the chair.

Jonetta was trying her best to be more open to people, starting with her family, but it was extremely challenging. Now Dr. Franklyn wanted to incorporate his parents? *They are Norman's friends, not mine!* She didn't want to meet new people nor have new friends, but one way or another, it was bound to happen.

CHAPTER 6

Familiar Faces and Places

Summer day camp for the Aldridge kids was the answer to their prayers. When Norman offered to pay the fees Colette agreed to allow Cornell, Lydia and Ruthie to attend while she went to worship at church with Delilah. All the praying in the world wasn't going to change Owen nor miraculously finalize their divorce. Yet, Colette attended church faithfully six days a week. The mornings around the house were completely chaotic. Nobody could ever find their shoes, back pack nor have their lunches ready. Georgia would quietly organize their clothes and separate their shoes by the front door. She even labeled their lunch bags with their names and made sandwiches on occasion, but somehow every morning something was always misplaced. Between the yelling, fussing, whining and sometimes even tears from Ruthie, Dawn became accustomed to staying hostage in her bedroom until the coast was clear. She emerged from her bedroom the moment she heard the front door slam shut in the morning. After they were gone, Georgia would roam about the house aimlessly for hours, but Dawn didn't mind her company.

Today, Dawn couldn't waste much time because she had a flight to catch to Atlanta later in the afternoon. She was anxious to attend the casting call of *Real Mistresses of Atlanta,* but knew there would be steep competition. Seems like these days everyone wanted a chance to act a plum fool on national television. Dawn had to admit this reality show was not her cup of tea, but she needed to work and she needed some attention. She had dated a few married men in the fashion industry before, but probably nobody the producers would be interested in knowing about since they weren't athletes or rappers. Nevertheless, she had her bags packed, flight booked and a wardrobe that would slay the competition.

When she reached for her phone to check the time there was a Good Morning text message from Dr. Franklyn. She had reached out to him after they met, of course. Dawn was no fool. She knew immediately that man wanted her. The feeling was mutual, he was smart, successful, handsome and hungry for a woman like Dawn. They had been keeping it a secret from Jonetta, well everybody for that matter, but especially Jonetta.

Dr. Franklyn thought that she had an emergency when she called the office insisting to speak to him directly. She had to disguise her voice and make up a name, "Ms. Moore", just to get past her mother who answered all the incoming calls. *No, I don't have an emergency, silly man. I want you!* After all, the last time she had sex was with Vine during Thanksgiving weekend. She thought they were going to reconcile, figure out their living arrangements in Atlanta, and get back to normal until he had asked Dawn to marry him. It was then that Dawn realized that, after being together almost four years, Vine still didn't know who she was. She had no interest in becoming a wife. The expectations and duties that came along with that title all but made Dawn want to crawl out of her skin. The commitment to one man alone was an unbearable thought. *Where is the fun in that?* She declined his proposal. Vine left to begin his acting career in Atlanta. And Dawn had been left horny ever since.

The men in Chicago were not as appealing, nor as successful as the men she met in New York. She had yet come across a man that piqued her interest or got her juices flowing just from conversation. Self-gratification became a regular routine when she could get some privacy from her nephew and nieces. But now she had her sights set on Dr. Franklyn taking care of her needs. Lately, their conversations graduated from cordial introductions and background stories to desires and dreams becoming realities. Dawn couldn't wait until he arrived to drive her to the airport later. She had the perfect short sundress picked out with flat sandals so she wouldn't tower over him so much.

Dawn immediately fluffed her hair, sucked on her bottom lip, lied back down, slightly exposed her breasts with erect nipples and snapped a sexy selfie. Dawn sent the photo, smirking to herself. *That'll get his morning going!*

Dr. Franklyn sent a text back: *Sexy… "Ms. Moore"*

Dawn smirked and headed downstairs to make a cup of coffee. Georgia was in the kitchen cleaning up after Colette's kids, as usual.

"Morning. Do you mind?" Dawn asked Georgia as she pointed the remote towards the television mounted on the wall in the kitchen. She knew that Georgia liked the house quiet so her thoughts could roam freely, but Georgia shook her head no. "Thanks. I just need some background noise, that's all."

"This morning's noise wasn't enough for you?" Georgia chuckled as she washed the bowls in the sink.

"It's good to hear you laugh." Dawn smiled as she tried to recall the last time she heard her aunt laugh or show any joy since her beloved Fred died. Fred was her joy, her world and without him she was lost. Georgia grunted as she stared out the window. Her hands suddenly stopped washing, and she stood frozen. Dawn stood on the tips of her toes, peering out of the window to see what caught Georgia's attention, but saw nothing. *What the hell is she staring at?* Dawn cleared her throat and it jolted Georgia back to washing the bowls.

"These hectic mornings must bring back memories for you since you and my mom grew up with lots of siblings, too." Dawn tried to spark conversation while she made a fresh pot of coffee.

Georgia shook her head and sighed. "It was much worse than this, believe me."

"Why don't you or Mama ever talk about your brothers or even your mother for that matter?"

"What's there to say?" Georgia shrugged, placed a third bowl onto the dish rack and wiped her hands on her apron.

"Well, I mean… it's just odd that they are never discussed. I know my grandmother is dead, but what was she like? Do I look like her? God knows I don't look like anybody else in this family. Technically, your three brothers are our uncles, even though we've never met them. Are they alive? Where do they live?" Dawn opened the refrigerator and searched through the unorganized grocery items for coffee creamer. She reached on the second shelf towards the back where it hid behind a bag of grapes.

"Every man for himself, that's how we grew up. Nothing much else to tell," Georgia replied dryly as she took a seat at the kitchen table. She stared at her hands and continued, "Once we were all old enough to leave the old shack, we did. I kept track of them for a while, but life gets in the way and…"

"And… what? You just stop caring about your family? I couldn't imagine…"

"Just give it a rest, Dawn!" Georgia barked. "You just don't know when to quit!"

Dawn closed the refrigerator, holding the coffee creamer in her hand with her mouth wide open and eyes even wider. "Well, excuse me for giving a damn!"

Georgia closed her eyes, clenched her hands shut. "Sometimes when you turn over old rocks, worms crawl out."

Dawn shook her head as she poured the coffee creamer into a mug. *Here she goes with these wise old sayings!* "This family is so full of secrets that I can't even ask a question to you or my mother without feeling foolish or being warned about asking at all!" The coffee maker hissed and bubbled. Dawn snatched the pot and poured its hot contents into her mug. She replaced the pot angrily slamming it on the base. She glared at Georgia, hoping she would offer more than reprimands to put her curiosity at ease.

"The more you pick at a wound, the longer it takes to heal, Dawn." Georgia stood up to exit the kitchen.

"Okay. Forget about the family we'll never know. Forget that you were the one last Thanksgiving who demanded that my mother tell us the truth. Forget about the nightmares that I keep having. Let's just forget the whole thing!" Dawn replied sarcastically, flipping her hand in the air as if it didn't matter. *Have it your way, lady!*

Georgia stopped in her tracks, spun around and approached Dawn. "Your mother told you what happened to our Aunt Betty Lou! She didn't kill her! She died of old age… So don't you dare take that disrespectful tone with me! If you're still having nightmares, it's because you are not satisfied with the truth!"

"But now I have nightmares about a baby boy, you know, my brother who died here…in the basement." Dawn sipped her coffee, raising her eyebrows. "Except…he's not dead in my dreams. He's

49

very much alive. It just makes me wonder who else could actually be alive in this family."

"See? The more we tell you, the more your mind wanders which is why you should just leave well enough alone." Georgia shook her head.

"I can't help it!" Dawn whined. "I want to know more about my family. Is that a crime?"

"Unless you're writing a book about this family, you don't have a real reason for your questions. You're just spoiled and used to getting your way. Right now, you're a grown woman having a little girl's temper tantrum."

"That has nothing to do with it, Aunt Georgia." Dawn dismissed her comment about being spoiled. She grabbed her coffee mug, glided past her aunt and continued, "Seems to me like you and my mother have things to hide and I'm the only one who can see straight through it. I believe in my dreams and I know they are trying to tell me something. I've never been wrong."

□□□□□

Dawn settled into the leather passenger seat in Dr. Franklyn's mineral grey BMW M2 Coupe and exhaled. She was headed to try her hand at reality television, but didn't know what to expect. Her thoughts raced, considering how her parents would feel seeing her on such a show. She would just reassure them it was all an act. Her sisters would definitely offer their unwelcomed opinions about being known as a mistress just for money. Where her previous career choices allowed her family to be proud, this would certainly bring shame to them.

"You look beautiful, as usual." Bishon eyed Dawn in admiration.

"Thank you, Shon." He had asked her to call him Shon, so she did. But in her phone she had his name as Doc, as in "Doctor Feel Good" because she hoped that's exactly what he was about to become in her life. She was trying to follow his lead, but it was a slow take-off compared to other men she had been with before. Even her Instagram Direct Message was full of unsolicited dick pics. Men she didn't even know were ready pounce on her, but Bishon was taking his sweet time.

"I still don't understand why I had to pick you up from here." Bishon said as he eyed the laundry mat curiously.

"I had a few items that I needed to handle before I hopped on the plane, that's all." Dawn shrugged and plastered a smile on her face. *Don't ask me nothing else, please...I'm not a good liar.*

"I hope it's not because you're embarrassed about where you live or anything."

"What? No! Not at all." Dawn laughed nervously and placed her hand on his knee, rubbing it softly. Bishon eased the car from the parking lot and headed to the expressway.

"If you ever need a place to stay, Dawn, my place is free."

"What?" Dawn screeched. "Shon, where did that come from?"

"I know we barely know each other, but you don't seem happy living with your family. You keep having nightmares and it's probably because you're in that house. And we're sneaking around like little teenagers. I understand that you don't want your mother to find out, but I'm a grown man."

"Shon... It's a little sudden." Dawn couldn't believe her ears. It was a dream come true actually, she would've hopped at the chance had it been anybody else, but the circumstances were too risky. Her mother would have a complete fit knowing that Dawn was dating her boss behind her back. But then again, it was just a job that her mother really didn't need anyway.

"We can move as fast or slow as you want. I'm just offering you an open invitation to my condo. You'll have your own room, your own space. Tell you what, when I pick you up from the airport on Monday night, I'll take you to my condo so you can see for yourself."

Dawn shook her head in disbelief. *Where have you been all my life?* "Sure. Okay, but..."

"I just want you to be happy, Dawn." Bishon squeezed her knee. "Promise me you'll just think about it."

"Okay," Dawn nodded, caressing his hand. "I'll think about it." *Damn! Why did you have to hire my Mama?*

They rode in silence the rest of the way to the airport. Bishon played his music through Blue Tooth. They were all R & B love songs. Dawn chuckled to herself. *We haven't even had sex yet! He's gonna be whipped!*

"Did you want to grab something to eat before you board the plane?" Bishon asked breaking the thick dead air lingering between them.

Dawn shook her head no and continued to stare out of the window at nothing in particular.

"Dawn, I hope that I didn't make you uncomfortable. I'm sorry if I did."

"There's no need to apologize." Dawn broke her silence. "I've never met anybody like you, Shon. My only concern is for my parents. Especially my mother. She hates to be deceived, although she has lived the majority of her life deceiving us!"

"What do you mean?"

Dawn shook her head and waved him off. "Long story, it doesn't matter. All I'm saying is, I appreciate the offer. Just give me some time."

"Of course," Bishon replied as he raised her hand to kiss it. "I understand about your mom. She does seem like a pistol!"

They shared a laugh. Dawn nodded in confirmation.

"I wish that I had a connection with my real mom." Bishon sighed.

Dawn had previously dodged this conversation a week ago when they were sharing stories about their childhood. Now certainly was not the time to bring it up again either. She wanted to give him something to think about before she boarded the plane, but this conversation would blow that chance.

"I wonder if she's feisty like your mom or if she's timid." Bishon continued as if he were talking to himself. "I've been thinking about her a lot lately, Dawn."

Dawn squeezed his hand. *He's getting too heavy with this conversation.* "Maybe you should just start your search. Seems like you won't be satisfied until you find your birth mom anyway."

"Maybe I will." Bishon replied, smiling. "You're right, Dawn. I should at least try because once my curiosity gets out of control it'll drive me crazy. I always try to satisfy my curiosity, just like I did with you."

"Oh, yeah?" Dawn cooed. *Now you're talking.* "Is your curiosity fulfilled yet?"

Bishon laughed, glanced at Dawn and place his hand on her thigh. "Not yet, but it will be soon. Trust me on that one."

Dawn liked the sound of that, leaned back in her seat and kept his hand right on her thigh.

When they arrived at Midway airport, Bishon guided the car into the Drop-Off lane. The line was long as usual. Dawn glanced at the time on the dashboard. She had two hours before her flight took off to Atlanta. *I'm in no rush.*

"I hate rushed good-byes." Dawn pouted as she stared out of the window watching people hop from their cars, grab their luggage, offer quick hugs and dash off into the glass sliding doors. She wanted a chance to talk to Bishon more, have a real kiss, and maybe even get a feel of what else he had to offer. *I hope he is offering a complete package.* Had they known each other longer, she would've made sure this morning that they were both satisfied before she hopped on a plane, and maybe even once more at the airport.

"I have a little time before my flight. Do you mind parking in the garage?"

Bishon quickly guided the car out of the drop-off line. "Not a problem at all."

"I want to chat with you a little longer. It'll help get rid of my jitters, too." Dawn squeezed his hand.

"You're nervous?" Bishon asked surprised. Dawn had always seemed so confident and sure of her next move. He didn't think being nervous about anything seemed part of her character.

"Yeah, I'm headed to the lion's den, Shon. Women can be very vicious, especially in this business. When they have their sights set on achieving a goal they won't let anything stop them."

Bishon nodded as he steered the car slowly to the lower level parking garage. "You'll do fine. But, honestly, part of me hopes you don't get the role. I want you right here in Chicago with me, not in Atlanta as somebody's mistress."

Dawn laughed. It did seem kind of ridiculous since he put it that way. "Is that what your offer was about? You want me all to yourself, huh?"

Bishon smirked and shrugged.

"Well, we see what happens. You'll be the first to know."

"Good. I can't wait to hear all about it." Bishon squeezed her hand. He found a parking spot between two vans, swooped in and turned the music down.

"I love talking to you, Shon." Dawn took off her seat belt and turned to face him. "You make me feel like I can tell you anything. I didn't even tell my mother which reality show I was auditioning for because she would have a stroke! But with you... I feel like there is no judgement." Dawn placed her hand on the side of his smooth face.

Bishon did the same to her face and replied, "No judgement here. You deserve the best, Dawn. I want to give you everything that you want. You're so sweet." He leaned in to kiss her soft lips, and Dawn allowed him. She opened her mouth slightly to welcome his tongue. She glided her hand up his leg until she felt what she had been dying to know. *Oh, thank God he's big and thick.* She stroked his erection through his jeans, and was tempted to swallow him whole but didn't have enough time.

Dawn broke their embrace, leaned back in her seat, opened her legs, pulled her dress up towards her hips, exposing her emerald green thongs, and slid her fingers up and down between her legs. She leaned over towards Bishon and replied, "I taste even sweeter." She put her finger in his mouth so he could get a taste of her sweetness. He sucked on her finger hungrily as he glided his hand up her thigh. Dawn moaned as he massaged her clitoris. After a few minutes of pleasure, she grabbed his hand, and stopped him from making her climax. *His seat should be nice and wet though.*

"I have a flight to catch."

◻◻◻◻◻

Dawn rolled her suitcase by the dresser, walked to the window and immediately opened the curtains allowing sunlight to rush into the small hotel room. It wasn't the Sheraton Hotel, but it was the best her Dad's money could buy. When she told him of the opportunity to audition, he gave her money, made her promise not to tell Jonetta nor her sisters and wished her well with a kiss on the forehead. Dawn was his baby girl, and there wasn't much that he wouldn't do for her. So there she was back in Atlanta. The last time Dawn was there it was for a fashion show almost seven years ago. Now the audition for a new reality show landed her feet back on the streets of Atlanta.

I need to freshen up and hit these streets. She walked towards the bathroom to see what it had to offer. As she checked behind the shower curtain to make sure the tub was clean her phone chimed. Just then it occurred to her that she hadn't let anyone know that she landed safely. *It's probably Mama.* She smiled when she saw it was a text from Shon.

Shon: Did you make it safely?

Dawn: Yes, just got to my hotel room.

Shon: How are the accommodations?

Dawn: It'll do for a two-day stay.

Shon: Need me to upgrade you?

Dawn: Aren't you sweet? I'll be fine, but thanks.

I might as well get this over with. Dawn sighed and dialed her mother's number hesitantly. She knew exactly how this conversation was about to go.

"Since when do you just hop on a plane without saying good-bye?" Jonetta barked into the phone.

Dawn cringed. "I'm sorry, Mama. I thought for sure Dad would let you know."

"He did, but that's beside the point!" Jonetta fumed. "Who gave you a ride to the airport?"

"A friend."

"Does this friend have a name?"

"Mama, I need to shower and get ready…"

"Fine. Have your little secrets. Good luck on this audition. What did you say the name of the new show was again?"

"I didn't." Dawn laughed at her mother trying to be slick by getting the name of the show.

"See you when you get back, missy."

Dawn looked at her phone, the call ended. "Well, I love you too, Mama!"

She placed the phone on the charger, turned on her Apple Music play list, stripped her clothes off, pinned her hair up and ran the shower. She looked at her sun kissed, copper-toned, naked body in the mirror and smiled. She decided to unpin her hair, allowing it to fall wildly past her shoulders and posed like a Goddess. *Damn! I'm gorgeous!* When she entered the shower the hot water saturated her scalp and it felt like all of her pores opened up at the same time. She used her new mint shampoo, followed up with a mint conditioner and her scalp tingled letting her know that it was doing its job.

Just as she was about to emerge from the shower, "Cranes in the Sky", by Solange came blaring through her phone. For some reason this song made her feel sexy, euphoric and sad all at the same damn time. She decided to turn the water to a lukewarm temperature and stay in the shower until the song came to an end. The water was rushing out of the shower head like a waterfall and she allowed it to rush down her body as she sang to the top of her lungs. The lyrics conjured emotions that she felt after Vine left for Atlanta. Dawn could relate to trying to push the pain away by any means necessary, it was a song of raw feelings for women in her generation. Even though she was certain that marriage was not for her and that it was best that they parted ways if that's what he really wanted, she still cried for a day after he left.

Not much for tears, Dawn turned to her reliable source of drugs which was hard to come by in Chicago since she didn't have any connections anymore. But once she had it in her possession, she found solace in a random motel room, turned off her iPhone and smoked a primo to her delight in peace. Realizing that since she was back in Chicago she just couldn't go randomly missing, otherwise her family would worry and call the police. So she had only stayed at the hotel for a day. When she turned her phone on there were nine voicemail messages and several text messages from her mother and sisters. Georgia knew that Dawn just needed time alone to grieve a love lost so she kept quiet about her disappearance. Once she was back in the house Georgia just gave her a hug, no questions asked.

It took almost two weeks for Dawn to bounce back to her normally bubbly self. Now Solange was invoking those grieving feelings again. *I hope I don't run into Vine down here. God only knows what emotions will fall out of my mouth.* She reached for more conditioner, lathered it through her hair and turned the water off.

"Time to switch this sad vibe!" She dried off with the hotel towel and changed the music list to Fetty Wap. With her hair wrapped in a towel she plopped on the queen-sized bed, gently rubbed on Shea Butter and Coconut Oil, a concoction she made for her skin. People always admired her skin tone and those lucky enough to touch her were in awe of how soft her skin was, but she credited that to her natural concoctions that she had been using since high school. She smiled at her reflection in the mirror when she walked past. Although she was aging out of her modeling era, she still had the goods and she knew it. Now it was time for the other goods she always carried were waiting on her in the toiletry bag. Two joints and a six ounce of Merlot.

Dawn called the front desk to request a courtesy wake-up call at seven o'clock so she would have enough time to wrestle with her hair and makeup. She knew from her modeling go-sees that a natural look for makeup was probably best, but considering the nature of the reality show she was going to step it up a bit. Her nails were short, painted a nude color just like she had been conditioned to wear them as a model all of these years. Dawn sucked her teeth, "I should've gotten some tips and a metallic polish. Soon as I get home we are getting an upgrade." She said to her hands as she pulled out her lighter and lit the tip of her joint, took a long drag and held it in as long as she could. When she exhaled, she fell back on the bed and stretched out all of her limbs. The spaciousness put a smile on her face because her bed in Georgia's house was only a full-sized bed. *I have to get my own place soon.* She took two swigs of the Merlot, closed her eyes, took another puff and allowed the melodic sounds of Galimatias to whisk her thoughts away. Immediately, Dawn felt lighter, relaxed, too relaxed. She remembered that she wanted to hit the streets, but she couldn't move. After another puff, the joint was losing its blaze so she tapped it out, placed it on the night stand and lied back down allowing "Ocean Floor Kisses" to drift her thoughts away.

In the morning when the front desk rang her room, Dawn shot straight up from her sleep. She wiped her eyes repeatedly, confused at first about where she was, then answered the phone. "Hello?" She scowled as soon as she heard the corny song playing as her wake up call. Slamming the phone back into the cradle she grabbed her phone to check the time. Yep, it was seven o'clock. Dawn went to grab her hair in frustration only to feel the towel still wrapped around her hair. "Ughhhh! It's still damp!" She scrambled to prepare herself for the day ahead. By the time she hopped in the cab waiting for her outside, she was flawless. With wing-tipped eyes, bronzed cheekbones and vibrant Heroine lips compliments of

MAC, Dawn felt confident and beautiful. Although her hair wasn't as poofy as she wanted it, the way the Atlanta humidity was set up, she let the back windows down and allowed it to work its magic on her curls.

When Dawn arrived to the location, it was a mad house. Not exactly what she was expecting, but she entered the lion's den anyway. The women were scantily dressed, looking desperate for a spot in the lime light. *I'm overdressed!* Dawn glanced down at her turquoise bodycon bandage dress and shrugged. The term mistress to her meant a dime-piece on the side, not a damn slut! Either these tricks got the wrong memo or Dawn was in over her head. She was about to find out.

The average looking white lady at the front desk checking the contestants wasn't friendly at all. Clearly, she was just doing her job.

"Name?" She said looking at a sheet of paper.

"Dawn Mi..."

"First name only. Dawn. Okay, got that."

"Age?"

"I'm thirty."

She looked up, eyed Dawn up and down and replied, "Twenty-six."

Dawn shrugged. "Okay."

She wrote that number next to her name and handed her plastic number card. "Your number is ninety-four. Have a seat over there." She pointed with her ink pen to a corner of the room where there were a group of young ladies sitting anxiously, some of them became better acquainted with nervous chatter. *Wow! This is hoodrat heaven!* Dawn was disgusted already, but decided to stick around since she had come this far. She stuffed the number card inside of her clutch purse, pulled out her iPhone, scrolled and chuckled at a few memes.

"Hey girlfriend!" A familiar voice said.

"Gideon? What the hell are you doing here?" Dawn hugged her old acquaintance, a hairstylist for a few fashion shows.

"Honey, this is an open casting call, and I'm here for it!" He laughed dramatically. "Come sit with me over here, girl." He grabbed Dawn's hand, leading her to a chair on the opposite side of the room.

"So, you're a 'mistress'?" Dawn asked anxious to hear his response.

"Well, girlfriend, you know that I don't kiss and tell, but..." he laughed wickedly. "I have been seeing a ball player for the past eight years."

"What type of ball player?"

"The NBA." Gideon shot her a look.

"Do tell!" Dawn leaned in closer.

"All I'm gonna say is, it would be a wonderful thing if his wife wasn't so sexually close-minded. But you know how you black women are about black gay men! Y'all would rather have us dead than gay!"

"An NBA player with a black wife? Wow! That surely narrows it down because there aren't many with a Queen on their arm!"

"So you were paying attention, huh?" Gideon slapped her knee. "If she would loosen up a bit, I wouldn't have to be his mistress, you know? We could be one big happy family. I'm already his secondary barber when he's on the road, but I digress."

"Does he know you're here?" Dawn's eyes grew wider.

"Chile, I told him already and this fool is ready to make an appearance as long as his face is blurred."

Dawn's mouth dropped open at that news.

Gideon howled laughing. He used his index finger to lift her chin. "Honey, the last thing you wanna do in Atlanta is give people the wrong impression about what's going in and out your mouth."

Dawn giggled, and nudged him in his rib. "Well, I'll say you have all the competition beat today."

"I don't have a competitive bone in my body. I am who I am." Gideon flipped his imaginary hair in the wind dramatically. "Who are you here to represent, missy?"

"Oh, nobody in particular. Nobody worth mentioning either."

"One of those old farts in the fashion industry, huh?"

Dawn grinned, embarrassed.

"We have to think of somebody else for you, honey. Like real quick, chile!" Gideon snapped his long fingers loudly.

Dawn laughed at his dramatic antics. "You might be right!"

"Look at this mess right here!" Gideon said loudly pointing at a young lady who just walked into the room wearing clear stripper heels, a white tube top that was barely covering her breasts and a red mini skirt that would show all of her goodies the moment she bent over.

"Shhhh!" Dawn nudged him again.

"I ain't worried about none of these hoes today!" Gideon rolled his eyes hard.

"And I'm not trying to fight none of them either!" Dawn said through clenched teeth.

"I got yo' back, girlfriend. Don't forget, I'm still a man." Gideon rolled his eyes and snarled at the competition. "I wish a bitch would try me!"

Before Dawn could respond the receptionist called out numbers 40 through 50 and several ladies formed in a line to enter another room. Gideon grabbed his back pack, stood and slung it over his shoulder.

"That's my cue," he announced. "It was good seeing you, Miss Dawn. I know I'll see you soon doing something fabulous!"

"Awwww... you're giving me goosebumps, Gideon." Dawn stood to hug him. "It was good seeing you."

Dawn went back to scrolling through her iPhone, growing bored with her timeline, she placed cordless buds in her ears to escape to some music. Dreezy and T-Pain were speaking to her soul, but then a cat fight ensued and security came to haul away two women still clawing at each other. *Oh, hell no! I'm too classy for this shit!* She got up quickly to leave.

"Excuse me! Are you leaving?"

Dawn looked at the receptionist and put on her shades. "What does it look like?"

"I'll need your number card back."

Dawn opened her clutch to retrieve the number card and tossed it on the desk.

My nerves are bad! Wish I had my damn joint right now! Instead she headed to the nearest coffee house that she saw en route to the audition on Peachtree Street. She ordered her favorite Passion tea cold, headed out the door to call for a cab when she heard her name called out.

"Dawn?" Someone called out again. It was a man's voice, familiar too. Yet Dawn was hesitant to turn around because with her history of sketchy past acquaintances, it could be anybody in Black Mecca. As she casually turned around to see who it was, she stopped in her tracks. Her mouth dropped open in disbelief. "Hi, Vine!" *Damn! I was hoping that I wouldn't run into your ass!*

Vine fidgeted as he managed not to spill the hot contents in his cup on himself and her as he offered a hug. "I thought that was you!"

"The one and only. Fancy meeting you at a coffee house, huh? Do you work here?" Dawn asked, smiling and it quickly faded when she saw a statuesque imitation version of herself exit the coffee house to stand next to Vine and a grab hold of his arm affectionately.

"No, I don't work here," he chuckled nervously. "I'm still with Tyler Perry Studios. What are you doing down here?" Vine continued the conversation, ignoring his companion.

"I had an audition for a new reality show." Dawn decided to follow suit and ignore this thing latching onto him, too.

"A casting call?" Vine questioned.

"Mmmm…hmmm…" Dawn replied as she pushed her sunglasses to the top of her forehead and gave Vine's companion a once over. They were almost standing eye-to-eye, both in stilettos, but Dawn's were more vibrant with tropical colors. Vine certainly had a type because they were almost the same complexion, save for the tan Dawn recently got from jogging on the lakefront and the fact that everything about Dawn was real. They also had the same taste in fashion because Dawn would've certainly rocked that sundress with open-toe stilettos, too. But unlike Vine's new interest, Dawn's mane was curly and natural, which she wore full on purpose to stand out from the competition. The humidity in Atlanta had done its job by increasing the size of her curls giving Dawn a Native-Caribbean appearance. *Atlanta must have been the capitol for hair weaves because everybody and they Mamas got one!* This one had a bone straight weave flowing for days with no end in sight and had the nerve to be swinging it like it was real. This thing had a face that was beat to the Gods, with false lashes on that were so long they could fan a fly away. *Everyone down here is fabulous and full of shit!*

"Oh, which one?" Vine inquired.

"Please don't tell me it's the Housewives of Atlanta? Chile, you don't want that mess in your life, trust me!"

Vine cleared his throat. "My bad… ummm… Dawn… ummm… this is Quinn."

"Ohhhh! This is the infamous Dawn?" Quinn flashed a devilish smile. "Nice to finally meet you in the flesh, honey!"

"Whatever that's supposed to mean," Dawn scoffed and rolled her eyes so hard that she almost strained a muscle. She took a sip of her iced tea as she tried to act unbothered.

"Oh, no, no, no! It's all good Miss Dawn!" Quinn laughed theatrically, placed a hand on a barely-there-chest, and tossed the weave around. "Vine couldn't stop talking about you when he first arrived here in The A. But I think that I've cured him now." Quinn placed a perfectly polished index finger on Vine's chin, turned his head and leaned in to plant a juicy, dramatic kiss on his lips.

Dawn scoffed, shifted her weight from the left hip to the right in total disgust. She visualized slapping the lip gloss right off of both of them. Instead, she narrowed her eyes at Vine, and shot a disapproving look.

"I see you've moved on in a drastic way." Dawn raised an eyebrow while she took another sip of her tea. The ice was beginning to melt rapidly in the heat while their conversation was heating up too. Vine lowered his eyes to the ground; he could sense that Dawn was on the verge of making a scene in public. But being the weak man that he always was he had nothing to say. In that moment Dawn tried to remember why she had been so in love with him in the first place. He was a spineless coward, easily manipulated by anyone who could get his nose wide open to try something new. *What a punk!*

"Well, it was nice to finally meet you, Miss Dawn. Hope you have a quick flight back to Chicago. Vine and I were headed…"

Dawn walked away before Quinn could even finish the sentence. She placed her shades on, tossed her tea in the street recycle bin and disappeared around the corner.

REBEKAH S. COLE

CHAPTER 7

Girl's Night Gone

Phyllis was actually glad that Dawn suggested they have a girl's night at her house when she got back into town. Although she was not sold on the reason behind it. Still, the week hadn't been so great since Damien was barely speaking to Phyllis. He was still in his feelings about her choosing to record on Facebook rather than indulge him with some long overdue sex. Although she had told her viewers last Friday that they would return to make the cod with lemon butter sauce, it never happened. Ever since then she had been trying to make it up to him during the week, but he wasn't biting at what she was fishing for. Damien kept his overtime routine all week instead of coming home on time. He was avoiding her. Phyllis knew this routine of his as well. He only parted his lips to have a conversation with her when necessary and he was extra nice to the twins.

It didn't get underneath her skin like it used to do, but this silent treatment routine certainly was getting old. By the time Friday rolled around Phyllis half-heartedly streamed live on Facebook while making sautéed asparagus, pan-seared salmon, and garlic couscous. But since her sisters were coming by later she figured that she would make enough for them as well. Lots of viewers were asking about the couscous, what type of grain it was, where she bought it and how it paired with the salmon.

"Listen up, you Food Fanatics, I see your questions pouring in, so I'll tell you this… You have to broaden your choices of grain." She told them matter-of-factly as she looked into the camera. "You can't eat white rice or white potatoes for the rest of your lives!

Upgrade your life by trying something new! I would've prepared quinoa, but one of my sisters don't like it, so I chose couscous instead. Her ass better eat it too!" She laughed but was serious. "Did you know that you can eat couscous and quinoa cold or hot? Toss it in a salad, or make a salad out of it by adding cucumbers, tomatoes, onions, red bell peppers, you know…make it look pretty! These grains get you full quickly, too! So that's your assignment for next week, Food Fanatics! Try a new grain and let me know about it. Send me a picture in my D.M., tell me how you and the family liked it! Okay?" She winked in the camera.

Phyllis enjoyed being on camera and having full blown conversations with the viewers on Facebook Live. It surely beat sitting in the house all day, watching television, doing chores, and preparing for the next week. A boring routine sometimes led to her over indulging in shots of vodka here or there. Streaming live kept her mind and hands busy. Some of her viewers had even suggested sending videos in to various cooking shows or local daytime television shows because she really knew how to connect with the audience and put a plate a food on display like chefs did in restaurants.

Earlier in the week she purchased Port wine and Sauvignon Blanc so her sisters could choose red or white wine with the dinner. Usually, a white wine was paired with fish, but whatever they chose, her taste buds were going to choose the Port wine since the alcohol percentage was higher. The clock on the kitchen wall indicated it was time to get the twins ready. Aunt Georgia had agreed to keep the twins for a sleep over with their cousins while she and her sisters had a girls' night. Phyllis was certain that Dawn did most of the coaxing because ever since Fred passed away Georgia seemed to be emotionally absent. Whichever way it went down Phyllis was certainly glad it did because she needed a break from Sabrina and Serena.

"Girls! Ready or not, you gotta get ready to go!" Phyllis called up the stairs. She waited at the bottom landing until she heard little feet scurrying around. A smile grew across her face knowing that they were just as excited as she was for this evening.

"Mommy, can I ride in the front seat?" Serena asked descending down the staircase, eyes wide and hopeful.

"I hate to break it to you, kiddo, but you have another six years before you can ride shotgun!" Phyllis twirled one of her ponytails as she walked past with her lip poked out. "You tried it though, huh?"

Serena shrugged as she headed to the closet to choose a pair of sandals. As soon as she settled on the strappy glitter, silver ones Sabrina snatched the shoe from her hand.

"I'm wearing those today!" Sabrina insisted.

"Hey! Give it back now!" Serena pushed her sister, knocking her off balance.

"Girls! I'm not going to tolerate..." Before Phyllis could finish her sentence Sabrina pushed her sister even harder, but Serena stood her ground. Phyllis snatched them both by their arms, almost lifting them off the ground. "Y'all must want me to get the belt!"

Their chests were heaving, ready for battle staring each other down.

"I'm sorry, mommy. Don't get the belt." Sabrina replied, lowering her eyes.

"Serena! You don't snatch things from anyone, ever! Do you understand me?"

She nodded, but still had her eyes fixed on Sabrina. Phyllis let Sabrina's arm go and bent down at eye level to look Serena dead in her eyes.

"I said, do you understand me, little girl?"

She sniffed and exhaled. "Yes, mommy."

"Now apologize to your sister and find another pair of shoes! The nerve..." Phyllis was interrupted by the doorbell. "Saved by the bell."

Phyllis peered through the door scope and was surprised.

"Mama! What are you doing here?" Phyllis asked opening the door.

"Well, hello to you too, Miss Phyllis!"

"Hey, Mama, sorry. Come in." Phyllis opened the door wider and stepped aside.

"Grandma!" The twins said in unison as they ran to give her a hug.

"Grandma is here to whisk you away to Aunt Georgia's and I'm going to be there with you tonight. Does that sound good?"

The twins nodded in an identical fashion. "Can we have pizza?" Sabrina asked.

"We can have anything we like!" Jonetta replied, pinching her cheek. "Actually, I was thinking about getting Italian Fiesta Pizza for all of us."

"Girls, go get your sleeping bags." Phyllis instructed them as she closed the front door. "So you're helping Aunt Georgia with the kids tonight?"

"Phyllis, you know good and well that Georgia isn't in the right frame of mind to watch six kids! I don't know whose hair brain idea that was so when I heard about it I offered my assistance as their *grandmother*, of course!" Jonetta snarled. "Why didn't you and Colette just ask me to watch all of the kids at my house?"

"Your house?" Phyllis teased half-heartedly. *Technically, that's my Dad's house.*

"Whatever, Phyllis." Jonetta scoffed.

"Aunt Georgia has been doing better lately. Dawn said she comes out of her room more and helps Colette with the kids in the morning."

"Like I said, I'm their grandmother." Jonetta raised an eyebrow, which usually meant she dared anyone to continue to debate her.

The twins reappeared with their backpacks on and smiles spread across their faces.

"We're ready!" The twins announced in unison.

"Okay, now listen, girls," Phyllis began bending down again to meet them at eye level. "Be on your best behavior. No fighting. Be kind to your cousins. No teaming up on each other. Share your things with Lydia and Ruthie or don't take them at all. Do you understand?"

"Yes, mommy." They replied together.

"Okay, give me kisses." Phyllis hugged them as they planted kisses on her cheeks. "Thanks for coming to get them, Mama."

"Dawn and Colette should be here shortly. Georgia is letting Colette drive her car. I certainly hope she returns it in one piece because I know you all will be drinking tonight. As a matter of fact, you girls be on *your* best behavior, no teaming up and no fighting!" Jonetta wagged her finger at Phyllis and cracked a smile.

"Scouts honor, mommy." Phyllis replied, crossing her fingers behind her back just like she used to when she was a kid.

"Mmmm... hmmm..." Jonetta eyed her up and down. "Come on girls, the castle is waiting on us."

Phyllis stood in the doorway until they pulled off, waving good-bye.

"Whew!" Phyllis fanned herself as she walked to the kitchen. Since she was done cooking for the evening, she let the sheet down separating the rooms and a gush of cool air whipped past her as if was waiting to break free. "Come on air, circulate! Circulate!"

A plate for Damien was waiting for him in the microwave oven whenever he got home from playing video games with his friends. He already knew the deal the moment Phyllis told him that her sisters were coming on Friday. It was fine by her anyway because they both needed space from each other. Before she could allow her mind to wander about their marriage lately, the doorbell rang.

"Hey big sis!" Dawn planted a kiss on her cheek and waltzed inside.

"Hi, Phyllis." Colette greeted her dryly.

I'm not going to let you get underneath my skin tonight, girl! "Come on in. Hope y'all are hungry. I've made salmon, asparagus, and..."

"We know," Colette interrupted. "I saw it on Facebook and I let Dawn know already."

"You know I'm all about that seafood life, so let's get to it because I'm hungry!"

Phyllis and Colette laughed.

"You're always hungry, Dawn! You're eating us out of house and home at Aunt Georgia's." Colette remarked. "Always the tiniest, but always the hungriest."

"Don't you get the Link card?" Phyllis asked.

"And? What's your point?" Colette snapped back.

"Like I said... I'm hungry!" Dawn widened her eyes at Phyllis, pleading her not to start being petty tonight.

"Okay, cool. Well, we can sit wherever you like." Phyllis gestured towards the dining room and living room.

"The dining room will work. Let's eat, drink and be merry!" Dawn suggested and flashed a smile across her face.

"Yeah, you must fill us in on Atlanta." Phyllis said, reaching for plates from the kitchen cabinet. "Start talking. I'm listening."

"Well, the audition didn't go so well."

Thank God! "Sorry to hear that, sis."

"No, you're not!" Dawn replied, laughing. "It's all good though. After I sat there, looked at the so-called competition... I was outta there! I'm way too good for that."

"You mean after the cat-fight broke out." Colette said intentionally to let Phyllis know that she already had the scoop on what happened in Atlanta.

Grow up, already! Phyllis let that comment slide for the sake of having a good evening. "I agree, Dawn. You are much better than being showcased as a mistress. Something will come your way that's meant for you." She handed Dawn some silverware, then proceeded to gather the food from the oven. "So does that mean we don't need to have this so-called anniversary party for our parents now?"

"I'll get the napkins and drinks." Colette offered. "Yes, I think we should still celebrate them. Why not?"

I hope that was rhetorical. Phyllis ignored her question and continued, "I have white and red wine, juice, flavored water, plain water..."

"I'll take the white wine!" Dawn yelled from the dining room. "I agree, we should still celebrate our parents, even though I'm not moving any time soon."

Colette grabbed the bottle of Sauvignon Blanc from the refrigerator and joined her sisters in the dining room. "So you only wanted to plan a party for them because you thought that you were going to move to Atlanta?" she asked, looking confused.

"Yes, girl. You should know by now that our baby sister is selfish!" Phyllis teased.

Colette shook her head. "Well, whatever we decide, it cannot be a surprise. You know Mama doesn't like surprises."

They all agreed.

After they were all settled at the table Colette led them in prayer and they got through dinner without any snide remarks or harsh words. It probably had a lot to do with Phyllis skipping out on having a glass of Port wine with dinner. Since its alcohol content was so high, she knew that it was best to only have one glass tonight. Surprisingly, Colette indulged in wine right along with Dawn. *Since when does attending church loosen you up?* Phyllis didn't think too much about it. She was just glad that her sisters were there and enjoying themselves.

"Come on, y'all. We're going to head to the living room to chill-lax and chit-chat." Phyllis announced as she cleared her plate from the table.

"Nobody says that anymore." Dawn teased as she followed Phyllis to the kitchen. "You can just say 'chill', Phyllis."

"Girl, don't try to school me like I'm old!" Phyllis laughed.

"I was still eating," Colette remarked as she appeared in the kitchen with her plate in hand.

"You were picking over your couscous like you were sifting through a pile of shit for a diamond." Phyllis said sharply, shaking her head. "You don't have to finish it if you don't like it. I promise not to put you on punishment like Mama used to do us."

"I was eating it!" Colette insisted. "I know that I'm the sister you were talking about in your little Facebook food segment today. So, I was eating the couscous!"

"No, you weren't." Dawn replied. "Just toss it. We're about to have some girl talk in the living room, so grab yo' glass and bring yo' ass." Dawn pranced to the living room, plopped down on the sofa and whipped out her iPhone to catch up on her timeline.

"Oh, so you tune into my show, huh?"

"It's not a 'show', Phyllis. You're just recording live on Facebook like everyone else does. It's nothing special." Colette replied, frowning her face.

Phyllis scoffed. "It's special enough for almost a thousand viewers to tune in every week. Don't be a hater all of your life." She winked at her sister, grabbed the bottle of Port wine, whisked past Colette who was still standing there holding her plate, and sat on the sofa across from Dawn.

"Hey, I thought you were on the wagon since last Thanksgiving?" Dawn teased Phyllis, but at the same time was curious.

"It's just wine for crying out loud!" Phyllis flipped her hand, dismissing the inquiry. "I am not an alcoholic for Christ's sake! Besides, you all act like I was the one with the addiction! That was Damien, remember?"

"Okay, your poison, your life." Dawn shrugged as she settled on the sofa with her empty wine glass in hand.

"I know you aren't judging, Miss au natural weed head!"

"Not at all," Dawn laughed, raising her hand in defense. "I'm just saying, smoking a natural herb does not destroy your life, nor your liver."

"Lacing it with cocaine certainly will though." Phyllis countered and raised her eyebrows.

"I don't do that anymore!" Dawn replied sticking her tongue out.

"Can somebody just pour the wine?" Colette whined as she emerged from the kitchen, finally joining them in the living room.

"My pleasure." Phyllis unscrewed the cap on the bottle of Port wine, filled her wine glass and clinked glasses with Colette. Dawn leaned forward with her empty wine glass and Phyllis poured her an ounce of wine. "That's all for you, little sis."

"Yeah, right! Gimme that bottle!" Dawn laughed, snatched the bottle from Phyllis and poured a generous amount into her wine glass.

"You really shouldn't mix light and dark." Phyllis warned them.

"I thought that only applied to hard liquor," Colette said, looking at Dawn to confirm, but she only shrugged her shoulders.

Phyllis scoffed and mumbled, "Don't say I didn't warn you."

"Well, I want to taste this one. Maybe we can use it for communion at church."

Dawn laughed, almost choking on her wine. Phyllis raised her eyebrows as Colette took her first sip, waiting for her response.

"Or ... not...Wow!" Colette blinked her eyes repeatedly. "That's pretty potent! The whole church will be drunk."

They all laughed at her revelation on the wine. Phyllis knocked back her first glass of Port wine within minutes. The rush of relaxation was immediately felt throughout her body. She reached to pour more into her glass as Colette updated them on her life as a secretary at the church. *Watching water boil would be more interesting.* Phyllis sipped her second glass of wine slowly, allowing it to linger on her tongue and rest on the inside of her jaws which caused her cheeks to flush. When she inhaled her chest

71

was on fire like she just took a shot of cognac. Yes, this was her favorite go-to wine to get the same feeling as hard liquor.

"Sounds like you are enjoying your new role at the church." Dawn remarked, trying to validate Colette since she needed so much encouragement these days.

Sounds boring to me. "So, Dawn…did you bump into Vine in Atlanta?" Phyllis asked, changing the subject on purpose. Colette noticed and shot her a look. If looks could even slightly injure these two would be full of wounds.

"Actually, I did." Dawn admitted. She mashed her lips together so no other words could escape because she was not in the mood to discuss that part of her trip.

"You did? You didn't tell me that part!" Colette replied.

Dawn shrugged. "It was nothing."

"Ha! See there!" Phyllis leaned forward, pointing at Colette. "You don't know every little thing that happened while Dawn was in Atlanta!" Phyllis retorted, sneering at Colette. She couldn't resist making sure Colette was called out on her pettiness from earlier.

"Oh, shut up, Phyllis! You're just jealous!" Colette retorted.

"Jealous? Of What?!" Phyllis demanded to know. She firmly placed her glass of wine on the cocktail table, pursed her lips and waited for her sister to respond. When she exhaled through her nose, it felt like a burst of flames escaped her nostrils.

"Jealous that Dawn and I have a closer relationship now that we live together. You're jealous that I have a job and you don't. You're probably even jealous because I have no problem getting pregnant!" Colette boasted as if it were her best talent between the two of them.

"I didn't have a problem getting pregnant either until Mama made me have an abortion!" Phyllis hissed and you could hear a bird poop. Phyllis certainly just dropped a shit bomb on her sisters. *Dammit! Loose lips!*

"Wait! What?" Dawn screeched. "When was this?"

Colette took a gulp of wine, eyes wide. "Yeah, when was this? And who were you pregnant by?"

Phyllis sighed, sat back and closed her eyes. She hadn't thought about that terrible time in her life in a long time. When Danny asked Phyllis to be his lady by the second semester of senior year of high school she was thrilled. But Colette decided to prove to her big sister that even a fifteen-year-old sophomore could steal him away from her. Even though Colette was only two years younger than Phyllis she passed her up in the physique department when they were teenagers. Phyllis still had a flat chest when she began high school, but Colette had blossomed in full bloom by the time she was a freshman. Although Phyllis had beautiful, round light brown eyes and creamy, fair skin it did not hail the attention as it did for Colette. They were always being compared to one another being so close in age. Colette was younger, but taller than Phyllis. Colette had long, sandy brown hair that flowed past her shoulders, but Phyllis had shorter, thinner hair and it was rarely raved about. When they were teenagers, Colette flaunted her long locks, especially when their mother pressed it out, making it touch the middle of her back. Colette won the hearts of many, including Phyllis' boyfriend, Danny.

It had cut Phyllis to the core that Colette would even think to betray her, especially when Colette knew how much Phyllis pined over Danny since freshman year. It had changed their sisterhood for good. Danny admitted that he was torn between the two sisters, but still wanted to take Phyllis to the prom. Phyllis looked to their mother to punish Colette for being a flirt on purpose just to prove a point. But their mother had said, "Well, there will be plenty more Danny's to come along. May the best sister win." With a flick of her wrist, that was the end of that conversation. Phyllis was devastated. A smirk grew across Colette's face and Phyllis remembered it well. *I should've slapped that smirk right off of her face back then!*

Even though Colette had no real interest in Danny, she felt like she had one up on Phyllis because she was able to get his attention. Eventually, Colette told him that she was not interested anymore because it was causing too many arguments between them, and well, he just wasn't worth it. Not to mention Phyllis had eventually stopped speaking to her over the ordeal. But it was too late. The only thing Phyllis could think of to keep Danny's attention was sleeping with him.

"Danny." Phyllis responded finally. "Remember him, Colette?"

Colette fidgeted, cleared her throat and lowered her eyes. "We were just kids."

"He was *my* boyfriend that you were hell bent on stealing!"

"Who? Her?" Dawn scoffed, pointing at Colette. "Did I miss something? Miss-Shy-and-Quiet over here tried to steal *your* boyfriend? I cannot even imagine that!"

"Don't let her innocent-church-act fool you, Dawn! She was a hot mess when we were teenagers. You were too young to really remember. The only reason she acts so meek and mild now is because she got with Owen when she was seventeen and he tamed that ass, didn't he?"

Colette glared at her sister with fury in her eyes. Phyllis held her stare boldly and matched her fury that had been buried for so many years.

"So you got pregnant in high school by some guy named Danny and Mama made you get an abortion at seventeen-years-old?"

"I didn't get pregnant on purpose. But yes, basically, I lost my virginity to keep him from liking Colette and got pregnant. The classic poster child for a teenage pregnancy." Phyllis took a gulp of wine and continued, "I was scared when I missed my period, of course. I didn't know what to do or who to tell. By the time I missed a third period I knew that I was pregnant for sure. So, I told Danny's stupid-ass and he told his mom just like the Mama's boy he was! Then his mom called our mom and well, tah-dah… no baby by Danny!"

"I'm sure it was for the best…"

"Dawn, I didn't want to kill my baby!" Phyllis snapped. "I was in love with Danny. I wanted my baby. I wanted him. But Mama took me to some jacked-up clinic for low-income people without insurance to get an abortion and I had complications afterwards."

"Complications? Like what?" Dawn asked concerned.

"Like the damn doctor didn't suck the whole baby out!" Phyllis shouted frustrated.

Dawn gasped. Colette cringed.

Phyllis continued with the details since she was already on a roll. "The head of the baby was left behind and still growing inside of me! So I needed emergency surgery at a hospital to rectify that whole mess. Now see how ridiculous you sound accusing me of being jealous of *that*?" Phyllis pointed her finger directly at Colette. "If being a "Fertile Myrtle" is your only claim to fame, then you have a lot of growing to do!"

Phyllis sat back on the sofa, glared at her sisters and fought back tears.

"Does Damien know all of this? Does he know that's the reason you had a hard time getting pregnant?" Dawn asked curiously.

"He thought that he was shooting blanks until I got pregnant with the twins." Phyllis admitted, shaking her head. *What's the point in telling him now?*

"Damn! I'm sorry to hear all of that. That's so fucked up, for real. All of these damn family secrets! Well, at least I'm not the last to know this time." Dawn remarked, shaking her head.

"That's part of the problem, too," Colette said. "Everyone is always protecting you, the baby of the family. Shielding you from what is really going on around you."

Phyllis and Dawn glanced at one another, confused.

"Hey! Leave me out of this!" Dawn briefly stood up to snatch the wine bottle from in front of Colette. She placed the bottle on the floor between her feet where she knew it would be safe from her reach. *Her ass is getting cut off!* Dawn remembered that it didn't take much for Colette to get tipsy and knocked up at the same time. She claimed that's how the last baby got here after a night of drinking with Owen. "And is that all you have to say after what Phyllis just shared with us? Who are you right now?"

"I didn't come here for a pity party!" Colette seethed.

"You got some nerve, Colette! The last time I checked, everyone was holding a pity party for you because you couldn't hold this last baby!" Phyllis hissed, leaning forward to deliver the last lash. "I guess your coochie finally gave out, huh?"

"Oh, please! You're a bigger fool than I thought." Colette laughed and waved her off. "I don't have *those* problems."

"What's that supposed to mean?" Phyllis demanded to know. "You just had a miscarriage, didn't you?"

"If you say so!" Colette responded.

Dawn clicked her metallic stiletto nails together trying to get her sisters back on track before it got really ugly. "Look, we just need to finalize the plans for our parents' anniversary. To hell with all this comparing coochies, pregnancies, abortions and babies!"

"I don't even know why we're doing this shit anyway!" Colette snapped. "They aren't even married anymore."

"Oh, the church lady is cursing tonight, huh?" Dawn scoffed.

"Must be nice being the baby of the family, huh?" Colette continued, with hooded eyes and slurring her words. "Nothing is ever required from you, Dawn. Nothing is ever expected of you. You're free to make mistakes, have people clean up after you and never rub it in your face. Must be really nice!" Colette took the last gulp of wine from her glass and chuckled to herself. She traced the rim of the wine glass with her finger, and then licked the remnants from her finger.

Dawn shook her head and began scrolling through her iPhone. *This drunk heffa better calm down!* "Don't come for me, Colette. You need to calm your drunk ass down, for real!"

"You have a lot of nerve coming for me and Dawn like this!" Phyllis stood over Colette wagging her finger in her face. "You messed up your life a long time ago with a fool and everybody warned you, including his Mama! Did you listen? No! So, unlike you, I ain't nobody's damn fool! YOU ARE!" Phyllis yelled loudly, clenched her fists as her body trembled.

Dawn jerked her head up to see the fury all over her sister's face while Colette sat nonchalantly nodding her head in slow motion. *Oh, shit!*

"Calm down, Phyllis!" Dawn pleaded, but it fell on deaf ears.

"Now you don't have a pot to piss in!" Phyllis ignored Dawn and continued, "But you're living with Aunt Georgia in an old house of horrors, full of kids running wild because… once again somebody is cleaning up after *your* mess! Our retired parents cleaned out your apartment after the fire, not you! Not even your worthless, poor-excuse-for-a-man, loser husband of yours helped after the fire! Everything was handled for you *and* your kids when you got released from the hospital. You got a new place to stay now, rent free and using Aunt Georgia's car whenever you want! So, it looks like you've been babied too!"

Colette struggled to get to her feet, clapped her hands slowly and sneered. "Who needs Facebook "On This Day" as a reminder when we have "Flashback Phyllis" to do it for us? You're beating that old-ass, dead horse again, girl! You wanna bring up Danny like I stole him or something. I didn't steal him from you, I just flirted a little. Nobody told your dumb ass to go get knocked up by him! And far as Owen is concerned, at least I finally opened my eyes and got some courage to leave my lying, cheating ass husband!"

"Good for you! It only took twenty years!" Phyllis gave a round of applause right in her face as they stood eye-to-eye.

"Hopefully, you'll do the same!" Colette retorted.

Dawn clenched her eyes shut and tried to pretend that Colette didn't just let those words fall out of her drunken mouth. Chills raced down her spine. *Oh, shit! She just went there! Damn! Mama has a big mouth! Shit!*

"What!?" Phyllis shouted, looking confused.

"You heard me!" Colette shoved Phyllis's shoulder knocking her off balance, creating distance between them. "Tell her Dawn!"

"Don't you dare put your hands on me!" Phyllis lunged at Colette, taking her down on the hardwood floors. She grabbed a chunk of Colette's hair while banging her head against the floor with every word she uttered. "You lonely, miserable, bitch!"

"Get off of me! You crazy, bitch!" Colette squirmed, trying to free herself from Phyllis, but she was losing that battle. Colette balled up her fists and proceeded to beat Phyllis on the sides of her head repeatedly.

Dawn stood frozen for a minute, hands covering her mouth. She could not believe that her sisters were actually fighting as if they were on an episode of some trashy reality show.

"WHAT THE HELL!? STOP IT RIGHT NOW!" Dawn grabbed Phyllis by her t-shirt forcefully, trying to pull her off of Colette, but instead ripped it. The sound of her clothes ripping, exposing her shoulder and left breast was enough to get all of their attention.

"Let me go, Dawn!" Phyllis snatched her arm away as she scrambled to her feet. She stuffed her breast back into her bra, tried to compose herself while catching her breath.

"Are y'all crazy!?" Dawn said with her hands on her hips. Colette moaned as Dawn helped her to her feet. She placed a hand on the back of her head, checking to see if there was any blood. There was none, but she was still furious as her chest heaved up and down.

"Tell me what, Dawn?!" Phyllis demanded, looking back and forth between her sisters. She held her ripped t-shirt together with one hand, looking as if she was pledging allegiance to the American flag. Tears were forming in her eyes, but she coughed trying to play it off.

"I cannot believe you two were just going at it like complete strangers!"

"Dawn! I know you heard me! Tell. Me. What?" Phyllis interrupted her. *She can just save that lecture shit and cut to the chase!*

"I…it's…well…" Dawn stammered as she stuffed her hands into her romper side pockets. She shrugged, shook her head and lowered her eyes. *Fuck! I need a damn joint!*

"For crying out loud, Dawn! Tell her what you saw!" Colette insisted as she grabbed the bottle of wine.

"Put my fuckin' wine down!" Phyllis demanded. Colette rolled her eyes, placing the bottle on the table.

Dawn jerked her head towards Colette and batted her eyelashes repeatedly. *This heffa got a lot of nerve! Mama should've never told you anyway!* "Listen, it might not be anything at all, really, Phyllis."

Phyllis folded her arms across her chest, raised an eyebrow, and glared at Dawn like she was about to pounce on her if she didn't spill the beans in two seconds flat. Colette sat down on the sofa waiting patiently to see Phyllis crumble at the bomb Dawn was about to drop on her.

"I saw Damien get into his car with… some chick." Dawn shrugged. "Doesn't mean anything. It was probably nothing."

"Not 'some chick', Phyllis. He was with Shante." Colette interjected, raising her eyebrows.

"Shante? *Owen's* Shante?"

Colette nodded. "Yep! And she's pregnant."

Dawn shot her a look of surprise. *I totally missed that part.*

"And if it's Damien's baby…then he'll know for sure that he wasn't the problem all these years." Colette remarked, covering her mouth as if she didn't mean to say that out loud.

"Would you shut up?" Dawn lashed out.

"Dawn, when was this?" Phyllis asked as her chest heaved. She was trying her best not to pounce on Colette again, but she was asking for it.

"A few weeks ago." Dawn replied, shaking her head as she glanced back and forth between her sisters. *This was supposed to be a fun girls' night in. I should've known better.*

"And you didn't think to mention it to me? And if this bitch knows," Phyllis said pointing at Colette, but kept her eyes steady on Dawn. "…that means Mama certainly knows! If Mama knows then that means Dad knows too! So everybody knows about my man and another woman, except me?"

Phyllis paced the floor. Her mind raced as fast as her eyes were darting back and forth. She wrung her hands over and over again. *Why would he sneak around with that whore?*

"Phyllis, like I said…it's probably nothing…"

"Get the hell out of my house!"

CHAPTER 8

Confessions and Confusion

Colette groaned, grabbing her forehead as she rolled over in her bed only to bump into Ruthie who was wide-awake, playing with a toy quietly. It was not the first time she had a hangover. No. But it was the first time she woke up with a hangover with a house full of kids. It was also the first time she had a fight with her sister as an adult. They had their fair share of fights when they were younger, of course, but nothing too drastic. Even when they fought about Danny, it was just a shove, but last night the shove led to a knock-down fight. This morning her body felt like she had been in a fight. Colette felt awful. The headache she had must have come from Phyllis banging her head against the floor because certainly wine would not have this effect on her. Word of their fight had probably spread like wildfire if Dawn had anything to do with it. And that was another headache she had to endure.

The last thing she remembered was the car ride home. Dawn lectured her about drinking too much and fighting with Phyllis, but she tuned her out and must have blacked out because now she was waking up in her bed. *How did I even get up the stairs?*

"Morning, mommy." Ruthie whispered, giving her a kiss on the nose.

Colette waved faintly and patted her head. She feared that if she spoke vomit would erupt all over Ruthie. She slowly rolled over to the other side staring at the window, trying to determine what time it was based on the sunlight beaming through the sheer curtains. It was morning, that was for sure, but she needed to know just how early it really was. Usually, an aroma of breakfast sausage, biscuits, bacon or pancakes would be finding its way to her bedroom by now. But how Ruthie sat in her bed expectantly was a dead give-away that nobody had cooked yet.

"Ruthie," Colette said above a whisper. "Go see what time it is."

"What did you say, mommy?" Ruthie pounced on the bed, repositioning herself to see her mother's face better.

Colette groaned painfully. "Stop moving the bed!" she growled, leaning over the edge of the bed.

"Mommy?" Ruthie shook her arm back and forth. "Mommy! I can't hear you!"

"Stop it! Get out!" Colette shouted, swatting her arm at the air. Ruthie scrambled to get off the bed, whimpering. Colette knew that she had hurt her feelings, but she needed the movement to stop before she hurled the contents swirling around in her stomach from last night all over the carpeted floor. The sound of Ruthie's feet stomping downstairs could be heard by everyone who was awake. Next, she heard the sound of adult feet coming up the stairs. *Must be Dawn. No, she wouldn't be up early at all.* Colette grabbed her head as she slung the top half of her body back on the bed. Once she was fully onto the bed, she covered her eyes with her hands. The room suddenly became a slow merry-go-round, her head was throbbing and somebody was talking. She spread her fingers slightly, peered through them to see Georgia standing in the doorway. Her mouth was moving, but Colette had not heard a word she was saying through her groans because Georgia always spoke softly.

"It was always better for Fred when he got it over with. Just do it. You'll be relieved."

Fred? Did she say Fred? Is she having one of her grieving moments? "What? I didn't hear you... What did you say?"

Georgia walked closer to the bed, slowly as if she was afraid to get too close. "I said...you should get to the bathroom and get all of that poison out of you. Fred always felt better afterwards. Go vomit, Colette." She reached into her pocket to retrieve two tablets and placed them on the dresser.

"Water?"

"Get some water from the bathroom. You need to get up, Colette. But don't take this medicine until after you've got the poison out of your stomach."

Colette groaned and rolled over.

"Your mother went home last night, but the twins are still here," Georgia informed her, hoping that would get her moving. "The children wanted cereal for breakfast. But I can make some toast and tea for you. Get yourself cleaned up so we can discuss what happened last night with Phyllis."

Colette flicked a thumb in the air to let her aunt know that she understood her instructions, but she wasn't about to move anytime soon. "What time is it, Aunt Georgia?" she mumbled.

"It's almost nine o'clock." Georgia replied impatiently because Colette had not budged.

Colette groaned again, clutching her stomach.

"Colette, you put a pot on the stove to boil, now everyone is watching the pot boil. We all know that a watched pot doesn't boil. No sense in delaying the process. We'll be downstairs waiting."

Who is "we"? Colette raised her thumb in the air again and closed her eyes. She heard the bedroom door close and exhaled into the pillow. The stench of her breath trapped inside the small air pocket between her face and the pillow finally sent her barreling from the bedroom to the bathroom.

After she emerged from the bathroom, she took the medicine and sat on the edge of the bed for a while thinking about everything that happened last night. The sounds of chatter and children's laughter traveled upstairs and suddenly Colette felt ashamed. *What will my children think of me now? How will my nieces feel when they find out that I fought their mom? Oh my God! What have I done?* Immediately, she fell to her knees and began to pray for forgiveness and healing between her sisters. She could easily blame the wine on her behavior, but she knew that was only part of her behavior. All she wanted was some validation from Phyllis, her big sister. Sure, she had made some terrible mistakes in her life with Owen but she was moving on with her life, making better decisions, even working at the church now. Why couldn't Phyllis just acknowledge that? A little credit would've gone a long way last night, but when Phyllis changed the subject as she was sharing her new role at the church and how good Pastor was being to her it infuriated her. *Why did she have to dismiss me like that?* There was always tension between them since they were children, but last night was all the bottled emotion, resentment, and hostility accumulated from over the years erupting into a full blown fight.

Colette felt like Dawn had a lot of nerve lecturing her about drinking too much when she was the Queen of recreational drugs and alcohol! The moment Colette decided loosen up a little and join her sisters with drinking and blurted a few curse words, she was judged. Even though Dawn was teasing her when she called her the "church lady", it still hurt her feelings. She wasn't Bible-thumping anybody nor damning everyone to hell. Colette was only trying to live right and move on from being abused by her husband, whom she hoped to be divorcing soon. Going to church lifted her spirits, especially after she lost everything they owned in the fire. Starting over had not been easy, even though having a place to stay was the least of her concerns, it was still frustrating not having a home to call her own. She didn't even know where to start or if she should find another apartment because her salary at the church wasn't enough to keep them afloat, and Owen wasn't offering any financial assistance especially since he had another baby on the way. But her sisters couldn't understand any of that.

In the past, she never once mentioned leaving Owen. Not even after the split lips, bruised arms, sexual abuse, public humiliation, ridicule and name-calling, Colette never threatened to leave him. This time she meant business. She was determined to get a divorce from Owen. She actually had a reason to now that a new love was blooming with the Pastor and she was finally employed for the first time in her life. So according to her, this part of her life was crucial, pivotal and exciting.

As she closed her prayer, she exhaled heavily and this time a whiff of minty breath greeted her nostrils. She wiped a loose tear away and stood to her feet. It was time to face the music. Once she got the nerve to get dressed, she headed downstairs with her family.

"Mommy!" Lydia ran to give Colette a hug and held on tight. "Do you feel better?"

Colette embraced her, smiling and glanced up at Georgia. "Yes, mommy feels a little better. Just a little."

"Your toast and tea is in the microwave. No jelly, no sugar or honey." Georgia rattled off anticipating the questions Colette was going to ask as soon as she saw how it looked and tasted.

"Thanks, Aunt Georgia. Where are the twins? I thought they were still here." Colette asked, looking around.

"They were, but Dawn took them home, of course." Georgia replied, turning her back on Colette as she reached into the refrigerator for a pitcher of cucumber water. "You know that Phyllis wasn't coming by like she planned after last night." She closed the refrigerator softly, pausing a moment to stare at Colette. Her face was etched with disappointment.

Another wave of shame swept over Colette as she glanced down at Lydia who was still wrapped around her waist. She patted her head, indicating that she could let go of her waist now. Once she walked away Colette called for Ruthie, who was in the living room, but she didn't appear. *I know she heard me.* "Ruthie! Mommy didn't mean to hurt your feelings. Come here."

Georgia waved her hand at Colette and whispered, "Leave her alone."

"The twins were being mean to me," Cornell said as he scooped a spoonful of cereal in his mouth.

"Good Morning, Cornell." Colette shook her head. She wasn't in a mood for tattle-telling. "I'm sure it didn't hurt your feelings too much, son." She patted him on the head as she made her way to the microwave.

He flashed a huge smile, looking just like his father, and shook his head. "Nah, I don't pay attention to silly girls. Besides, Aunty Phyllis sent over some cartridges for my Nintendo DS. I was too busy learning the new games, but the twins were mean, though. Especially Serena! That's the evil twin." Cornell nodded to himself.

"Where's my baby?" Colette asked, changing the subject.

"I put her in the bouncer after she ate her breakfast," Georgia said, gesturing towards the living room.

"I can get her, Mama!" Lydia offered. She enjoyed her role as a big sister and always jumped at the chance to show how she could be helpful.

"Please don't, baby." Colette grabbed her by the arm before she could dart past her. "She's peaceful now, so just let her stay in there." The last thing Colette needed was to tend to a baby while she was trying to recover from a night of drinking and fighting.

She placed the plate of dry toast on the table with a cup of herbal tea. "Is this your special tea, Aunt Georgia?"

Georgia nodded without looking in her direction and turned her attention to the children. "Cornell, you're all done. Now you and Lydia, go join your sisters in the living room. Don't turn up the television too loudly."

They dashed towards the living room arguing about who was going to have control over the remote control.

Oh, God! Here we go. I'm so not in the mood to be lectured.

To her surprise, Georgia finished clearing the table quietly, only glancing in her direction once. Colette cleared her throat nervously, reached for her tea, sipped slowly and cringed at its bitter greeting. As she munched on the dry wheat toast her stomach did a somersault. She wasn't sure if it was because she was hungry or if her body was rejecting the idea of food. Either way, she kept on chewing because she was going to need all the strength she could muster to get through the afternoon. Pastor was expecting her to fulfill her duties, all of them, by the end of the day in preparation for Sunday morning service. The church bulletin took up most of the time because it required lots of formatting, editing, adding color and rewording submissions or rejecting them altogether. There was no way that Colette was going to convince Pastor that scripture: "*For a whore is a deep ditch; and a strange woman is a narrow pit.*" from Proverbs 23:27 actually belonged in the church bulletin. She would just deal with Sister Templeton and her scripture of choice later. Now she felt foolish for getting drunk last night knowing full well that she had work to do at the church today.

Finally, Georgia pulled out a chair, wiped it off with a red and white dish towel and took a seat at the table. She folded her hands, stared at them for a moment and began the dreaded discussion.

"Colette, I'm not your mother, so don't expect a lecture from me. I was not around when you and your sisters were younger, so I don't know the dynamics of your relationship now. But I will say, from what I heard, I am very shocked at *your* behavior. I've noticed the tension between you and Phyllis before..." Georgia paused for a moment, staring off into space. Colette had gotten used to these moments and knew not to interrupt. As she patiently waited for her aunt to complete her thoughts, she mindlessly traced the rim of the tea cup with her finger. After a brief moment, Georgia leaned forward and continued, "Sometimes alcohol will wake up an ugly side that we never knew lived inside of us. Fred, as sweet and loving as that man was to me, became an evil, verbally abusive bigot when he drank. I hated that ugly Fred."

Colette looked up swiftly, shocked by that news. "Really?"

Georgia nodded. "And from what I heard about how you behaved last night, sounds like you don't need to drink either."

"I don't know what Dawn told you, but I was only telling some truth that nobody wanted to hear. But I didn't start the fight!"

"You sound like one of your children right now," Georgia pointed towards the living room where the sounds of bickering children filled the air. She excused herself from the table and headed towards the living room to diffuse the situation. Just before she disappeared around the corner she turned to look at Colette and said, "Fix it before it's too late."

☐☐☐☐☐

During the drive to the church, Colette had time to think without the constant baby-babbling from Delilah in the backseat, thanks to Georgia keeping all the kids at home. She glanced in the rearview mirror several times during the ride, making sure that her hair was in place and that her eyeliner wasn't running. She didn't want to look anything like what she had been through the night before. *Pastor won't know the difference.* A hot shower, fresh breath and a tad-bit of makeup lifted her spirits. The meds finally eased her headache, but her stomach was still unsettled so she stopped at the gas station for a sports drink, muffin and breath mints to help ease the nausea.

She kept hearing Georgia's voice ringing in her ears, telling her to "fix it" and it only made her angry. Why should it be on her to fix anything? She was simply telling the truth. Phyllis did have a jealous streak in her, that was no secret. But now that Colette knew why Phyllis had complications conceiving, she felt really awful. She shuddered at the thought of having that conversation with their mother. Although she was showing a warmer side towards her daughters now, Jonetta was nothing nice while they were growing up. It was no surprise that an abortion was the result considering

Jonetta didn't have a Christian bone in her body, but to have your seventeen-year-old daughter have a horrific experience like that made Colette want to cry. Her thoughts lingered on her three daughters and chills ran down her arms. *There's no way I'd force them to have an abortion.*

She shook her head in disbelief because all these years she never knew any of that happened to Phyllis. She did recall Phyllis being away for a few days, but Jonetta said that she was at a "sleepover" or something along those lines. Now she knew that it was actually an extended stay at the hospital due to a botched abortion job. Her stomach churned again. At a red light she opened the sports drink and gulped it down. Her cell phone interrupted her thoughts and she grimaced when she saw her mother's face flash across the screen.

"Hi, Mama." Colette answered, putting the call on speakerphone so she could continue driving.

"I have no idea what has gotten into you, but I heard all about it, missy. You have some explaining to do! I didn't keep your kids just so you could go fight your sister! You're lashing out at the wrong people, Colette. What is going on with you?"

Colette sighed heavily as she accelerated the car when the light turned green. She kept her eyes steady on the road, thinking of a way to end this conversation quickly. *Everybody wants to blame me! I'm not going for it!*

"Wow! Phyllis must be crying to anybody who will listen! Did she tell you that she knocked me to the floor and was banging my head over and over again?"

"She told me that you pushed her first and she retaliated to defend herself." Jonetta replied, pointedly.

"Mama, did Phyllis also tell you that she told us that you forced her to have an abortion when she was only seventeen-years-old?"

"What! That is not true!" Jonetta argued.

"It really made me wonder… Did you make a subtle suggestion for her, too?"

"What are you implying, Colette?" Jonetta demanded to know.

"I'm pulling up to the church." Colette lied. She had another five minutes before she arrived at the church, but needed to end the call quickly before she said something to her mother that she regretted. "I'm going to say a real special prayer for you, Mama. Bye!"

Once in the parking lot, she sat in the car for a few moments collecting her thoughts before she greeted Pastor. He always seemed to sense when something was bothering her and she adored him for it. Owen never picked up on her moods nor cared enough to inquire even if he did notice. She flipped down the visor to glance at herself in the vanity mirror one last time before she entered the church. A rap at her window startled her causing her to jump. It was Sister Templeton. *Does this lady live at the church?* Colette forced a smile on her face and waved. She turned the ignition off, gathered her purse, sports drink and opened the car door.

"Hi, there Sister Templeton," Colette pleasantly greeted her as she eased from the driver's seat. "You startled me for a minute."

"Only a guilty mind would be on edge while sitting in a church parking lot," she replied flippantly.

Colette scoffed, "I beg your pardon?" *What is she talking about? I know good and well word about the fight with Phyllis didn't spread to my church!* Colette proceeded to enter the church, walking swiftly on purpose and Sister Templeton followed her, trying her best to keep up with her pace.

"That's between you and God." Sister Templeton waved her off. "What I want to know is, are you going to put that scripture in the bulletin today for Sunday service tomorrow? I was thinking it would be perfect because…"

Colette stopped dead in her tracks before proceeding to the Pastor's office. She had about enough of this woman pestering her. "Listen, Sister Templeton, it is my job update the church bulletin with announcements, inspirational memos, and *appropriate* scriptures. Pastor will not appreciate any member trying to micromanage me doing my job, which I do well."

"So you didn't even show him the scripture that I wanted printed?"

Colette exhaled sharply. "I used my sound judgement and wisdom that God gave me. Pastor has enough on his plate already leading the congregation. Now if you'll excuse me, I need to get to work."

Sister Templeton shifted her thick hips and just barely folded her short, fat arms across her huge chest. "We'll just see about that!" She looked Colette up and down nastily, then sped past her, almost shoving her out of the way in the narrow hallway.

Colette tried to catch her before she knocked on his door but it was too late. Sister Templeton hammered on his door repeatedly until he opened it. When Pastor snatched open his door the expression on his face spoke volumes. He wasn't pleased at all.

"Pastor, I really hate to bother you, but…"

"Then don't!" he barked, removing his reading glasses.

"Pastor, I'm so sorry about this." Colette said standing behind Sister Templeton who was blocking the entryway to his office.

His face softened when he addressed Colette but his tone remained the same. "What is going on here, Sister Colette? You know I don't like to be interrupted when I'm writing my sermons." Whenever Pastor was upset, his words were rushed and mashed together with his Haitian accent more pronounced. Now was one of those times as his thick accent echoed in the air.

"Sister Templeton wanted a scripture in the bulletin that I thought was inappropriate." Colette explained. "I had no idea that she was going to come banging on your door to interrupt you, Pastor. I'm so sorry for this intrusion on your time with the Lord." Colette shot a look towards Sister Templeton hoping that she would get the hint.

"How is a Bible scripture inappropriate?" Sister Templeton argued, eyeing Colette up and down again.

Colette pursed her lips and replied slowly so this old woman could hear her clearly once and for all, "Proverbs twenty-three verse twenty-seven is not being approved for the bulletin!"

"Sister Templeton, I have to get back to my sermon," Pastor replied in a softer tone, but clearly still annoyed. "If Sister Colette doesn't think it's appropriate, then that's the end of discussion." He walked back to his desk and flipped through the Bible as if he were looking for the scripture Colette had just referenced.

Colette nodded in confirmation. She felt justified with her decision especially since Pastor had just backed her up. She adjusted her posture, standing taller and smirked at Sister Templeton.

"Oh, I see what's going on here!" she huffed and folded her arms again. She continued loud enough for the Pastor to hear, "The new girl gets to have her way around here just like Alyssa did! You see where that got her, don't you?" She narrowed her eyes at Colette with all the hatred she could muster.

This lady is relentless! "We have work to do. Now if you'll excuse us," Colette replied and squeezed past her to enter the office. "Have a good day, Sister Templeton."

"Bunch of whores," she mumbled and walked off.

How dare you? Colette was mystified by her accusations and strong language, especially in the house of the Lord. But more importantly, she wasn't a whore! She had only been with one man in her whole life and that was her soon-to-be-ex-husband, Owen. But Colette decided not to respond because she was still recovering from the fight with her sister from last night. Lord knows that she didn't need to come to blows with one of the elderly women of the church. That would be too ugly and a scandal that she would never recover from once the gossip began. She closed the door swiftly and exhaled.

"Rough day?" Pastor asked as he rounded his desk. He sat on the edge, opened his arms and smiled.

"Yesssss..." Colette rushed into his arms where she often found comfort. He embraced her inhaling her scent and smoothing her hair. Colette moaned a sigh of relief. *Thank God somebody has my back.*

"Don't let the old crows in this church bother you. They are just jealous of your position and your beauty. You're not a whore. I would never allow whores to ever get this close to me in my church." He kissed her forehead, lifted her chin up, looked into her eyes and grew concerned from the look in her eyes, "What's wrong?"

Colette shook her head and buried her face into his neck. Tears began to flow uncontrollably and it caught them both off guard. It wasn't her plan to cry on his shoulder today, but the moment she gave him a hug she knew that it was inevitable. He led her to a chair where she sat sobbing for a moment while he grabbed a box of tissue from the corner of his desk. Colette wiped her tears and nose repeatedly until the tears finally stopped flowing.

"I'm so sorry, Pastor," she apologized whispering. "Sister Templeton really angered me with her snide comments. I'm really sick of the gossip about Alyssa, too."

"What did you hear?" Pastor asked grabbing her shoulders, searching her face.

"It's just church gossip about who the father of her baby could be from the church. A couple of deacons' names were mentioned and... yours..."

Pastor cleared his throat nervously. "It's just gossip. Don't let that bother you," he pulled her close again. "What else is troubling you, Sister Colette?"

"I just have a lot going on right now with my family." Colette explained the fight and conveniently failed to mention drinking too much wine, of course, because she didn't want him to judge her too harshly.

"You've sinned gravely against your family, Sister Colette," he said firmly.

"You think it's my fault, too?" Her eyes welled with tears again.

"Well, based on what you've told me, you pushed your sister first. You provoked her to wrath against you. Yes?"

Colette hadn't thought about it that way until now. Pastor was right, she did push Phyllis first, but she provoked her to wrath with her words. She shrugged and agreed. "I guess."

He stood in front of her then rested on the edge of his desk as if he were in deep thought. "Before we proceed with our work today, you need to repent so you can have a clear mind, body and spirit with the Lord. Yes?"

Colette nodded in agreement.

He placed his thick hand on her shoulder and continued, "Now, get on your knees for prayer, Sister Colette. I will anoint your head with oil as I pray over you." He reached into his pocket to retrieve a small, glass bottle that was filled with oil. When he twisted the cap off it had a roller on the top and the fragrance reminded Colette of Egyptian Musk oil that the Rastas usually sold at the African Festivals. "I am going to pray over your whole body for protection."

Colette emerged from the chair and slowly dropped to her knees, locking eyes with the Pastor. She knelt before him and her heart was racing with anticipation because she didn't know what to expect. Of course, whenever she prayed she knelt on her knees, but she never knelt before a man. She closed her eyes and he began to rub the oil on her forehead in a circular motion before he even began praying.

"Lord, anoint Sister Colette with the spirit of peace in her mind," he said, rubbing the oil in a cross fashion like they do in Catholic churches for Ash Wednesday. "Anoint her lips so only words that represent you escape from them. Keep her lips pure, soft and on reserve." He rolled the oil over lips. "Anoint her tongue that she remembers to use it to edify her duties as an obedient woman of God doing your will. Stick your tongue out."

Colette did as he instructed still keeping her eyes closed. She felt his finger slide up and down her tongue in a soft, slow motion three times.

"Put your hands on my knees, Sister Colette."

Colette obeyed, but she closed her mouth.

"Keep your mouth open until I finish," he instructed.

Colette dropped her mouth open immediately.

"Lord, anoint her hands to be used for obedience, talents, and nurturing as a mother, secretary and woman." He rubbed the oil on the back of her hands as her palms rested on his knees. When he finished with her hands, he placed the cap back on the oil and put it on the desk. Next, Colette felt his hands on her face rubbing the oil into her forehead and cheeks while her mouth hung wide open. He traced her lips twice with his finger, pressing firmly the second time around. Colette noticed the rhythm of his breathing increased right along with her heart rate. He cupped the sides of her face with his thick hands and finished praying. "Lord, I want Sister Colette to remain in my flock doing your work and lots of work for me and with me. Allow your will to be done between us. Amen."

"Amen." Colette said softly. She kept her eyes closed and remained kneeling in a praying position before him when she felt his hands guide her head towards his lap and she followed his lead. She rested her head in his lap as he caressed her hands.

"Sister Colette, you are far too beautiful to fight anyone," he said softly as he guided her left hand up his leg. "Use these hands for something more purposeful."

Colette popped open her eyes and gasped when she felt a huge bulge. She tried to scurry to her feet, but Pastor had a grip on her hand and the back of her neck.

"Sister Colette, this is a natural reaction to a woman as beautiful as you. No need to be alarmed," he chuckled. "I am still a man, remember?"

Colette remained on her knees frozen, staring eye to eye with what looked like a snake that was trying to force its way out of his pants. "Pastor, I apologize if…"

"Shhhh… You've apologized enough for one day. Yes?" He held her face in his hands as he gazed down on her. "You are something special. I have been praying for a woman like you."

Colette suddenly felt a rush of excitement causing a huge smile to grow across her face without her permission. *Quit grinning so hard.* Her heart raced as she held onto his hands and gazed into his eyes.

"We have a lot of work to do today. We might be here all night if we don't get started. But I think it's best we begin once we have relieved ourselves from the stressful demons interrupting our day. Yes? We need to be in a good spirit when we do the Lord's work."

Colette knew that it was only a matter of time before they were honest about their feelings for one another, but she didn't expect it to happen here, at a church, in his office. Colette nodded, unable to form any words as she tried to catch her breath. *What is happening?*

He leaned back, unbuckled his brown leather belt hidden beneath his big belly, unzipped his pants and kept his eyes steady on Colette as he fully exposed himself.

"Good girl. I think you are ready now to use your talents, Sister Colette."

CHAPTER 9

Closer than Close

At work on a Saturday was the last place on earth Jonetta wanted to be, but there she was filling in for Kaiya who called off sick. She would rather have her foot up Phyllis and Colette's ass after she received a call from Dawn this morning. These two have been like oil and vinegar since they were toddlers. Jonetta recalled the time they were getting the living room remodeled and there were exposed outlets everywhere. Colette wobbled in the kitchen where Jonetta was cooking, wide-eyed with her mouth open and Jonetta noticed a welt across her cheek. When she asked Phyllis what happened to her sister a guilty look spread across her face. Jonetta knew Phyllis was up to no good so she snatched her by the arm and Phyllis immediately told her that Colette "licked the wall". Jonetta instantly knew from the welt that extended from the corner of Colette's mouth up her cheek that Phyllis made her put her mouth on the socket. Her one-year-old baby got electrocuted. Phyllis was only three-years-old at the time.

There had been other numerous times that Jonetta could remember fights between them, wicked things done to one another, but that incident stuck out in her mind first. Based on her conversation with Dawn she seemed to think that Colette started the fight, but Jonetta knew that Phyllis probably provoked her. She also had a sweet side of her like when she stayed by Colette's bedside at the hospital after she was in a fire last year. But Phyllis always had a way of getting even with anyone who wronged her. *What am I going to do with these two grown ass women still fighting?* Her thoughts were mangled this morning on top of being stuck at work.

Jonetta didn't let on too much that she was completely irritated by being there because Dr. Franklyn kept thanking her every time he walked a patient to the front lobby. On Saturdays, he only saw six patients at the very minimum anyway and so far they only consisted of cleanings, one filling and a new patient consultation. So far, her workday was smooth sailing compared to weekdays. Besides, Dr. Franklyn had ordered lunch for them today and by the time their lunch arrived he was just finishing up the last patient for the day.

Jonetta put the two bags of food in the supply room on the counter when they arrived, but the aroma still lingered in the waiting area teasing her empty stomach. She sipped on piping hot black coffee, hoping it would curve her appetite, as she surfed the internet for new sandals but only found boots for the fall. *It's not even the end of August yet!* She shook her head and kept scrolling when the last patient appeared with gauze stuffed in his mouth asking for his next appointment. She happily provided a few dates and times that were available and jotted down the date and time that the patient agreed to with a couple of nods.

"Have a good weekend and heal well." Jonetta said as she hurriedly escorted the patient to the door. She locked the door, flipped the sign to read CLOSED, and exhaled.

Dr. Franklyn called the front desk to invite her into his office for lunch. She checked her smartphone to see if Norman was on his way, but only found messages from Phyllis and Dawn providing details about how the fight began. *Colette think she's off the hook, huh? She's got another thing coming!* She sent a text to Norman letting him know that she would be ready in an hour.

A whiff of her favorite lasagna and Greek salad combination greeted her as she rounded the corner to enter his office.

"Come on in and dig in!" Bishon had already emptied the bags of their contents and laid out a nice spread on the extra table in his office by the window.

"Thank you for ordering lunch, Doctor Franklyn," Jonetta said as she entered his office, clasping her hands together.

"If we are going to break bread together, I insist that you call me by my first name or at least my nickname," he said, raising his eyebrows and waited for her response.

"Will do, Bishon." Jonetta conceded. "Your whole name is… unique. Do you have a middle name?"

Bishon laughed. "Who needs that with a name like mine?" He gestured towards his desk where he cleared a space for Jonetta to sit and eat her lunch.

Jonetta smiled as she gathered her food, grabbed plastic ware, a bottled water and took a seat opposite of him at the desk. "Even the last name spelled with a Y instead of the traditional way is unique. I suppose your people were trying to separate themselves from the slave master's original spelling."

They shared a laugh.

"You know, I never thought of it that way," he pondered for a moment. "Or maybe this spelling *is* the original spelling." He stuffed a ravioli into his mouth as he gave Jonetta something to think about as well. He flicked aside the walnuts on his salad into a corner by themselves.

"Don't like walnuts?" Jonetta asked.

"I'm allergic to them." Bishon replied as he continued searching for more in his salad.

"My daughters and I are allergic, too." Jonetta nodded. "They make the roof of my mouth feel like it's on fire."

"Same here," he responded, frowning. Finally, he grew tired of fishing them out, placed the lid back on and pushed it to the side.

"Where are your people from?" Jonetta inquired, slicing her lasagna into perfect sections as if she were about to share it with six people.

"I don't know, exactly." Bishon released a slight chuckle, took a gulp from his bottled water and shook his head.

Jonetta paused slicing, cocked her head to the side and stared at him for a moment. "Young man, how is that even possible?"

"Well, I was adopted as a newborn. I don't really have a clue who or where my birth parents are," he explained casually. "All I know is that I was dropped off at a church. I had lung complications, could barely breathe. The church secretary found me and rushed me to a hospital. A few weeks later, she and her husband became my mom and Dad. Now, I know all about Stanton and Barbara Franklyn's background, of course, but nothing about my own."

Jonetta sat back in her chair and suddenly felt empathy for Bishon. She spent many years resenting her parents, especially her mother for having too many children. It seemed as if each time her father returned from one of his jobs, she popped up pregnant again. It's not like any of the pregnancies made him stick around any longer than he had before. But at least she knew who they were and where they were buried. "That's some story, Bishon. Well, be glad that you're an only child. My daughters have been fighting since they were born. Lately, they've been at each other's throats, fighting like animals."

"Who? Dawn?" Bishon asked concerned. "Is she okay?"

Jonetta paused for a moment. *Whoa, there buddy! You only met her once. Calm down.* "Dawn is fine. It's my other two that have lost their minds."

Bishon exhaled, relieved. "I'm sorry to hear that."

"Me too! They've been fighting like cats and dogs since they were little." Jonetta shook her head disgusted. "Anyway, getting back to you. Have you ever tried to look for your birth parents?" Jonetta inquired. Finally satisfied with her portion sizes, she placed a forkful of lasagna in her mouth and nodded. *This is so good! Norman will have to eat this for dinner tonight.*

"Of course, a while ago, but…" he shook his head.

"What happened? Stanton and Barbara didn't like the idea?" Jonetta presumed that if anybody, his mother would not appreciate him searching for someone who abandoned him.

"They are fine with it for the most part. It was uncomfortable for me, actually. All of these thoughts of doubt and what-ifs began swirling in my mind." He used his hands in a circular motion wildly on the sides of his temples as his eyes grew wide. "It made me feel inadequate, unwanted and unsure of myself. As you can see, Ms. Jonetta, I'm pretty self-established and I plan on opening another dental office later this year. I'm not lacking in self-confidence. And I'm certainly not familiar with any of those feelings, so I gave it a rest."

Jonetta nodded. "Impressive for a young man your age. But don't give up on finding your mother. You never know what made her drop you off at the church and thankfully she did. Right?"

Bishon shrugged, "You're right. I guess it could've been worse like being dumped in an alley or aborted altogether. My mother said she doesn't mind me doing the research, but..."

"Then do it!" Jonetta encouraged him as she cut the onions and tomatoes in her salad. "That way all of your curiosity will be satisfied."

"I am curious," Bishon admitted. He placed the lid back over his food and wiped his hands on a napkin carefully.

"I'm sorry if you lost your appetite talking about finding..."

"No worries," he reassured Jonetta. "But now I am seriously considering searching for her again."

"You should, Bishon," Jonetta replied softly. "You'll have a family of your own one day and you'll want to know even more then. Especially when you have children. You'll wonder about their features, their behaviors and sadly, as much as you love Stanton and Barbara, you won't be able to attribute any of those traits to them."

Bishon drummed his fingers on his desk as he let her words sink in. "That's true... I definitely want a family one day."

"Knowing your *real* family, especially your mother, is very important." Jonetta nodded her head repeatedly. "Just imagine, she's probably wondered all these years what happened to you, too. You probably are not an only child either. Bishon, becoming a mother is the hardest job in the world."

CHAPTER 10

The Proposal

"So you mean to tell me that you haven't felt a real dick since Vine?"

"Nope. I haven't," Dawn chuckled and shrugged. "I guess that comes with the territory of being single, I suppose. But now that Shon is in the picture that may change soon."

Chena leaned back on her pillows uncomfortably. Dawn could see that she was pondering something and waited for her to respond.

"What's up with that anyway? I'm surprised you haven't jumped his bones by now."

"I want to, but…" Dawn stared at the floor and fidgeted. "I'm kinda afraid he'll fall too deep in love with me. He plays love songs for crying out loud! He even offered his place to me if I needed to crash… Shon moves too fast in one area and not the other. It's like he wants me to commit to him only, which feels to me like he's a bit controlling. He even told me that I would never have to work again because he could take care of me. Honestly, Shon is offering everything I need. A place to stay, lots of money, and frequent dick." Dawn counted off the three offers on her fingers.

"But?" Chena nodded, urging her to continue her thoughts.

"But it's just too soon." Dawn shrugged. "And my mother works for him!"

"Well, I might have a solution to that problem," Chena replied with a wicked grin.

"What? Getting my mother another job?" Dawn laughed and shook her head.

"No, your dick problem."

"It's not necessarily a problem...I can get dick." Dawn retorted with a wink.

"Girl, please, you know you're aching to have that hot raw dog up in you!"

Dawn let out a loud howl, nodded her head in agreement. "But when I can't have it, that's what my vibrator is for. Although it certainly lacks warmth!"

They laughed together.

"Well, you do know that when I'm gone, I'll be replaced," Chena began. She clasped her hands together and her expression grew solemn.

"Oh, stop it!" Dawn couldn't bear the thought of losing her best friend. A hard lump grew in her throat immediately at the thought.

"I'm serious, Dawn. My days are numbered. You know that men cannot be alone for too long. Raffi will eventually want to remarry, or have some in-house hoochie around my son. If I'm going to be replaced, I want it to be you."

Dawn stared at her best friend, studied her face. She was serious. Chena didn't bat an eye. *This medication is making her lose her mind!* "You cannot be serious! What medication do they have you taking?"

"I am serious," Chena replied without blinking. "It's not like you and Raffi are strangers. After all, he was your boyfriend first."

"Yes, but we never..."

"I know, you told me. He told me, many times before. It was just a high school crush. I know! I know! But it just makes sense to me. You would finally get to feel a real dick and I can die in peace knowing it would be you raising Shiloh rather than a complete stranger. I would rest easy knowing that you were in my house, in my role, and being a good woman to my husband and son."

Dawn stood, paced the floor shaking her head in bewilderment. Her mind raced at the thought of basically becoming Chena, it turned her stomach. Dawn looked at Chena and felt pity for her. It had actually come down to this moment. She was dying and desperate.

"Please don't make this awkward request about my sex life, okay? I'm perfectly fine with my vibrator and using condoms with a random dude. Trust me on that."

"It's killing two birds with one stone, though." Chena continued, propping herself up on another pillow. "Dawn, I gave it a lot of thought."

"But I'm not interested in killing any birds!" Dawn contested while adjusting the pillow so it was square in the middle of her back. Dawn was ready to strangle her friend if she didn't shut up about her sex life and this ridiculous request! "I hope that you didn't discuss this with Raffi! Have you discussed this with Raffi?"

"No, I wanted to run it by you first." Chena repeatedly smoothed out her blanket mindlessly.

"Good, don't mention it to him," Dawn advised. "Don't ever let him know that we had this discussion. You don't want to give him a free pass to coochie-land."

"Raffi is going to do what he wants anyway." Chena admitted pointedly. "I'd rather it be with you, Dawn."

Dawn placed her hands on her narrow hips defiantly. "Would you please stop saying that? It sounds disgusting!"

"Right now it does, but the more time you spend with us the more natural it will become, I'm sure of it."

"What do you mean 'us'? I know you're not suggesting that I move into your house now! And why do you sound so convinced that I'm going to agree with this bullshit?"

"You need a place to stay. You don't want to move in with Shon or your parents. You want a sex life, but you don't want one with Shon. I'm simply offering you an alternative plan. Move in with us, become familiar with my husband and son, and take care of them in every way they need. Are you going to deny your dying best friend of her last wishes?"

"Uhn-uhn, heffa! Don't do that!" Dawn wagged her long, slender finger in her face. *Her manipulative ass gotta lot of nerve!* "Don't pull that sympathy shit on me!"

Chena laughed and shooed Dawn away.

"This shit is not funny, Chena!" Dawn plopped down on the end of the bed, frustrated with her best friend. "Why would you even suggest something like this anyway?"

"You're right, it's not funny, but it makes sense when you think about it."

"To whom?"

"Come on, you cannot tell me that after all these years you are not the least bit curious about Raffi. You never sealed the deal back in high school. Now here's your chance."

"Because I was not a loosey-goosey back in the day like you were!" Dawn slapped Chena's foot. "Hell, I'm still trying to catch up to you! But thank God we didn't have sex in high school because he ended up marrying you!"

"I've seen the way he looks at you when he thinks nobody is watching." Chena admitted lowering her eyes. "Sometimes, I think he wishes he married you instead."

Dawn took a swig of her Croix and almost choked. "What!?"

"If you aren't curious, he certainly is," Chena said and raised what was left of her thinning eyebrows. "Dawn, I *know* my husband. If I offered you on a platter, he would lick it clean."

"Oh, come on! Give Raffi a little more credit than that!" Dawn knew that Chena was certainly right about her suspicions, but defended him anyway. Since Dawn had been back in Chicago she had noticed on more than one occasion how Raffi gawked at her. She could feel his eyes all on her body, undressing her. Dawn used to be so in love with that man, more than she let on back then. She dismissed her feelings for him by reasoning it was just a high school crush, nothing more.

Before Chena was diagnosed with ovarian cancer, she had her head so far up his ass that she knew when he was about to take a shit! That joker swore he was always too tired or too busy to help her with their son, Shiloh. She might as well be a single parent as far as Dawn was concerned. Dawn remembered that she was thankful that she dodged a bullet. *Raffi probably strains his eye muscles with his wandering-eye-ass*. But that was none of Dawn's business until her best friend made it her business. At one point Chena had the notion in her mind that their marriage was perfect, until she was diagnosed and she could no longer put on a façade.

Chena pursed her lips and cocked her head. "Come on now, Dawn. You know I'm right. It's not like he's been the most faithful husband. You were probably next on his list anyway."

"I don't want your husband, first of all!" Dawn said to be perfectly clear. "Whatever we had back in the day was nothing more than a crush. Second of all, you know that I travel all the time, spur of the moment trips here and there so I'm the last woman to recruit to be in a domestic role. That's the very reason I didn't want to be with Vine, remember? Now I'm running from Shon for the same reasons. Do you ever listen to me?"

"You're the perfect woman for my family," Chena said, smiling as if she heard nothing that Dawn just explained. "You'll see."

☐☐☐☐☐

"I think it's a horrible idea for you to move in with them," Jonetta said.

"Chena needs my help, Mama. They have a big house in Olympia Fields, and I need a place to stay. Besides, I'll be closer to you and Dad now," Dawn explained. She desperately wanted her mother's approval for some reason, but she knew that she was batting zero.

"Dawn, it sounds like a marital mess is about to take place with you at the center of it!" Jonetta warned. She wasn't impressed by that little cherry-on-the-top that Dawn added at the end by being closer them. That was only a benefit if Dawn was going to be useful to them and Jonetta doubted that very seriously since she was always leaving town.

"Well, I can't wait to pack my bags and get away from that house!"

"Two women under one roof? Ha!" Jonetta scoffed. "Dawn, that's every man's dream. I bet it was his idea, too! He was in love with you as a teenager. I'm sure he can't wait to have you in house, watching you, waiting for his opportunity to pounce on you! If you're just looking for a place to live, you're better off just coming to stay with us."

Not a chance in hell! "Mama, please! It's nothing like that with Raffi!" Dawn tried to sound convincing. "This was all Chena's idea. You know that she is sick and not getting any better like they thought she would. She just needs help in her final stages. I've never had a friend die on me before and I just want to help."

"Soon enough she's going to be sick of *you* walking around looking beautiful in front of her husband. You're healthy, able-bodied and taking her place as the mother and wife. This isn't going to end well, Dawn. Just mark my words."

103

Dawn sighed. "It's better than living with Aunt Georgia, who's almost mentally absent from this world, and Colette with her kids. And to think she had another one on the way! I hate to say it, but it's a blessing in disguise that Colette didn't…"

Jonetta cleared her throat and glared at Dawn. "Your sister has been through a lot, Dawn. But I agree she didn't need another baby by that asshole."

"Yeah, well, even you bailed out on us, Mama!" Dawn reminded her mother that as soon as she got an offer to leave that house she jumped at the chance.

Jonetta couldn't deny that truth. "Nobody in their right mind would ask a beautiful woman like you to live with them! I hope she's been a good friend to you like you are being to her."

"Of course she has been! Mama, this is Chena that we're talking about."

"I know who we're talking about. Your best friend who married your high school sweetheart. I haven't liked her since, truth be told. You simply cannot trust a friend who would do such a thing. But you don't seem to be too bothered by it. Well, just don't say that I didn't forewarn you when the shit hits the fan, okay?"

"You'll be the last person to know if it does, Mama."

"You should've hopped on that hot cocoa train when you had the chance!" Jonetta chided. "Vine is on the cover of magazines and being interviewed on television left and right!"

Dawn cringed at the mention of his name. *Give it a rest!* She felt like her head was going to explode if her mother kept mentioning that man's name.

"Mama, you never liked Vine."

"That's neither here nor there. That boy was so in love with you!"

"And he wanted to change me, too! I cannot be domesticated and controlled like a puppet. You *know* me, Mama."

"Vine wanted you to become a wife, *his* wife. It's part of life, Dawn. But now you're about to go play a wife role for your friends' husband?" Jonetta frowned up her face and shook her head. "Do you actually listen to yourself sometimes? This doesn't make sense at all! Sooner or later you'll have to grow up and stop running from natural occurrences."

"I'm not running! I'm back!" Dawn was on the defense, frustrated that her mother was disapproving of her next move. She leaned back on the plush pillows, twirling her coils with her lips poked out. "Besides, I don't know how to be a wife. I don't even know what that looks like on a daily basis!"

"So why are you so quick to go play a wife and mother for Chena's family?"

"She's my friend! I just want to help her, Mama. But honestly, I don't know what I'm getting myself into because I never saw a happy marriage play out before my eyes because you and Dad divorced when I was a toddler."

"Oh, okay, so it's my fault?" Jonetta placed her hands on her hips, fed up with Dawn's excuses.

"You're missing the point, Mama." Dawn sucked her teeth and closed her eyes in frustration.

"And you missed the gravy train! You should've sucked it up and rode that hot ticket. Vine's career is on the right track and your career could've exploded simply by being seen on his arm in the public eye! You would've been that talk of social media with your beautiful skin, hair and fashion model experience! The right people would've been clawing just to get you in their circle!"

Dawn grew silent and Jonetta smirked. She knew that would give Dawn something to think about. Dawn loved the attention; always have since she was a toddler. Forget the fact that she was the baby and was going to get all the attention anyway, based on birth order alone. To hell with those facts! Dawn had to be the center of attention. Always dancing, singing, walking around the house in heels. She was the center of everyone's attention that translated to her career choices. Dawn craved attention and felt lost without it.

"I have a career too, Mama. However, I'm not going to use people to get where I want to be in life."

"I don't know why not," Jonetta replied. "That's how things have been done since the beginning of time."

Dawn sighed. "Mama, at the end of the day, I want to take pride in my accomplishments without someone throwing it in my face that if it weren't for them then I wouldn't be who I've become. No, thanks!" Dawn threw her hands in the air. "Besides, my career is far from over. It's just beginning."

"Yes, but you could be so much further ahead of the game had you accepted Vine's engagement ring."

"I saw Vine in Atlanta, and trust me… I'm soooo good on him. Trust me on this one, Mama!"

"Oh, now we're getting somewhere. Do tell."

"Mama, I really hate to break it to you, but Vine is gay!"

"Say what?!" Jonetta smashed her cigarette in the ashtray.

"I guess you would've been happier if I married Vine just to find out that he's gay, stay married in a fake marriage just for success and appearances sake!"

"Don't be so dramatic, Dawn." Jonetta rolled her eyes. "How did you find out that Vine was gay? That can't be true. Did you see him while you were there? Is that why you've been in a foul mood since you've been back?"

"I wouldn't just lie on Vine to shut you up, Mama. Come on, now," Dawn sighed. "Of course I saw him. I saw it with my own two eyes. He's with a transvestite now who looks very similar to me… except, it's a man. Quinn, as in Quentin."

"What the hell? You're kidding me! You really broke that boy's heart, Dawn."

Dawn laughed. "No offense, Mama, but I probably broke his… manhood. He's so green, I wonder if he knows that Quinn is a dude. But anyway, look at this family and its history with marriages and kids. It kinda sucks on all levels. There's always a financial problem, someone seeking a peace of mind or getting some freedom, and having options."

"What type of options?"

"Quite frankly, Mama, I cannot be with one person for the rest of my life! So it's probably best that I save everyone the heartache and disappointment now," Dawn admitted. "I like having options of men to choose from. I'm single, carefree and loving it!"

Jonetta threw her hands in the air, shook her head growing tired of the conversation. Trying to convince Dawn that she was making a terrible mistake was falling on her stubborn, deaf ears. "To thy own self be true," Jonetta replied. "Owen certainly doesn't mind having options and Colette allowed it. Phyllis and that Damien with their money problems sickens me! He's probably cheating on her too."

"What makes you say that?"

Jonetta raised one eyebrow and folded her arms across her chest. "If he's not gambling anymore, then what's the issue now? Only one thing it could be. You cannot just stop a bad habit without picking up another in its place. It's just human nature. He replaced his gambling with something... or someone else."

"Mama, have you discussed this with Phyllis?"

"For what?"

Dawn gave her mother a disappointing glare. "Because she's your daughter?"

Jonetta shrugged.

"Did you tell your sister that you saw her husband with that whore Shante?"

"Touché!"

"Look, Dawn, all I know is...sharing a man will only lead to a whole bunch of trouble. Trust me! I've seen that movie before a few times with different characters, but I know exactly how it ends every time."

CHICAGO, IL
1969

Jonetta was tired all the time now keeping company at her aunts' house and entertaining at Mr. Lucky's. It was becoming too much although the money was good and she could afford fine clothes, but her body ached and her soul was conflicted. The expensive minks and jewelry were from Mr. Lucky, her lover and pimp. He usually bought nice things for her after she would catch him with another woman... or whore who lived in his house. "It's part of the business, baby. I don't love them, but they have to show me appreciation from time to time." He explained. Jonetta said she understood, but didn't like it all the same. What Jonetta didn't understand was that Mr. Lucky was not anybody's man, he was a business man and that made him everybody's man.

Her aunts questioned her whereabouts on nights she should have been working at their house. They also questioned her fur coats she flaunted. "We don't even own more than one mink, Netta." Betty Lou said with a tinge of jealousy. Jonetta made up all types of lies that eventually she couldn't keep up. She decided to tell the truth and just suffer the consequences, whatever they may be. After a year's worth of savings and skimping on money that she earned, Jonetta figured she could afford her own place or just move in permanently with Mr. Lucky. The opportunity finally came when Betty Lou asked her again about her whereabouts one evening. "I'm beginning to think you're working for somebody else!"

"I don't. I have a man who loves me and provides everything I need," Jonetta replied frankly.

"Is that right, missy? And who might that be? It can't be that he thinks you're so pure and innocent. At the rate you're going flashing all these expensive jewels and furs, he's probably your pimp, but you're just too dumb to realize it."

Jonetta scoffed and glared at Betty Lou with as much hate as she could muster. Betty Lou knew she struck a nerve. "Pure and innocent? Oh, you mean like you?"

"Don't get smart with me! You mind your manners. I'm still your aunt."

Jonetta rolled her eyes and replied, "Mr. Lucky is my man." There. She said it. The cat was out of the bag. She was snide about it on purpose to hurt Betty Lou. Had she been more street smart, Jonetta would have said it while standing to defend herself for what was coming next. But she sat at the kitchen table and glanced at her nails thinking she was due for a manicure.

"Who did you say?"

"I think you heard me the first time," Jonetta replied still looking at her nails.

"You little bitch!" Betty Lou lunged at her neck and held a tight grip. She shook Jonetta trying to choke the life out of her. "I'll kill you! He's mine!" Jonetta clawed at her aunt's arms trying to release them, but Betty Lou had a vice grip around her neck. Finally, Jonetta kicked her in the shins and Betty Lou stumbled backward. Jonetta coughed and tried to catch her breath, but Betty Lou was back at her. This time she grabbed a huge chunk of Jonetta's hair and threw her on the floor. Jonetta grabbed her aunt's ankles and yanked hard causing her to fall flat on her ass. Betty Lou hit her head against the cabinet when she fell and she saw stars. Finally, she whimpered and grabbed the back of her head. When she saw blood on her hands, she cried even harder.

"Get out!"

Jonetta stood to her feet and said, "Gladly!"

"He's just using you! He doesn't love you. You're a stupid little whore!"

Jonetta spun around and replied, "Betty Lou, if he loved you so much he would've married you long time ago and you'd be having his baby instead of me."

Betty Lou's mouth flew open and she screamed, "Get the hell out and never come back!"

Although Jonetta lied about being pregnant, she knew that announcement would cut Betty Lou to the core of her soul… and it worked. After she told Mr. Lucky what happened, except the pregnancy lie, he allowed her to live with him. He never "visited" Betty Lou again. Adelle tried to reach out to him, but he thought it would be best to cut all ties with the aunts. He did love Jonetta, but did not have any intentions on marrying her nor having any children with her. She was good for him and for his business. That's all.

It seemed that her daughters never listened to her sound advice. *Raffi and Chena are only going to use you!*

CHAPTER 11

Nobody's Fool

She felt so stupid. Maybe she was the one living in the fantasy world thinking that her husband is supposed to be faithful and honest. Maybe she was the unrealistic one and he was the one living in the real world. *What will my family and friends think when they find out that our husbands are sharing a side chick? Hell, they probably already know!*

When Dawn and Colette dropped the bomb on her about Damien and Shante, she was unable to control her breathing and tears. Back and forth, she weighed her options. *Call him now, he'll play dumb. Wait until later and look him in the eye. Call him now and, he'll turn it around on you! Wait until later... he'll turn it around on you!* Finally, she gave way to her secretly hidden vodka that was waiting for her in the basement door. After a few straight shots, she mustered the courage to pick up the phone. Her hands shook as she scrolled through her contact list on the phone. Once she landed on his name it occurred to her that his name wasn't stored under "Babe" or "Hubby" like most women did their significant others. It was just plain ole "Damien".

She wiped away tears and took a deep breath. *No, just wait until he comes home.* As her breathing increased, her tears began to flow from anger. She sat on the sofa, rocked back and forth with the phone clutched to her breasts and cried. Her thoughts led her to seeing Damien playing the dumb role when she confronted him. *Lord, please let him just tell the truth so I won't have to kill him!* She had not had an asthma attack since she was a child, but at that moment, she felt one coming on strong.

What could he possibly want with that hoe, Shante? It could be nothing, just like Dawn said, but Colette said the bitch was pregnant! By whom? Damien or Owen? There was no real explanation for any of it in her mind. Now what was she supposed to do? If she kicked him out, she would be forced to use her funds until she found a job. And how long would that take considering the job market these days? She didn't even want to think about going back into the workforce. When she worked downtown, men flirted with her all the time! Although she would be flattered and sometimes even tempted, she remained faithful to Damien. Hell, if she could keep her legs closed, why couldn't he? Did Damien think she wasn't capable of the same thing? *Am I this naïve and so trusting of him?*

Just because she put on a few extra pounds after the twins didn't mean she wasn't sexy anymore. She was sexy alright! Her creamy, walnut skin, almond eyes, small yet full lips, high cheekbones and a button nose to boot were God's perfect creation. Her hair was thick and long, just the way Damien liked it. Since she had been home, her wardrobe only consisted of shorts, yoga pants or capris, t-shirts and tank tops. Not very sexy, but still no excuse for his behavior. She bit her cuticles until they bled. Although it stung, she needed that little distraction for the time being while she sorted her life out. Right now, she didn't want to be a mother. She didn't want to be a wife. She just wanted to be Phyllis Miller again. She balled up on the sofa allowing a river of tears to stream down her face. She tasted the saltiness as the tears crept through the corner of her mouth.

Phyllis had nothing but time on her hands to think the situation through clearly. But every time she came to a conclusion it involved bodily harm. It didn't seem so unreasonable considering the circumstances. She poured herself one more shot of vodka before placing the jug back onto the basement steps. She wondered if she should call her mother to get the twins until she sorted things out with Damien. But she wasn't prepared to go into too much detail about what happened. Hell, she didn't even know what was really going on based on what Dawn said. *He was in the car with Shante, Owen's side chick, of all people! I can't even make sense of this shit!* Phyllis didn't know exactly what she was going to do, but she didn't want to say too much too soon only to look like a fool later.

Eventually, she climbed into bed after she got tired of waiting on Damien to bring his sorry ass home. The alcohol forced her mind to shut off, and her eyes closed. When she opened her eyes again, Damien was the first thing she saw grinning in her face. His breath reeked of beer as he whispered in her ear, "I'm home, baby." Phyllis jerked her face away and pushed him away from her. He laughed as he kissed her neck, grabbing her breasts, giving them a firm squeeze.

"Stop it, Damien!" Phyllis pushed him away, but she wasn't using as much force as she thought because thanks to the vodka. She couldn't bear to look at him so she shut her eyes closed and tried pushing him away again.

"Nooooo..." he groaned. "We have the house to ourselves and I'm feeling good, baby. I want allllll of you..." Damien began singing John Legend's "All of Me" totally off key. "Don't you want alllll of me?" He swiftly climbed on top of Phyllis, slowly gyrating his hips on top of hers. When Phyllis tried to push him away again, she felt his skin. She opened her eyes to see a full view of his erection. He had already taken off his pants in anticipation to go for the kill.

"I know you want me, baby." Damien massaged between her legs through her panties.

Yessss...

"You've been trying to get some of this good D for a minute."

Yessss...

"And, I'm gonna give it to you, baby."

Yessss... give it to me! No... wait...stop!

Phyllis moaned as he lunged down to nibble on her neck. His locs fell on top of her face, hitting her repeatedly and she grew irritated. "Get off of me!" She clamped her legs shut as she remembered that she was supposed to be mad at him. *Question him about being with Shante. Get to the damn bottom of things!*

"Stop it, Damien!"

"Have you been drinking, baby? It's cool if you have... 'cause I've been drinking, too!" Damien continued kissing her neck, holding her hands down as he worked his way down to her exposed nipple. "Why is your shirt ripped, baby? Take this shit off!"

Yessss... take it off...

Damien lifted her shirt along with her bra over her head without any fuss from Phyllis.

As his hands explored her body, she arched her back and spread her legs again, welcoming him into her space. Damien didn't hesitate to slide her panties to the side to dive into his wife. Over the next few minutes, Phyllis moaned, panted, and finally cried. Her vodka-induced emotions were all over the place. She hated and loved it all at the same time. She missed his touch and hungry desire for her. It had been so long, so she gave in easily because she knew it would be a long time coming once they had their talk in the morning.

When they finished making love, Damien passed out on his side of the bed while Phyllis stared at the ceiling wide-eyed with their sweat clinging to her clammy skin and their evidence of sex between her thighs. She was wide awake now with thoughts swirling in her mind about the mixed message she just gave Damien. Forget the fact that they just had mind-blowing sex she still wanted answers regardless.

Phyllis eased from their bed and went into the master bathroom, softly closing the door behind her. Once she turned on the light and caught a glimpse of herself, she was disgusted. A pained expression grew across her face. *This wasn't the plan at all!* After knocking back shots of vodka plus two glasses of wine, she knew that her head would be pounding the next day. She opened the bathroom cabinet, popped four pills and downed them with water.

As she plopped on the toilet to relieve her full bladder, she rehearsed in her mind how she would begin the conversation in an accusatory tone, but now that they made love, it would come across as if she was insane! She debated if she should say anything at all just to keep the peace between them. *Plenty of women turned a blind eye to their cheating husbands,* she reasoned. Nevertheless, that would be living a lie. It would take too much energy for her to put on phony smiles, nodding in agreement with him, and playing nice while keeping her mouth shut. *No! I'm not one of those weak ass women!*

She felt the rage boiling inside of her again. *Why was he with that bitch at all? Does he know who she is? Of course he does!* She visualized herself taking a baseball bat right to Shante's belly and one to the skull. This was followed by an even clearer vision of her clawing at Damien's face, peeling his smooth caramel skin and drawing blood until the white flesh appeared. Without even realizing it, Phyllis was grinding her teeth as the wicked thoughts took over her mind.

When she pulled open the drawer to look for her feminine wipes, a pair of scissors were staring at her. That gave her a completely new idea. His pride. His crowning glory that took over a decade to grow, long and beautiful. *How dare you cheat on me?* She cleaned herself, snatched the scissors from the drawer and slammed it shut. "Shit!" She was so caught up in her devious thoughts that she forgot to be quiet so she wouldn't wake him. She paused for a moment, holding her breath to listen for movement from the bedroom. She exhaled softly when she didn't hear any signs of him moving.

As Phyllis slowly opened the bathroom door, she peered through the darkness to see Damien still sleeping on his left side. She could only chop away at the right side of his head, but in her anger it didn't matter because she wanted revenge. She quietly tiptoed to his side of the bed, gingerly lifting two of his locs. She licked her bottom lip she attempted her first cut. *Dammit!* The locs were thick. She grimaced struggling cutting through them, but once she got a good angle nothing stopped the madness. Phyllis was trying to be quiet as she could while she unevenly snipped away at his locs. *Got me out here looking like a damn fool!* Some were short, some mid-length, and some were cut sideways as her heart raced, partly out of anger and fear that he would wake up. *Of all people to creep with!* She held on to a few of the locs in her hand as she steadily cut his hair, but most fell onto the floor or in the bed. With one side of his head with short locs and the other side with long, Damien wouldn't have a choice other than to get it all cut off. He was going to be furious in the morning when he got a good look of himself in the mirror, but she didn't care right now. She had to teach him a lesson.

Finally satisfied with her handiwork, she crept back to their bathroom, dumped a handful of his locs in the bathroom wastebasket, grabbed her smartphone and pillow off the bed and headed downstairs to the living room. The clock on the wall read 3:20 in the morning. She groaned. Her mind was too active for her liking, so she carefully opened the basement door and took another swig of vodka from the jug. The fiery sting was racing down her throat and felt like it singed her stomach. She clutched her stomach, flopped on the sofa and tossed the throw blanket over her hoping to finish sleeping.

In the morning, she jumped from her slumber when she heard someone yelling her name repeatedly. She lied on the sofa frozen not really knowing what to do next. It was Damien. He was awake. Wide-awake and aware. Fear shot through her body. The damage was done. She couldn't undo any of it. Before she could gather her thoughts, Damien flew down the stairs screaming.

"Phyllis! What the fuck did you to me? Why did you do this?" His eyes were burning with fury as he held a fistful of his locs, shaking them in the air. "We just had a great night... I'm so... confused...What the fuck? Why would you cut off my hair? Answer me, dammit!"

Phyllis recoiled only for a moment at the sight of him. As he stood there with half of his hair looking like "Sid the Science Kid", it was almost comical and she had to catch herself from laughing. *He might choke the shit out of me if I laugh.*

"Have you lost your fuckin' mind, Phyllis? Answer me!" Damien rushed towards her as if he was about to hit her.

Phyllis jumped from the sofa, stood to her feet with her fists balled just in case they came to blows. She yelled in his face, "You can't cheat on me and get away with it! Not now! Not ever!"

"What? I haven't cheated on you!" Damien responded confused as his nostrils flared. "Is that why you cut my locs off!? You think I'm cheating on you?"

"Dawn saw you getting in the car with that bitch Shante! Don't even try to deny it, Damien! She saw you!" Phyllis folded her arms across her chest and pursed her lips.

"Is that what this is about?" Damien shook a fistful of locs in her face. "You think that I would cheat on you with Owen's side chick, so you cut off my hair? You are fuckin' CRAZY, Phyllis!" Damien threw his hair to the floor and stared wide-eyed at Phyllis.

"Why were you with that bitch knowing full well she is a homewrecker?"

"You are something else!" Damien shook his in disbelief. He touched the right side of his head where she cut his locs short and tears welled up in his eyes.

"I'm listening." Phyllis jerked her neck and placed her hands on her hips.

"I was out looking for a place to call our own! Shante is a realtor, remember?"

"That whore is *not* the only realtor in all of Chicago, Damien!" Phyllis shouted. "Try again, but this time don't insult my intelligence!"

The expression on his face was of pure disgust. His eyes glazed over with hurt. He shook his head repeatedly, rubbed his beard and exhaled. "I don't feel like I actually owe you an explanation because this time YOU fucked up, Phyllis! But... to put your mind at ease and so I can watch you eat humble pie later I'm going to explain this to you one time, and then I'm done!" Damien pointed his finger in her face and began to explain, "For your information, I ran into Owen and Shante while I was WORKING! You know, the job that I have to keep a roof over our heads and food on the table? Yeah, I was *working* when I saw them and he was just shooting-the-shit, asking about the family and how we liked this new house. That's when I mentioned how I really didn't like it and how I wanted to buy a house for us since I could probably afford it now that I got a promotion as a manager!" Damien paused for a moment to let that news sink in. Phyllis expression was priceless. She was about to say something but he held his hand up to her face and continued, "That's when Owen mentioned that Shante was a realtor and could give us a family discount. I took her card and she's been sending me several houses to look at ever since. One caught my eye in Hyde Park and she showed it to me. That's probably the day Dawn saw us because that's the only time we were together because I've been too busy working!"

Phyllis shot her eyes to the ground from embarrassment. It all seemed like a reasonable explanation now, but she still had questions.

"Why didn't you tell me any of this before? When did you get promoted?"

"I wanted to surprise you with all of it!" Damien explained furiously.

"Damien, don't you think that I should be involved on deciding where we live?" she asked softly.

"Get the fuck outta my face, Phyllis!" Damien flicked his hand, dismissing her and walked away towards the stairs. "That's all you have to say for yourself?"

"Damien! Come back!" Phyllis pleaded.

He stopped in his tracks, whirled around and yelled, "What do you want? You can't even apologize when you are dead wrong! Look at me! Now I have to spend my Saturday finding someone to fix the mess you created! You know how long it took me to grow out my locs and you just go and chop them off the minute you think that I cheated on you? Your ass didn't even bother to ask..."

"Damien... if you are telling the truth, then I'm terribly sorry..."

"Did you say 'IF'? If I'm telling the truth!? You know what..." Damien walked towards her and pointed in her face, "I want you to get the fuck outta my house!"

"What?" Phyllis shrieked in disbelief.

"You heard me! You fuckin' bi..."

Phyllis gasped. *I know he didn't!*

"Ohhhhh weeeee..." Damien placed his fist up to his mouth. "I almost called you out of your name, girl... You better go now, Phyllis! I swear to God! You better get your shit and get the fuck out before it gets too ugly around here!"

CHAPTER 12

Freedom Fight

Colette stood on her feet immediately when she heard the front door open. Her racing heart leaped in her throat, her stomach did a flip. She had been anticipating his arrival and the confrontation about their divorce. As she heard Owen down the hallway, she scurried to get the paperwork to present to him. *This should be quick and easy.* She could hear the pounding in her head growing louder and louder with every step he took.

"Wassup?" Owen said standing in the living room with his hands wedged in his pockets. He grew his jet black hair out long enough to slick it in a ponytail with a braid. With a gold chain dangling low on his t-shirt and baggy jeans, he looked just like a playboy, every woman's nightmare. *What did I ever see in him?* Colette imagined that Delilah's hair would be just like that once she got older. She could see a piece of all of her children in his face as he stood there looking dumbfounded, which made it even more difficult to discuss their divorce.

"So you just let yourself in these days, huh?"

Owen shrugged. "It's not like you weren't expecting me. So, wassup?"

"You know what I want to discuss, Owen. I told you over the phone."

"Well, let's talk about it then." Owen took a seat on the sofa, spread his legs wide open along and draped his long arms across the back of the sofa. To his surprise, Colette sat in an armchair across the room from him. "Why are you way over there? Come here. Sit next to me." He patted the sofa cushion softly.

"I'm good right here." Colette refused, rolling her eyes. Owen looked surprised at her response. She didn't look herself either. Her turquoise blouse with chiffon ruffles and white shorts with sparkly sandals complimented her well, but it wasn't her style. At least the style that Owen was used to seeing. It was like she had a make-over since the last time he saw her. Even her eyes were determined, her posture confident and her voice steady with authority.

"Look, Owen, it's pretty evident that things are over between us. We don't have property or assets to argue about, so this should be easy. All you need to do is sign the papers so we can move on with our lives."

"But…we do have kids." Owen leaned forward and rubbed his hands together as if he had a good idea swirling in that empty brain of his.

"And? You can see them whenever you want. You know that! There's a whole section in here about visitation." Colette remarked, flipping through the pages. "Although you never really commit to seeing your children like you should." She raised her eyebrows waiting for his response to that truth.

"What about child support? Is that in there too?"

"If you look through the papers you will find out. Now, will you please sign the papers?" Colette placed the document on the table and slammed a pen on top of it.

"You must have some new man or something. Usually, you'd be sweating me to be a family or begging me for some money. I see what this is about now! You and this new nigga wanna live happily ever after with *my* kids. Is that it?" Owen jumped off the sofa standing over Colette.

"Stay away from me you bastard!" Colette blurted, surprising herself and Owen. That's not what she wanted to say. That was not how she wanted to approach him, but that was her first reaction. She stood to her feet to show him that she was not going to be afraid anymore, although she was.

"Would you calm your ass down?" Owen held his hands up in defense. "This ain't even that type of visit, Colette. I came to talk about this divorce thing and see my kids. Where are my damn kids anyway?"

"They are outside playing. You probably didn't recognize them because you haven't seen them in so long!"

Owen jerked his neck and sucked his teeth. "Shut yo' ass up talking crazy to me! I can recognize my own damn kids!"

"Can you just sign the divorce papers?" Colette pointed to the papers on the table.

Owen folded his arms across his chest, stared at Colette for a few seconds before responding. He gave her a once over and nodded his head. "I could want us to get back together, but you won't even give me a chance to talk."

"I don't want to hear nothing you have to say about us, Owen! It's over!" Colette screamed. *Calm down, girl. Don't get him worked up.* She couldn't help it. She clutched her shirt as she felt a sharp pain shoot through her chest. When her breath quickened Owen became concerned and tried to calm her, but Colette resisted and swung on him.

"What the fuck is wrong with you!?" Owen grabbed her arm to prevent her from swinging again.

"I know all about you getting that bitch pregnant! How could you?" She slapped him in the face with her other hand. Owen's eyes bulged as he grabbed her by both wrists. They stood staring at one another in silence. Colette felt his rapid pulse on her wrists, both of their heart beats were creating a dance-worthy rhythm accompanied by their heavy breathing. He was completely thrown off guard by her discovery.

"Who told you that shit?" He growled, shaking her.

"You're a liar and a cheater, Owen!" Colette's voice cracked. She tried to keep her tears from falling because she didn't want him to think that she was weak. "We have four children, a lifetime of memories, and I thought we had a future, but you threw it all away! We could never get back together. There is no US! Now let me go, Owen!" Although she had rehearsed repeatedly what she would say to him, this was the result. She saw Owen become enraged and feared what would follow. He was furious now. The thought of losing his family for good angered him. He let go of her wrists with a push. Colette stumbled backwards, but remained standing. She quivered fearing knowing what was next, but this time she was ready to fight back.

"I was ready to come back to you! I told your ass that I was coming back!" Owen stepped closer to her and pointed in her face. "But when you lost my baby...I didn't see the point anymore. It

120

would just be the same ole bullshit! So, yeah, I'm starting a new family with Shante!"

"I didn't lose the baby, Owen." Colette replied calmly. She squinted her eyes and folded her arms across her chest as she let those words sink in.

"What the fuck are you saying?" Owen leaned his head forward as if he was straining to see her clearly. "What the hell are you talking about, Colette?"

Colette pursed her lips and cocked her head to the side. "I didn't *lose* the baby." She repeated slowly so he could understand this time. For once she felt like she had the upper hand and it felt good.

"You fell down the stairs on purpose?!" Owen grabbed her by the shoulders, shook her over and over trying to understand. "You crazy bitch! You killed our baby? Answer me!"

Colette let out a wicked laugh as he shook her. Finally, she pushed Owen with both of her hands as forcefully as she could to get him away from her. They were both breathing heavily. "Just sign the damn divorce papers and get the hell out of our lives!"

Owen took his hand and slapped her as hard as he could across her face. Colette lost her balance and went face first into the mantelpiece ledge. She let out a scream when she hit her head. Blood began to trickle down into her right eye. She wiped it away with the back of her hand and became enraged seeing all the blood on her hand. Her vision was blurry as the blood streamed into her eye. Not caring what came next, she lunged at Owen scratching and clawing his face. She smiled when she felt his flesh tear open with each swipe of her nails.

"Get off of me! You crazy bitch!" Owen yelled, trying to catch her hands.

"Mama! Stop!"

Colette's body froze when she turned around to see her son.

□ □ □ □ □

"He's not taking it well," Colette said, massaging her forehead. "I think he blames me for everything."

"Cornell is a big boy. He just needs time to process everything," Georgia replied, leaning over to pat her knee. "Some fresh air will do him some good. I saw him take off on his bike towards the park."

"Everything happened so fast. One minute Owen I'm trying to get him to sign the divorce papers, the next minute we're arguing and he slaps me. I fought back this time, and that's the part Cornell saw when he walked into the kitchen. Then he called the police. But I was only fighting for my life!"

"Finally!" Jonetta replied, blowing out a cloud of smoke.

"Netta..." Georgia admonished.

"No, I agree," Colette interrupted. "Yes, Mama, finally I stood up for myself and I feel good about it."

"Well, you don't *look* good. Your lip is swelling by the minute, your eye is blood shot red, and you have a cut on your brow. Maybe we should take you to the hospital. You probably need stitches."

Colette shook her head. "No, I'm not going. This is nothing. I know how to fix myself up."

Jonetta and Georgia shared a glance of disbelief.

"What has gotten into you lately, Colette? First, you're fighting with your sister, now Owen. You've got to know which battles to choose, and which ones you can actually win."

"I'm just tired of everyone treating me like they can walk all over me! I've reached my breaking point!" Colette yelled. She winced at the pain that shot through her face where Owen slapped her. The bag of frozen peas was only making her skin numb, but swelling of her bottom lip began to feel heavy when she talked.

"Georgia, where were you when all of this was happening?" Jonetta demanded to know, eyeing her sister. She was still in her housecoat as if it were seven o'clock in the morning.

"Netta, I was taking a nap." Georgia answered shrugging her shoulders.

"As usual." Jonetta remarked, rolling her eyes.

"I just hate that the police had to get involved," Colette admitted.

"Why?" Georgia and Jonetta asked simultaneously, shocked by her admission.

"Because Owen is still the father of my children. I don't want him in jail. I just want him out of my daily life!" Colette explained as if they were stupid. "I'm glad he left before the police got here. I can't press charges anyway because I messed up his face pretty badly."

"Oh, child…" Georgia sighed, shaking her head.

"I wish the cops would've gotten here sooner to bash his head in!" Jonetta blurted out, puffing on her cigarette and squinting her eyes as she allowed the smoke to escape through her nose. "Now you have your father out there looking for him. It's no telling what he's going to do to Owen! After your father saw your face, he's likely to kill that man! It would've been better if the cops got to him first. But your silly-self told them not to press charges! He's a dead man walking now!"

"Mama!" Colette shouted, covering Ruthie's ears. "Would you please stop?"

"Come on, baby. Aunt Georgia is going to make mommy some special tea. You wanna help me?" Ruthie nodded and grabbed Georgia's hand. "I'm going to check on Delilah and Lydia, too." Georgia announced as she led Ruthie into the kitchen, glaring over her shoulder at Jonetta.

"I really wish you wouldn't speak like that about their father in front of them, Mama!"

"Oh, yeah? Well, I really wish *their* father would keep his hands off of *my* daughter! You're their mother for God's sakes! Cornell should always side with you, not that loser! You have to do a better job of teaching your kids that their loyalty is to you, always!"

Colette pressed the gauze on her forehead harder, and exhaled sharply. *I don't need a lecture right now!*

"Look at you! Just go in that bathroom and take a good look at yourself!"

"No!" Colette refused because the way she felt was enough indication of how she really looked.

Jonetta jumped up from her seat, snatched Colette by the arm, and dragged her into the bathroom. She grabbed Colette by the shoulders and shoved her towards the mirror, "I said LOOK!"

Colette slowly raised her eyes to the mirror. She removed the gauze, whimpered, holding back strained sobs until her reflection in the mirror spoke a silent truth. She sobbed covering her face. Blood from the cut above her brow began to seep into her hand.

Colette looked at the blood on her hand then looked at herself in the mirror. "Look what he did to me."

"Out of all the black men in Chicago, why couldn't the cops just kill this one today?"

Colette gasped at her mother's vicious comments. Her bottom lip quivered as she let out a loud cry. "Mama, please!"

"I wouldn't shed a tear! Not a single one! Do you hear me?" Her words were purposely spiteful to shock Colette back into her reality.

Colette wailed, slowly collapsed into her mother's arms. Jonetta sat her down on the toilet seat, lifted her chin so she could get a good look at her wound. She sucked her teeth because she knew that it would have to be stitched which meant a long night in the emergency room at the County hospital.

"Make sure this is the last time he ever lays a hand on you, Colette. If you don't, I will!" Jonetta looked at Colette directly in the eyes to make sure that she understood what she was saying.

Colette nodded as she tore tissue off the roll. She wiped her nose and winced from the stinging pain shooting through her face every time she touched it.

"What were you all arguing about anyway?" Jonetta folded her arms across her chest and sighed waiting for Colette to gather her composure.

"I told him that I knew about Shante being pregnant."

"What? Never mind…" Jonetta replied shaking her head. "I don't even want to know how you know that!"

"I heard about it at church." Colette shrugged. "Then we argued about the baby…" Colette wiped her nose with the tissue wincing again.

"Which one?" Jonetta asked concerned.

Colette sobbed, shaking her head. She didn't want to talk about it.

"What did you tell him?" Jonetta asked anxiously. "Colette! What did you say to Owen?"

Colette refused to answer her mother. All she could hear was the pounding of her heart in her ears and felt it in her throat. She winced as she felt the gash above her brow separate. *Maybe I do need stitches.*

"Look at me, dammit!" Jonetta shouted lifting Colette's chin. "You and I both know that your uterus is stronger than a mule's back. Owen knows that, too. He's an idiot, but he's not stupid. You had better stick to your 'miscarriage' story because if he ever found out the truth…"

"It's too late. I told him…" Colette wailed. She buried her face in her hands again. "Mama, I feel so guilty about what I did."

"Why on earth would you tell him what you did!?" Jonetta threw her hands in the air. "You really know how to make matters worse than they have to be, don't you?" Jonetta paced the small space in the bathroom, shaking her head. "But who could blame you? Look at the misery you're in all the time with him! The four children you have are enough to prove you love somebody. It's time you love yourself, Colette. We're all relieved that you didn't have another baby by that asshole! But you didn't have to tell him *how* you lost the baby!" Jonetta patted her daughter's shoulder, but Colette snatched away.

I know she's not blaming me? Jonetta glared at Colette, trying to read her, but she couldn't tell one way or the other what that snatch was about. "What's your problem?"

"Seems like you encourage your daughters to get rid of their babies if you think it means being miserable and stuck with a man for the rest of our lives." Colette finally admitted, sniffing. She kept her eyes forward not wanting to look at the expression on her mother's face.

Jonetta huffed. "Phyllis was seventeen-years-old! What do you expect a mother to do? Your situation was different. I didn't force you."

What did Colette expect her to do when she came to her mother crying her eyes out? With baby Delilah latched onto her boob sucking for dear life, she had expressed regret and not wanting another baby by Owen. Quite frankly, Jonetta was glad that she felt that way. The feeling was mutual throughout the family. Well, save for Norman and Georgia who think all children are a blessing from God. Jonetta strongly disagreed. Some children were downright Satan's spawn that came with guaranteed debt for eternity.

When Colette asked her mother to visit one afternoon, she was in shambles. Jonetta was concerned that Colette suffering from the baby blues again, like she had with Lydia. Most women suffered from it after a pregnancy, but her hair had an oily texture with a stench as if it hadn't been washed in weeks. All of their clothes were unkempt and the kids looked as though they had not had a bath in days. Colette held onto her latest blessing, Delilah, so tightly that she began to choke on her milk, but Colette had not seemed notice. Jonetta quickly took her granddaughter from her arms to examine her for bruises, a diaper rash or any signs of neglect. After burping her granddaughter and lying her down on her Queen-sized bed, Jonetta went to the kitchen, poured a glass of Jameson neat, gulped it down and popped a peppermint in her mouth.

Even after Jonetta snatched the baby from her arms Colette just sat with a tear stained face, staring at nothing while her exposed breast leaked milk all over her clothes. At first Jonetta thought it was just the hormones talking, but Colette was serious. She confessed that she really did not want to go through another pregnancy. She wanted a divorce from Owen, but if she kept the baby, nine months was enough time for Colette to be suckered back into whatever lies and deception he had to offer. Colette admitted that she was just not strong enough to go through with it and get a divorce. She knew it, and everybody else knew it too. Colette needed to end it in every way possible. Jonetta saw a piece of her daughter dying, she understood all too well.

CHICAGO, IL
1967

Jonetta had been down those steps more than a hundred times, but this day she lost her balance. She took a long tumble and landed on top of her stomach at the bottom of the stairs. She wailed and tried to reposition herself, but her left leg bent sideways and it caused her more pain. The aunts came rushing down the stairs to her aid.

"Oh, God! What have you done?" Betty Lou exclaimed. "How many times have I told you to be careful on these steps?"

Adelle gasped as soon as she saw Jonetta's twisted leg. "Let's move her on the floor; she's too heavy to carry back up the stairs." Adelle and Betty Lou counted to three and moved her on the cold, concrete floor. Jonetta winced and stiffened from the pain that shot through her body. It felt like fire from the waist down until she felt something warm gushing between her legs. The pain sharpened feeling like someone was repeatedly stabbing her. She screamed with tears streaming down her face.

"Something's happening down there," Jonetta managed to say between quick deep breaths. Betty Lou lifted Jonetta's smock and gasped, "I'm going to call Doctor Scott." She darted up the stairs quickly to call the doctor whom helped their girls get out of "trouble". Adelle squeezed Jonetta's hand. Jonetta cried out in pain. She twisted and flinched every time the pain ripped through her body, which seemed like every minute. Adelle cried with her and kept reassuring her that she was going to be just fine, until she heard Betty Lou returning.

"The doctor said he would get here as soon as he could. In the meantime, let's see what we can do for this girl." Betty Lou was beside herself with fear, but she did not to let on. She was the level-headed one, always in control.

Adelle hung her head because she knew what was happening. The fluid the baby needed to survive was slowly making a puddle on the floor. If the doctor did not arrive in a matter of minutes, the baby would not make it into the world alive. She wiped her eyes with her sleeve, biting her bottom lip to keep it from quivering.

"Adelle! Snap out of it and help me!" Betty Lou yanked her arm hard forcing her off the floor. They rushed to the laundry area to gather towels.

The last thing Jonetta heard was hushed whispering between the aunts before she finally fainted from the pain that shot through her body once again. When she woke up an older white man was checking her pulse from her wrist. He cleared his throat and announced, "We have to get this baby out of her or it could cause her complications not to mention death."

"What?" Jonetta said trying to rise up on her elbows. "What's wrong with my baby?"

"Lie down, dear," Adelle whispered. "The doctor is here now, everything will be fine."

"But ... my baby..."

"Doctor, give her something to relax her and keep her quiet," Betty Lou demanded.

"I can't. I need her to push the baby out," he said and lifted Jonetta's head off the cold floor. "Lean up some more on your elbows, young lady. Miss Adelle, come support her head. Miss Betty, spread her legs."

Jonetta yelped in pain. "My leg! Don't touch my leg. I think it's broken."

"There's no doubt about that." Dr. Scott replied, adjusting his eyeglasses. "It definitely is broken, probably in two different places. We'll worry about that later. Right now, I need you to push this baby out."

"What? But I'm not ready! It's not time yet," Jonetta cried in confusion. She looked at her aunts for an explanation; there was none.

"Hold her down," Dr. Scott instructed. "No time for talking. Bear down really hard, young lady."

Jonetta shook her head, refusing to push her baby out. It was too soon, she had three more months to go.

"Listen to me! It's either you or this baby! You can have more children if you let me save your life now!" Dr. Scott explained, frustrated that Jonetta couldn't comprehend what was taking place.

Jonetta whimpered, letting his words sink in. She certainly didn't want to die on this cold floor in a basement, but she didn't want her baby to die down there either. She took a deep breath and pushed as she was told, but nothing was happening, only excruciating pain. Her body felt viciously ripped apart. Sweat poured down her forehead as she panted, and yelled. She squeezed Adelle's hand harder with each push, but Adelle never let go. After a few more minutes of pushing finally she felt her baby leave her womb.

Jonetta panted, thankful that it was all over. The doctor's eyes met Betty Lou's, then he glanced at Adelle. He never looked Jonetta directly in the eyes, though. Adelle whimpered like a scared child.

"Well?" Jonetta said between deep breaths. Her eyes were wide and expectant. "Is it boy or girl? Why isn't the baby crying?"

"You have yourself a boy, young lady," the doctor announced. Jonetta smiled weakly. "But I'm afraid he is premature."

"What are you saying?" Jonetta wailed desperate for an answer. She glanced back and forth between her aunts who were quiet and kept their eyes low. The doctor wrapped the baby in a towel and handed him to Adelle while he managed to stabilize Jonetta's leg. Adelle walked slowly up the stairs with the baby.

"Now for this leg," Dr. Scott directed the conversation to Betty Lou. "We can save it, but she won't be able to walk for a few months."

"Dammit! Don't talk about me like I'm not here!" Jonetta screamed. "Answer me! What happened to my baby? Please, somebody tell me!" She looked frantically back and forth between her aunt and the doctor. Their silence caused fear to race through her like a bolt of lightning. Jonetta began to whimper.

Betty Lou stood, folded her hands in front of her, with a cold expression and replied, "He died. We will make arrangements." She was always thinking ahead. "But now the doctor needs to tend to your leg, or do you want to lose that too?"

Jonetta covered her mouth and cried. She stretched out her arms towards the staircase where Adelle had quietly escaped out of sight. Whether he was dead or not, she wanted to hold him in her arms for a few days just to look at his sweet face, but they snatched him away.

"Bring back my baby! Adelle! Adelle!"

Jonetta was living in a house of horrors and her aunts were the orchestrators. She clawed at Betty Lou's ankle, snatched the hem of her knee length skirt causing Betty Lou to lose her balance.

"Get off of me!" Betty Lou kicked at Jonetta as she tried to hold onto her skirt. "Would you give her something, please? She's delirious for Christ's sake!"

The doctor reached for the syringe he had prepared and gave Jonetta a shot of medicine in the shoulder. "She should sleep well. Keep giving her this medication every four hours for the next week. Call me when you run low and I'll supply more. She needs to heal from the inside out and that will take time."

"How long, Doctor Scott?" Betty Lou asked annoyed.

"Months, Miss Betty. Three at the very least," Dr. Scott replied as he packed his medical bag neatly. "Ladies, I bid you a goodnight and good luck."

Days later when Jonetta was feeling more like herself instead of drug induced, she insisted that her son had a proper burial so his soul could rest. "He deserves a name, too," Jonetta had told her aunts. "His name is Henry." Adelle agreed and told Jonetta that her son was underneath the mulberry tree in the backyard.

□ □ □ □ □

A piece of Jonetta died that day. She purposely didn't think about the accident that caused her to lose her son. It was too heavy a burden to bear. A broken leg, loss of a child, and being stuck in a cold, damp basement for months was enough to make anyone lose their mind. Maybe Jonetta did lose a bit of sanity. The very reason she was sent to Chicago in the first place had been forced out of her body, displacing her once again. The irony of it all made her angry enough to want to hop all the way back home. However, going back to Pennsylvania wasn't an option. She knew that she stood a better chance in Chicago than she ever would back home. So many painful, suppressed memories came flooding to her thoughts ever since she opened up to her family last year.

But Jonetta did not under any circumstances ever encourage Colette to throw herself down a flight of stairs. The same basement stairs where she lost her son many years ago. All she did was share her story with Colette. She accomplished the mission all on her own. Now Owen knew the truth about his fifth child.

"He thinks I'm a murder, Mama. But I was just depressed and desperate."

"I know you were." Jonetta muttered, as she lowered her eyes and picked at her cuticles.

"Owen is never going to sign the divorce papers now." Colette tilted her head up to the sky, exhaled. She was deep in thought about her next move.

"Being married to that asshole a few more months won't make a bit of difference after all these years anyway. We can worry about that fool some other time. You need stitches, Colette."

"I have to call Pastor to tell him what happened." Colette ignored her mother on purpose. "I cannot go to church looking like this."

"Why do you tell that man all of your business?" Phyllis asked irritated. "You haven't even been a member of that church long and here you go telling all of your business to complete strangers. He's not a priest and he certainly is not God!"

"That man has been a savior to me and the kids. I'm employed because of him. I can bring Delilah to work with me because of him. He is kind and allows me to be creative without criticizing me. He's the one who had his lawyer draw up the divorce papers for me, and for free!"

"Everything comes with a price, Colette." Jonetta shot Colette a look. *I taught her better than that!*

"He is a man of God, Mama! And the best thing that has happened to me and the kids in a long time!"

"My goodness! It sounds like you're in love with this pastor!" Jonetta folded her arms across her chest, completely baffled by her daughter's admiration for this man.

Colette pressed harder against the gash with gauze and shrugged. "Pastor Paul has shown me what love really looks like and it feels good, too!"

Jonetta couldn't believe her ears. "Who did you say?"

Colette repeated herself, "Pastor Louis Paul. Do you know of him?"

CHAPTER 13

Deceit in the DNA

Her stomach had been in knots ever since she learned that her daughter was falling for the same man who had raped her many years ago. Jonetta had been thinking about a way to break the news to Colette, but thought the better solution would be to get rid of Big Louie once and for all. When he showed up on her doorstep last year unannounced after three decades Jonetta almost crapped herself. A self-ordained pastor, who was probably pimping out his members in the church to the highest bidder, was now swindling her daughter! Out of all the churches in Chicagoland, what was the likelihood that her daughter would all of a sudden want to find God and end up at his church? It was a horrible nightmare on repeat. Just as she was putting her family back together again, her past seemed to rear its ugly head to destroy them completely.

If that wasn't bad enough she just had to tell Owen that she purposely lost their baby! What an idiot! After Colette fell down the stairs and lost the baby, she ended up in the hospital for a few days and Jonetta wanted to be right there when she opened her eyes. She had a feeling that Colette had done the unthinkable and wanted to make sure the medication wouldn't have her confessing her sins to Owen. The words of wisdom that Jonetta shared with her that day obviously had escaped her mind. Jonetta shook her head as she skimmed through her closet looking for something to wear. *I don't have time for this! I have bigger fish to fry!*

The last thing Jonetta wanted to do was go make nice with the Franklyn family. But she had promised Norman that she would attend the dinner. They decided to meet at the Chicago Cut Steakhouse on the Riverfront for dinner early evening. Around that time, the summer heat gave the city a break from what seemed like scorching torture. It was actually a perfect summer evening to have dinner outside without sweating through the whole meal. Still, Jonetta insisted on riding with the air conditioner on the whole ride downtown to keep her hair from swelling. She had been quiet the whole ride downtown while Norman played jazz music. Jonetta half-heartedly accepted the Franklyn's invitation. On the one hand, Bishon was a decent man and she grew to like him as a person. On the other hand, their connection didn't have to move past the office as far as she was concerned. He was adamant about everyone meeting over the past few weeks; he wouldn't let it rest, so she finally agreed to dinner.

When they arrived at the restaurant, The Franklyn's were already seated, drinking spritzer water and conversing among themselves. A tinge of jealousy shot through Jonetta seeing them as a family. *Why can't my girls get along like this?* She took a deep breath and cleared her thoughts as she extended her hand to greet Stanton and Barbara.

"Nice to finally meet you, Jonetta." Barbara greeted her with a huge smile. Her coffee stained teeth were shocking to Jonetta considering her son was a dentist. Surely, he could've fixed that for her easily. *Good God, woman! Let your son help your teeth before you die.*

"Jonetta," Stanton extended his hand, squeezing hers firmly. "Heard so much about you."

"All good things, I hope." Jonetta shot Norman a look. She had hoped Mr. Motor Mouth didn't tell them her personal business that she intimately shared with her family. *I will kill you in your sleep, Norman!*

"Of course," Norman replied as he pulled out her chair. "Have a seat, Netta."

"Doctor Franklyn," Jonetta nodded and patted his shoulder as she took a seat next to him.

"He's just Shon outside the office," Barbara remarked, laughing as if she had just told a joke.

Jonetta cleared her throat, reached for her glass of water and sipped through tight lips. *You're the one who named him after a dog that you couldn't afford!* She glanced over the wine menu first because that's exactly what she was going to need in order to get through this dinner. After glancing over the dinner menu, she decided to order something heavy on the stomach so she wouldn't get drunk so fast. "I'll have the Bone-In New York strip, whipped potatoes and grilled asparagus." Jonetta told the waiter when it was her turn to order.

She plastered a smile on her face as Barbara rambled on about the joys of raising her son, praising his accomplishments as if she was about to auction him off to the highest bidder. Stanton and Norman recalled some of his basketball games and that conversation turned into sports, and that's when they really lost her. The breeze was a reminder that the humidity had mercy on them as it swept gently across their skin. Jonetta inhaled sharply as her thoughts drifted back to Colette. *How in the world am I going to fix this mess?*

"Do you agree, Jonetta?" Barbara asked, sipping on a glass of Chenin Blanc wide-eyed waiting for Jonetta to respond.

"I'm sorry, what?" Jonetta cleared her throat.

"Barbara and I have been very honest with Shon about his adoption. But his mother thinks it's quite alright for him to seek out his birth mother. What do you think about that?"

Jonetta glanced at Bishon to see what his expression revealed. She didn't want to let on that they had already discussed his adoption and how she encouraged him to look for his birth mother. He raised his eyebrows expectantly as he nodded encouraging her to engage in the conversation. Everyone patiently waited for her to answer.

"It doesn't sound like you're too thrilled about the idea, Stanton." Jonetta deflected the conversation back to him, not wanting to get in the middle of their family affairs. Her mind was quite cluttered, full of concern about Colette for now.

"Well, it's unnecessary if you ask me. You never know who this woman is, or what her life is like after all these years. Sometimes it's just best to leave well enough alone!" Stanton cut angrily into his Porterhouse steak; the bloody juices flowed freely onto the plate.

"I'm fine with it. I don't feel insecure about Shon finding his real mother. I know that I did my job and I did it well. I can never be replaced." Barbara remarked confidently as she sipped her wine pleased with herself.

"Yes, you did mother and nobody could ever take your place." Shon reached for her hand and squeezed it gently. "I love you both for raising me as your own son. But I am curious, naturally, about who my birth parents are and where my features come from and how it came down to abandoning me. The issue is that there is no record of my birth. I was just placed on the doorsteps of a church."

"It wasn't on the doorstep, Shon. You were lying in a box in the vestibule of the church lobby." Stanton corrected his son's version of his arrival in their lives. "Back then the only women who were desperate to get rid of their newborns like that were either drug addicts, prostitutes or runaways. Your umbilical cord was still attached to you so you know that you weren't delivered at a hospital. It was probably in an alley somewhere. You were born early and needed medical attention because you were so scrawny."

"We believe that one of the local brothels dropped you off, son." Barbara interjected, trying to smooth things over. "They were known for doing that if one of their girls got into trouble that way. Then all of a sudden, we would have a new lady visit church services, probably trying to get word of what happened to her baby or to see if a newborn would suddenly appear. It was very common back then. And of course, the church had a No Questions Asked policy."

Norman cleared his throat and glanced at Jonetta. She ignored him. *Don't you dare open your stupid mouth!*

"Which is precisely why he doesn't need to go snooping around!" Stanton snapped. "Just leave it alone, son."

Jonetta tried to recall if there were any women in her aunts' brothel back then who were expecting then mysteriously disappeared or returned without a baby. *No, my aunts made sure that their girls were taking precaution.* Of course, she couldn't reveal that her aunts ran a brothel close to where the church was and that she was once a prostitute, and that her family still lived there, so she just offered her advice. "Well, if your curiosity won't let you rest, then you should search. Just keep your findings to yourself since your parents are divided about the topic. You wouldn't want to break up their happy marriage just to satisfy your curiosity, would you?"

"Oh, don't be ridiculous. Stanton will come around. He could probably ramble off a few addresses of local brothels." Barbara shot him a look. "Anything for his son, right, honey?" She nudged his elbow, smiling like a Stepford wife.

Stanton grunted. "Do they serve beer here?"

"Well, our children certainly have a way of keeping our lives interesting in our old age, don't they?" Norman chuckled nervously. "Our daughters keep us on our toes. Throw our grandchildren into the mix and I feel like I'm the ring master in a circus act."

Jonetta watched as they laughed at Norman's corny joke. Her eyes fell on the napkin in her lap, once again thinking about Colette and Big Louie. *She has my grandchildren around him!* A pained expression grew across her face.

"Grandchildren would be a wonderful addition to our family." Barbara raised her wine glass towards her son.

"I have to find a wife first, Mother."

"Well, it's definitely going to happen, son. Maybe really soon, too! Jonetta, your daughter is so gorgeous. I can see why Shon is so fond of her." Barbara remarked, stuffing two Brussels Sprouts in her mouth.

Jonetta noticed that Bishon stiffened, as he diverted his eyes to an almost empty plate. Norman cleared his throat and shifted in his seat. Jonetta glanced back and forth between Barbara and Stanton who were nodding in agreement, smiling like they had won a jackpot. She raised her eyebrows, stared at Norman with a plastered smile on her face. *What the hell did she just say?*

"Thank you." Norman replied, breaking the awkward silence.

Jonetta placed her fork down, reached for her glass of Amarone and decided to take a long gulp before responding. She emptied the glass, set it on the table and chose her next words carefully. "You've met my daughter? Which one?" She asked blinking her eyes several times. Norman knew that look meant one or two things were about to happen. He touched her knee underneath the table to calm her, but Jonetta jerked away from his touch. As the wine raced through her body, her cheeks flushed and the hair on the back of her neck raised. She stared at Bishon with bewilderment as she waited for an answer.

"Yes, of course, we met Dawn. They've been dating a while now…" Barbara replied, looking confused.

"Mother..." Bishon interrupted, shaking his head. He cleared his throat and continued, "Mrs. Miller, yes, Dawn and I have been seeing one another. I do apologize that you had to find out this way. We were going to..."

"You were going to what? Tell me on my lunch break at work? This is quite some news that you all just dropped on me!"

"Mrs. Miller, I have nothing but respect for you and your family. As my Mother said, I am very fond of Dawn. Mrs. Miller, when I first met her at the office I was totally blown away by her beauty..."

"Wait. Why are you only addressing me?" Jonetta swiftly directed her attention to Norman who was biting his bottom lip. "You knew about this too?"

Norman shrugged. "Jonetta, they are grown. It's not my business to tell."

Jonetta laughed incredulously at the irony. "Oh, really? You're always so quick to tell everyone's business! But you neglected to tell me that our daughter was dating my boss? Your friend's son? It just slipped your mind, huh, Norman?" Jonetta threw her hands in the air. "Oh, that's right! Dawn is your favorite. You're always protecting her little dirty secrets! Is there anything else anyone would like to share with me tonight?"

Stanton glanced around the restaurant at the other patrons as Jonetta grew louder. She was drawing attention to their table, but she didn't care.

"How long have you two been sneaking behind my back?" Jonetta demanded to know.

"Now hold on Jonetta," Stanton interrupted, becoming irritated. "Shon is a grown man. Now maybe you hover over your children's every move, even though they are grown ass adults, but we know that we raised Shon properly, therefore we trust his decisions. We don't require explanations from our son about whomever he wants to date and neither should you!" Barbara nodded in agreement, as she rubbed her husband's shoulder.

"Like you said, Shon is a grown man. Right now, I'm speaking to him, not you, Stanton!" She pointed her finger in his direction, making her point very clear.

"Netta, this is not the time or place." Norman tried to reason with her calmly. "Can we discuss it some other time?"

Jonetta shot him a look, Norman returned a pleading look for the sake of arguing in public.

"What are you so angry about, Jonetta?" Barbara asked annoyed. "We just gave Dawn a compliment, which is also a compliment to you and Norman. What's wrong with them dating one another? Is there something we should know about Dawn?"

"What the hell did you say?" Jonetta snapped. "You know what...I'm so done with this conversation! Doctor Franklyn, consider this my resignation!"

"Netta! Don't be ridiculous!" Norman pleaded.

Jonetta stood up, smoothed her linen skirt and huffed. "Norman, I told you this was a bad idea! I'll be in the car." She swiftly grabbed her purse and left the restaurant.

□□□□□

Back at home she paced the patio back and forth, taking long drags on her cigarette frequently looking up to the sky as if waiting on an answer from God. "These children are going to be the death of me!" Jonetta fumed. "Colette, falling in love with the very man who raped and beat me! God, I hate him! It's like a sick joke they're playing on me! I wonder if he knows that Colette is my daughter!?" Jonetta spun around, wide-eyed waiting for Norman to answer. He shrugged, looking bewildered. Jonetta cocked her head to the side and snarled, "Oh, now you don't know anything? You didn't know Colette's pastor was Big Louie? The devil himself!" Jonetta demanded answer with her hand on her hip.

"No, I didn't know, Netta! I've never been to the church! How the hell would I know?"

"Because you talk to Colette regularly. Not once did she mention his name?"

"Netta, you seem to forget that none of us knew the man's name. You didn't even tell us that he stuck around to become a local pastor of a church! All you told us was somebody from your past showed up demanding the house as a form of pay off from some debts that had nothing to do with you! That story still doesn't seem right to me." Norman rubbed his beard, remembering last Thanksgiving.

"I know what the hell I said!" Jonetta snapped. "It was bad enough that he forced me to give up my house over something that had nothing to do with me. Now he's after my daughter, too! Ohhhh, hell no!" Jonetta growled. She was hotter than coals burning on a grill.

"Netta, you never made peace with your past. Now it's disrupting your present life and possibly your future if you don't come all the way clean with the truth!" Norman admonished in vain, as Jonetta waved him off. "Now, you've been ranting about this for the past few days. When are you going to tell Colette who her pastor really is?"

"Soon… when the time is right…give me time to think!" She pulled a long drag from her cigarette. "Then Dawn's little sneaky ass has been running around behind my back with Doctor Franklyn! She better not be living with him after I offered her to live with us! She doesn't know Bishon Franklyn from a can of paint! I'm going to cuss her ass out tomorrow! Now Phyllis is at Georgia's house, too! What the hell has gotten into these girls? They are trying to give me a heart attack!"

"You're taking it too personally, Netta." Norman leaned back in the patio chair, watching Jonetta pace back and forth. She waved him off again, turned her back and continued to smoke.

"I should've stayed at Georgia's. I should've never moved in with you. They have just gone wild ever since I moved out."

"Netta, you sound like a control freak. You do know that our daughters are not little girls anymore. They don't need us to hover over them! What do they call that these days? There's a term for it…" Norman snapped his fingers trying to remember the term. His face lit up as he remembered. "Helicopter mom! Yeah! That's it. That's what you are… and well, have always been I guess. If you are not in some type of control you feel out of control. You only have control over yourself!"

Jonetta spun around, flicked her cigarette towards the grass and marched towards Norman with her face twisted. "You know what, Norman? After you decided to move out I was left to raise three girls by myself! So yes! I became a 'helicopter mom' as you put it because I didn't have a choice!"

"I left because you wanted a divorce! But that's neither here nor there. Netta, it's time to let it go now. You've done your job.

The girls will be alright. They're just finding their way in life, that's all."

"I've tried to keep control as long as I could. Now it's time to put a stop to what I cannot control!" Jonetta was sizzling mad as she marched into the house and tried to slam the sliding glass patio door, but Norman caught it just in time. She was done listening to his reasoning, but he wasn't done having a talk with her. *You've got a lot of damn nerve telling me how to be a parent! Where were you?* Anger was taking over so much that her head was pounding.

"I'm going to take a shower. Stop following me!" Jonetta lashed out and Norman halted his stride.

"I'll be waiting for you when you get out. We're not done talking, Netta!" Norman yelled up the stairs.

Jonetta slammed her bedroom door shut while he was still talking. The buttons on her blouse weren't cooperating so she pulled them loose and they went flying all over the floor. She threw the blouse, bra and skirt into a clothes hamper and stood in the shower. The tile was cold against her skin but it felt good since her blood pressure was up. Eventually she turned on the water to shower. When she emerged Norman was sitting in a chair across the room in his flannel pajamas.

"I brought you some tea." He announced pointing to the tea cup on the nightstand. "It's your favorite Chamomile."

Jonetta exhaled, reached for her robe on the bed, and began rubbing lotion on her skin. "So I guess you aren't going to give me any privacy, huh?"

"You ain't got nothing I ain't seen a hundred times before, old lady!"

Jonetta chuckled. "Why aren't you upset with our daughters, Norman?"

"I'm more so concerned about Colette, not Dawn nor Phyllis." Norman admitted. "Dawn is bouncing back from heartbreak. Phyllis is just humiliated right now. Damien will forgive her and she'll go back home. But Colette…" he sighed, rubbing his clean-shaven chin. "She is so fragile. But she seems to be in a happy place right now and if we destroy that for her with this awful news she'll only end up angry with us. We have to come up with a wise plan to drop that bomb on her."

"I'm still going to have a talk with Dawn tomorrow. But you're right, I have to think of a way to break the news to Colette. And Phyllis... I don't know what to make of her situation with Damien because it just doesn't make sense." Jonetta lifted her leg onto the bed, rubbed lotion between her toes up to her thighs and repeated with the other leg. She looked up to see Norman watching her carefully. "There's nothing new to see here, remember?" She remarked heading towards the bathroom with smirk on her face. When she came back into the bedroom she was wearing a silk, rose-colored nightgown with her salt and pepper hair flowing. Her scent drifted across the room and Norman smiled at her warmly. She aged beautifully, her peanut butter skin glowed and her body was still in good shape.

"Thank you for my tea," she replied taking a few sips. "I'm exhausted."

"Me too. Goodnight, Netta." Norman got up to leave the bedroom.

"But I don't want to be alone." Jonetta admitted as she placed the tea cup down and turned to look at Norman.

Norman stopped in his tracks, turned to study her face. Those words were music to his ears, but he had to make sure that he heard her correctly. "You want me to stay?"

Jonetta nodded as she pulled the blanket back and patted the bed.

He climbed into bed to cuddle next to her. They had not been this close in decades. Jonetta didn't want to admit it but his arms wrapped around her felt really good. She exhaled, allowed her body to sync with his in a spoon position, and closed her eyes.

"Don't get any ideas pressed against my nice ass, Norman." Jonetta teased.

"Who me? You were always assertive, taking the lead, performing acts of pleasure on me," Norman recalled. "I always wondered how you knew those techniques." His belly vibrated on her back as he laughed heartily.

"Is this a complaint?" Jonetta asked seriously, and popped open her eyes.

"No, an observation," Norman replied, clearing his throat. "Sometimes, a man wants to take the lead, feel like he's in control of sexually dominating a woman and usually a woman allows him to do just that. But you… Like I said, you always took control in the bedroom. I always thought women want to feel desired, but you hardly ever gave me the opportunity to express that."

"What's your point, Norman?" Jonetta asked through tight lips, still waiting for him to get to the point of his babbling.

"It just all makes sense now, that's all." He shrugged and rubbed her shoulder.

"What makes sense?" Jonetta asked slightly tilting her head up.

"That you were…" Norman paused, choosing his next words carefully. "…trained to behave that way with men."

"I see…" Jonetta mumbled.

"I mean, you just didn't know any better, that's all I'm saying," Norman replied, softly. "All you ever told me was Mr. Lucky was sometimes rough with you. I didn't know that he was…pimping you. Had I known all of that happened to you, I would've loved you in a different way," Norman admitted, sweeping her hair up from her neck.

Jonetta inhaled sharply. She was not expecting that admission. It evoked emotion that she wasn't ready to revive just yet. Shedding tears on Thanksgiving in front of the whole family last year was enough to last for the next few years as far as she was concerned. But right now she felt a tear escape from her eye and land on the lilac pillowcase.

He continued, "I feel like we never experienced the love that could've been sparked between us. Actually, I'm feeling kinda robbed."

Jonetta exhaled finally. *You just had to ruin it.* "It's all about you, Norman."

"No," Norman replied, squeezing her around her narrow waist. "It's about us." He held her closer as whispered in her ear.

Now she had goosebumps and tears. His words were sincere, but she had to get a good look at his face. She repositioned herself to face Norman. His eyes welled with tears as he caressed her face. After an awkward moment passed, Jonetta broke the silence.

"I don't know what you want from me…"

"I want you," Norman confessed. "I want the Jonetta who was full of hope, desires, and love, not who those monsters created."

"I was eighteen years old, Norman… and by the time I met you it was already too late. I don't even remember who she is or what she wanted in life. But it certainly wasn't to be raped, sent away in shame to start a whole new life in a strange city and become a prostitute! That much I'm pretty sure of, Norman. But I'm not sure that I can dig deep to give you what you want. I'm too old for that shit!"

"Alright." Norman rubbed her shoulder, seeing that Jonetta was becoming irritated. He didn't want to press her anymore and ruin the moment. The last thing he wanted to do was upset her while they cuddled. "But won't you at least consider going back to work? I mean, you don't have to quit just because our daughter is dating your boss."

"Absolutely not! If he needs an official letter of resignation, I will type it up in the morning. I quit and that's final!" Jonetta replied.

"Alright, alright." Norman sighed, but held her tighter. "Well, for the record, I'm here. I never stopped loving you. We had a life together, a family, and I miss all of you tremendously. I was devastated when you wanted a divorce. I was raised to keep a family together. Keeping my distance all these years was counterproductive," he admitted rubbing his chin again. "I was hurting too back then. But I'm not trying to force this now. I offered my home to you as a fresh start because I didn't want you to be tormented living in that house. I still love you, Netta. You're more than welcome to stay here as long as you want. Hopefully, this time it'll be forever."

CHAPTER 14

Pleasure Principle

The photo shoot went exceptionally well. Dawn was a natural in front of the camera and as usual the cameraman fell in love with her. She missed life as a model. When her former agent, Marcie Saxton, in New York called to tell her that she was in town, she also invited her to a photo shoot for the K-Mart fall catalogue. Now that was the life she was accustomed to and it felt so good to do exactly what she loved, while rubbing elbows with some of the best in the business. Good ole Marcie Saxton had always treated Dawn well while she was in New York. She was one of the best talent agents and could get her clients to auditions at the last minute because of her reputation and connections in the business. Now she was squeezing Dawn in for a photoshoot in her own city.

Since Dawn was a last-minute add-on for the shoot, Marcie reminded her that there were no guarantees to that her photos would appear in the ads, but she still paid her for the day. Of course, Dawn wanted the exposure as well because just about everybody in America would see the Back-to-School ads in the Sunday paper, but time was money and money was what Dawn needed lately since she had not been working as she expected. Just getting to the photoshoot on time required Dawn to beg Georgia to use Fred's beloved Mercedes S-600 because Colette still used her car every day, as usual. However, Dawn knew that Georgia kept the Mercedes securely in the garage, only turning on the engine once a week, usually on Wednesdays.

Whenever Georgia disappeared from around the house, it was usually because she was in garage just sitting in the car listening to music. She deserved her moments alone with memories of her husband; everyone understood and didn't bother her. Asking to use or borrow anything of Fred's took a lot of nerve, but Dawn was desperate. She promised to take good care of the Mercedes when Georgia handed her the keys. However, she failed to tell Georgia that her New York driver's license had expired two months ago on her birthday. *I have to renew my license soon!* Dawn carefully drove around the city making sure that she gave herself enough time to get where she needed to be so she wouldn't be caught speeding. Marcie wanted to grab dinner after the photo shoot, but Dawn knew she had other duties to fulfill with Chena.

If it had been anybody else, Dawn would've cancelled on them in a heartbeat just to have dinner with Marcie, but she was homeward bound to play Mama, sister, and wife to Chena, Shiloh and Raffi. "I cannot believe that I'm doing this!" Dawn blurted out, frustrated that she was playing the very role that she denied with Vine. Although, she was thankful that she did after running into him in Atlanta, still this domestic shit was getting underneath her skin. Dawn had been cooking, cleaning, and keeping up with Shiloh's summer camp schedule and play dates along with occasionally helping Colette with her kids. She knew that she needed a change and the more she thought about it the more she wanted to take Bishon up on his offer to crash at his place. Then again, how would she explain to anybody exactly where she was living?

When Bishon pulled into the parking garage to his condominium in the south Loop she had no idea that he lived right across from Soldier Field. On the elevator ride up, she tried to contain her excitement as it took them to the twenty-first floor. She nuzzled her nose into his neck and kissed him just for being great. *This is the type of life God wants me to have!* She had already decided on the elevator ride that she was going to allow Bishon to touch her, taste her, and feel her body inside and out as long as he wanted.

Bishon didn't hesitate to blow her mind. He took his time with her and kept reminding her that they had all night. Nobody even knew that she was back in town and she liked it that way. No interruptions. Dawn had never met any man that didn't try to pounce and dominate her in the bedroom, but Bishon treated her delicately like he was examining a fragile, delicate flower. Dawn figured that he learned that skill from being a dentist, but it worked for her in the bedroom too. She found herself calling Uber rides frequently, at his expense, just to be in his space. The more time that Dawn spent with Bishon, the more enticed she was to become his woman. Living with him would mean that she would be far enough away from her family, watching the sunrise and set in peace with the whole place to herself while he was at work. Not to mention she would definitely have access to cash and possibly her own credit card. The way Raffi was blowing her up since this morning, that's exactly the escape she needed right now.

Dawn glanced at her phone vibrating in the passenger seat. "Dammit, Raffi! What the hell do you want now? I'm on my way!" She yelled in the air and slapped the steering wheel. When she flipped the phone over, she saw that Bishon had sent a text with a link attached. She glanced back at traffic before she tapped it to see what it was. YouTube opened to a video of a young brother begging some chick to send her location to him. She played it, liked it and decided to connect it through Bluetooth so she could blare it through the speakers. "Let's see what this Mercedes sound system can do!" A wide smile spread across her face as she turned up the volume and grooved to the song "Location" by Khalid. *Definitely adding this to my music list!*

"Ohhhh, okay, Doctor Bishon Franklyn. You wanna know my location, huh?" Dawn smirked while she guided the Mercedes through traffic and made a detour towards Bishon's office. Her phone vibrated again with another text from Bishon.

Bishon: Send me your location…

Dawn refused to respond. She pulled up in front of the dental office ten minutes later instead. Even though Raffi and Chena were expecting her any moment, she wanted to remain in his good graces just in case she needed to move in unexpectedly.

"Have a seat… right here," Bishon pointed to his lap as he leaned back exposing his full erection. He was happy to see her.

"Right there?" Dawn asked seductively as she pointed to his lap.

"Yeah, come take a ride." Bishon reached out to pull her closer to him. "You look beautiful."

Dawn hiked up her floral sundress and straddled him. "Thank you, Doctor."

Shon cupped her butt with his hands, feeling the warmth of her skin. "No panties, huh? Bad girl!" He slapped her left cheek and guided her down until he was fully inside of her. Dawn let out a loud moan and he quickly covered her mouth. "Shhhh…shhhh…" He slowed down her motion by grabbing hold of her hips. He moved her back and forth to a slower rhythm, but thrusted deeper. Dawn moaned again, louder than before.

"Dawn, you gotta take this ride in silence today. Please. I still have people out there."

Dawn nodded her head in agreement, panting as she slowly guided him in and out of her warmth. The stickiness of their sex was creating moisture underneath her and Bishon took notice immediately. "Damn, you are so wet! You missed me?" He took his middle finger and slid it up and down her the middle of her butt.

"Yessss…" Dawn moaned in pleasure and began riding him faster.

"Slow down, girl!"

Dawn shook her head no and smiled wickedly. "This has to be a quickie today, Doctor Franklyn."

"Ohhhhh… shiiiiiii..." Bishon grabbed her waist tight. "I'm about to cum…"

Just as Bishon released inside of Dawn, Kaiya busted into his office.

"Oh, my God!" Bishon exclaimed in pleasure and astonishment. "Oh, my God! Close the door!"

Kaiya gasped and slammed the door shut. Dawn laughed, pleased that she saw them fuckin' because she knew that Kaiya had a little crush on him.

"That'll teach her to knock." Dawn snarled.

"Please, get up sweetheart," Bishon pleaded squeezing her shoulders. "I've gotta get back to work and smooth this over."

Dawn put her full weight on him, refusing to budge. "No," she pouted, locking her fingers behind his neck.

"Dawn, seriously, get up." He lifted her off of him, reached for a tissue to clean himself.

"What's the big deal?" Dawn asked annoyed. "You're the boss! Who is she gonna tell?"

147

"The board, the partners!" Bishon shook his head. "This was totally unprofessional and out of character for me!"

Oh, my God! He's freaking the fuck out. Dawn folded her arms in disgust. "Fuck her! You deserve a little fun! Lighten up!"

"Dawn, I have to get back to work." He handed her a tissue and gestured for her to clean herself.

"Fine!" Dawn snatched the tissue and cleaned herself. "I'm so glad that my Mother doesn't work here anymore. That little snitch would tell on us for sure!"

"If you move in with me, we won't have to sneak like this anymore." Bishon remarked.

"I really like your condo, Shon. Just give me some time to get things situated and smooth things over with my Mother."

"You only like my condo?" Bishon inquired.

"You're alright, too." Dawn replied laughing.

"I'll see you later tonight. Right?" Bishon walked over to her and planted a kiss on her forehead.

"That's the plan, Doctor."

                                                   □ □ □ □ □

Dawn drove deep in thought with tissue stuck between her legs and chuckled to herself as a flash of Kaiya's expression popped into her mind. Her phone rang breaking her thoughts.

"I'm on my way!" Dawn answered impatiently.

"You were supposed to be here an hour ago!" Raffi barked into the phone.

"I had a stop to make unexpectedly, Raffi. I'm on my way now."

"I just finished giving her a sponge bath. Chemo was a bitch today!" Raffi fumed. "She's resting now though. Shiloh is getting hungry…"

"I'll be there to start dinner and help with Shiloh, as promised." Dawn ended the call abruptly.

What have I gotten myself into? I'm starting to feel like a damn maid! Since things were crazy at the house and her mother was still pissed about her secretly dating Bishon, Dawn decided to move in temporarily with Chena and Raffi, to help them out, she reasoned. And because she truly did love her best friend. And this is what

best friends do, right? However, it was really a way of escape
from her family friction, but moving out only proved that she
jumped right from the frying pan into the fire. When Dawn pulled
in their driveway twenty minutes later, she sighed heavily. A wave
of regret swept over her as she searched in the glove compartment
for a napkin, found one and wiped vigorously between her legs.
She pulled out fragrant lotion from her purse and rubbed it on her
thighs to mask the scent of sex. *That should work.*

"See? Told you I'd be here!" Dawn announced gliding past
Raffi who held the door open for her. "Let me use the restroom,
then I'll get dinner started."

Raffi didn't say a word, instead he watched her carefully as she
disappeared into the first floor bathroom.

"Fuck my liiiiiife!" Dawn whispered to her reflection in the
mirror, pulling her hair from the roots. She grabbed a hand towel
from the cabinet, lathered it with hand soap and cleaned herself.

When she emerged from the restroom, Raffi had already placed
on the counter what he wanted for dinner. "Alfredo shrimp pasta
with broccoli and bread sticks?"

"Yeah, and a salad with croutons. You can handle that, right?"
Raffi remarked snidely.

Dawn sneered at him and began preparing the meal for them.
During dinner Raffi poured glasses of whiskey for him and Dawn.
He watched Dawn carefully interacting with Shiloh as he sipped
the whiskey through his full lips. Dawn felt him staring at them but
ignored it as usual. Shiloh was so helpful around the house and he
often spent time in his mother's room reading to her or updating
her on the latest drama in middle school. His birthday was fast
approaching in September and he didn't let a day go by without
reminding all of them.

"Shiloh, is it still cool to have a cake for your birthday?" Dawn
asked.

"I dunno." Shiloh shrugged. "I guess."

"What's your favorite? Chocolate? Yellow? Marble?"

"Usually mom bakes a cake for me. But it's no biggie because
I'm about to be thirteen! I'm not a baby anymore. I don't need a
cake. I need money and gifts!"

Dawn and Raffi laughed.

"That's my boy! You have to ask in order to receive." Raffi gave him a high five.

"Well, if you change your mind, let me know. Maybe we can bake a cake together?"

"Nah, it's cool, Aunty Dawn. I was only doing it to make ma happy."

Raffi and Dawn shared a glance.

"I understand, Shiloh." Dawn shook his twists with her hand. "Let me know if you change your mind."

"Why don't you go see if your mom needs anything right now? If not, you can take the rest of the evening to do whatever. Just chill out, son. Cool?"

"Aight, cool!" Shiloh said, giving his father a fist bump. He headed upstairs in a dash to spend time with his mother.

Dawn finished rinsing the dishes, dried her hands on a dish towel, and began loading the dishwasher.

"You never did say what happened in Atlanta." Raffi said out of nowhere.

"What do you mean? I told you the audition sucked. I'm glad that it didn't work out."

"Nah, I mean, like… what really happened?"

"That's what really happened." Dawn remarked with her back turned to him. *What the hell is he getting at?*

"Did you see your ex when you went?"

"What?" Dawn turned to face him, jerking her neck. "Where is that coming from? Since when do you care about Vine?" Dawn began loading the plates in the dishwasher again to avoid his glare. For a moment, she thought she was seeing double and shook her head, but her blurred vision remained.

"I don't. I care about you." Raffi replied and leaned back in his chair as he watched her bend over. "Well? Did you see him?"

"Yeah, I did…" Dawn said as she closed the dishwasher door. Goosebumps raced down her arms which caused her nipples to tighten. *What is going on? I must be coming down with something.* She looked down at her chest and it was prickled with goosebumps.

"I fuckin' knew it!" Raffi slammed his hand on the table.

"You knew what? Why are you trippin'?" Dawn frowned up at his behavior.

"You've been acting weird since you got back! I knew you saw that bastard!"

"And so what if I did?" Dawn shrugged. She licked her lips seductively for no reason at all and glowered at him. "What's it to you, Raffi?"

Raffi jumped up from his seat and rushed towards Dawn, grabbed her elbow. "Did you fuck him? Tell me!"

"Raffi! Let me go!" Dawn demanded as she tried to snatch away from him, but he had a tight grip on her and it turned her on. *What the hell is going on here?*

"Answer me!" Raffi pulled her closer to him as his chest heaved. His liquor-laced breath was hot on her face.

"That's none of your business!" Dawn replied as she leaned closer to his lips. "Now let me go!"

Raffi released his grasp, breathing heavily, but refused to move from in front of her. They stood almost nose to nose not saying a word. She smelled his whiskey laced breath and throbbed between her legs. *What the hell is my body doing? Don't do this Dawn. Don't do it.*

"Dawn, lower your voice before you bring too much attention to us down here."

"What the hell has gotten into you?" Dawn asked angrily. "You smoke half of a joint and have some whiskey and this is the result?"

"You drive me crazy, Dawn!" Raffi admitted, biting his bottom lip.

"Lower *your* damn voice, Raffi." Dawn pushed his left shoulder, creating space between them. "Get a hold of yourself!"

"I can't," he whispered, lifting her hand to his chest. "You feel that? My heart is racing just at the thought of you with another man. It drives me crazy!"

"I'm not your woman anymore, Raffi…" Dawn stroked the side of his face. "Where is this coming from after all these years?"

"It may have something to do with this…" Raffi removed a baggie from his pocket and waved it in front of Dawn.

"What is that?" Dawn blinked trying to regain her focus.

He giggled like a child.

"What is it, Raffi?"

"I laced my weed with some Ecstasy and put the rest our drinks." He snickered like a little boy confessing his dirty deeds.

"What the hell?" Dawn slapped his chest. "It's no wonder why I'm feeling like…"

Raffi dove in, grabbed her by the back of her neck, and forcefully kissed her. Dawn gave in kissing him back at first, then wiggled herself free and stormed off into the first floor bedroom. She was conflicted. *What am I doing?* He followed quickly behind her. Before she could slam the door in his face he pushed it open, knocking Dawn off balance. He closed the door behind him and locked it.

"Don't tell me that you don't want me, too, Dawn. I know you do."

Dawn slowly backed away from him and stumbled on the bed. "Look, whatever you're feeling it's not real, Raffi. You drugged us! It'll wear off soon. Besides, your wife is upstairs in her sick bed!" Dawn reminded him hoping that would snap him back into reality.

"Chena told me what she wanted us to do." Raffi confessed, smiling. "She's cool with it."

"Oh, my God!" Dawn slapped her forehead in disbelief. "Don't listen to her. She's not thinking clearly."

"Dawn, just let the drug take over you. Don't fight it." Raffi walked towards her slowly. "All these years…I've wondered if I made the right decision. I know it hurt you when you found out…"

"No!" Dawn shook her head. "It was a long time ago."

"Dawn… Yes…please…Just listen…"

"No!" Dawn stood up, but Raffi pushed her back down on the bed and climbed on top of her. He wrapped his hand around her neck firmly, but passionately. Dawn lied there frozen looking Raffi into his eyes. Eventually, her body went limp, willing as she felt like she was melting under his spell. She closed her eyes and it felt like her body had elevated from the bed. *This is magical…*

"Dawn, I never meant to hurt you by marrying Chena. I thought you were never coming back. I've always wanted you. I need you to know that."

"Raffi…please…" Dawn grabbed his hand trying to ease his grip from around her neck.

"I'm right here. Just trust me." He slid his hand from around her neck, grabbed her breasts in his large hands, caressed them through her dress, squeezing her nipples firmly. Dawn moaned with pleasure. Raffi closed his eyes and exhaled a sigh of relief that she was not fighting him as he caressed her. "You're so soft just like I imagined." He grabbed the cups of her sundress and ripped them apart, exposing her breasts. Dawn gasped. Raffi swooped down and hungrily sucked her nipples from left to right, back and forth he went. It turned Dawn on completely. She caressed his soft locs as his lips explored her body. He took his t-shirt off and his muscular, hairless chest and ripped abs made Dawn throb.

"My God, Raffi…" Dawn ran her hands from his chest to his stomach.

Raffi smiled, lifted her dress, and glided his hand across her smooth, bare skin. "Take this dress off and let me see all my dessert."

Dawn lifted the torn dress over her head and tossed it across the room. She sprawled across the bed, legs and arms wide open. Her body was just as beautiful as his and she wanted to show him what she had to offer. "Your dessert is ready, King Raffi." Dawn opened her legs wide and grabbed her breasts.

"Damn, Queen! Your body is bangin'! That's just how I like it." Raffi slid his finger inside of her and Dawn winced. He kept thrusting as he unzipped his jeans with his free hand. Finally feeling her moisture between his fingers, he took his jeans off and stood in front of Dawn so she could get a full view.

"Damn!" Dawn exclaimed. *I should have fucked him long time ago in high school! Chena would have never had the chance to marry him!*

"Come here," he commanded. Dawn sat up, he clutched a fist full of her hair and leaned her head up to look at him. "Get on your knees and taste your dessert."

Dawn didn't hesitate as she dropped to her knees, ran her hands up and down his ripped abs and took him whole. Raffi moaned as he rapidly guided her head with both of his hands. "Oh shit, Dawn! You trying to make me bust already? I knew you were a bad girl!"

Raffi allowed Dawn to continue showing off her skills a few seconds more before he repositioned her, bending her over. "Grab your ankles." He instructed in a hushed tone.

Dawn obeyed him without question. She was so anxious to feel him after so many years of wondering. *We are long overdue anyway!* Raffi spread her cheeks open trying to determine if both places were available for him to explore. Pleased with his choices he went for what he really wanted and moaned when her warmth welcomed him. Dawn let out a deep moan as he pushed himself as far as he could go inside of her. Raffi let out a medley of curse words as he pumped faster. The ecstasy had their hearts pumping, feeling exhilarated, and uninhibited. Dawn closed her eyes, bit her bottom lip and tried not to wail in pleasure.

"You taking all this dick, Dawn! Shit! I knew you wanted me!" Raffi grabbed her hair by the roots, causing her to arch her back.

"Fuck me, Raffi!"

"I'm fuckin' the shit outta you!" Raffi released her hair and grabbed her hips tight. "You feel that?"

"Yesssss...." Dawn moaned loudly.

"Shhhhh....I'm about to..." Dawn felt him throb inside of her before he could finish his sentence. Raffi quickly pulled out as if he remembered suddenly that Dawn wasn't his wife. He slipped his tip inside of her ass as he finished releasing himself. Dawn moaned with pleasure as Raffi throbbed inside of her, closing her cheeks tight around his tip. He slid himself up and down her crease as he lost his erection.

"You like that?" Raffi asked smacking her butt.

"Yessss..." Dawn moaned and arched her back more.

"You gonna be my little freak whenever and wherever from now on." Raffi wiggled her cheeks up and down and chuckled. "Look at that ass bounce!" He smacked her on her butt again then collapsed on the bed pleased with himself. He swept his hand gently across her face, clearing her wild hair from in front of it. He pulled her in to kiss her lips then instructed her, "Get a towel and clean me off."

Dawn grabbed his t-shirt from the floor, threw it on and went to the restroom to get a towel for him. *Shit! Did that just happen? Wow!* She looked at herself in the mirror and shook her head. *It's what Chena wanted.* She lathered some hand soap on the towel, cleaned herself first. When she caught her reflection in the mirror again she felt guilty, not because she had just slept with her best friend's husband, but because she had just fucked Bishon earlier. *Thank God Raffi didn't taste me. He would've been tasting Shon!* Dawn shuddered at the thought. When she returned Raffi was sound asleep. She locked the door behind her and decided to check her phone.

Bishon called once and sent two text messages asking to send her location. Dawn sighed knowing that she would have to come up with a clever lie. Thankfully, she had until morning to think about it. She placed her phone on silent mode, got back in the bed and wiped Raffi down. He woke up from the warmth of the towel, grabbed her hand, and pulled her towards him.

"Come here. Lay on my chest." He held her close and kissed her forehead.

In the middle of the night, Dawn woke up to Raffi inside of her again. She opened her eyes to see him in the dark, but could barely make out his face. After blinking repeatedly until her vision became clearer, she saw the whites of his eyes glowing in the dark, and then his white teeth appeared. Raffi was smiling.

"I can't get enough of you," he admitted, panting.

Dawn raised her knees to her chest allowing him to go deeper. She gasped as he hit her spot. *This man knows what the fuck he's doing!*

"Right there, Dawn?" He pressed on her pelvis with the palm of his hand while he thrusted.

"Yessss…" she moaned with pleasure.

"Right there?" Raffi asked, pounding faster. Minutes passed as he kept the same pace. He wrapped his hand around her neck and Dawn gasped. "Just relax." He told her as he gently squeezed his thick hand around her neck. Asphyxiation was something Dawn was not accustomed to during sex, but she knew about how it increased the sexual experience. She closed her eyes, relaxed her muscles so she could embrace the euphoria. She quickly began to lose consciousness as he squeezed tighter. *Shit! This feels so good and scary…at the same damn time…* Before she could plead for air, she felt him throbbing inside of her again. He finally collapsed on top of her out of breath.

In the morning when she rolled over on her stomach, Raffi was already awake watching her sleep. She reached for her phone on the nightstand to check for messages. There were three missed calls from Bishon and several texts from other people. Dawn sucked her teeth, placed the phone back and closed her eyes. *Dammit! Now I gotta think of a damn lie to tell Bishon.*

"Good morning, beautiful Queen." Raffi cooed as caressed her butt.

Dawn smiled and buried her face in the pillow.

"Don't try to be shy now." Raffi climbed on top of her back and kissed her neck.

"You drugged me last night asshole!"

"And I'm gonna do it again, until you give it to me on your own." Raffi began grinding against her butt. "You loved every minute of it. Admit it."

"What did we do?" Dawn moaned with regret.

"Exactly what were supposed to do a long time ago." Raffi laughed and began dry humping her. "And exactly what she wanted us to do. Remember? This was her idea."

She felt Raffi grow erect on her butt and she swatted him away. "No, Raffi. I'm so sore."

"You sore? Where?" he asked still kissing and grinding her, holding her hands down above her head.

"Everywhere." Dawn whined.

"Poor baby. How about right here?" He lifted his hips and forcefully poked at her until he found his way inside.

"Raffi, please... Stop...The drugs have worn off now." Dawn tried to free her hands, but he had a tight grip on her wrists. She winced as he pushed himself further inside of her.

"I told you last night, you're my freak now."

CHAPTER 15

Fix the Focus

When Phyllis pulled up to the curb, her angry thoughts about Damien came to a complete halt as soon as she noticed a BMW parked in front of the house and a man standing outside with a notepad and pen. *Who the hell is this?*

"Can I help you?" Phyllis asked immediately as she emerged from the car.

"Hi, this house was on a list of possible brothels in this neighborhood back in the fifties and sixties." The stranger began his introduction as if he were a friendly tour guide.

Phyllis maintained a stern face as she walked closer to him on the sidewalk. She folded her arms across her chest and cocked her head to the side. "Like I said, can I help you?"

"Oh, right. I'm Doctor Bishon Franklyn," he extended his hand.

"Phyllis." She shook his hand firmly to send a message that she wasn't a weak woman.

"Nice to meet you, Miss Phyllis. I was adopted and I'm just doing some research on possible places my birth mother may have lived… if she was… you know…a working girl…" He gestured his head in the direction of the house. "Do you know if there are any living relatives who still live here? It may be a long shot, but…"

"Is it just me, or does this conversation seem extremely off-the-wall?" Phyllis shook her head in disbelief. *He needs to hurry up with all this rambling!* The sun was making its presence known as singed her skin. She grew irritable by the minute as she felt perspiration forming under her breasts and on her forehead.

Bishon laughed. "I know it's not every day a total stranger pops up asking these types of questions, but…"

"Ya think?" Phyllis raised her eyebrows and shifted her weight still folding her arms across her chest.

"Listen, if this is a bad time… I understand. I can come back another…"

"No," Phyllis interrupted. "I don't think so Mister…uhhh…"

"*Doctor* Franklyn."

"Look, *Doctor* Franklyn, my aunt lives here. She's pretty old and still in mourning from the passing of her husband. It's not a good time, period." Phyllis replied with finality. "And if you haven't noticed, it's like ninety degrees today. So, I'm in a rush to get inside."

"Oh, I'm sorry… I just…"

Phyllis held her hand up impatiently. "My aunt is fully aware that this house used to be a brothel. That's not earth-shattering news around here, okay? From what I've been told, there were numerous women coming and going in this house. There is no possible way after…" she paused, sizing him up. "Forty plus years that she would…"

"Forty-eight." Bishon interjected and flashed a smile.

"After forty-eight years, we would not know anything about who your mother could be even if she did live here. I'm sorry. Good luck." Phyllis proceeded to walk away, but Bishon grabbed her by the arm. Phyllis was appalled.

"Miss Phyllis, please, I've done extensive research, contacted several people and they are pretty sure that a young pregnant girl lived here in the late sixties. I'm just asking for a moment of your aunt's time."

"Can I have my arm back?" Phyllis snatched from his grip.

"I'm so sorry." Bishon released his grip immediately. He hadn't realized how tight he was holding onto her. "I'm pretty desperate."

"You sure are! You just show up here to a complete stranger's home claiming it used to be a brothel, which we already knew. But what if we didn't? You just come dropping bombs on people like this! Who does that?" Phyllis reprimanded him as if she were talking to the twins.

Bishon dropped his eyes to the ground for a moment. "I

apologize, really. I just need answers…"

"I guess common sense can't be bought, huh, Doctor Franklyn? We can't help you." Phyllis harshly interrupted his plea.

"You can't or you won't?"

Phyllis ignored him and began to walk towards the front door.

"Just hear me out, please. I spoke to a, ummm…hold on…" Bishon flipped through his notebook frantically. "I spoke to a Lorraine Hickman, who also lived here for a while. Does that name ring a bell?" he asked loud enough for Phyllis to hear.

She stopped dead in her tracks.

CHICAGO, IL
1992

"Mama, telephone!" Phyllis yelled down the hall to her mother. When there was no answer, she stomped down hard on the ashen hardwood floors while she proceeded to her mother's room, but not before she glanced at herself in the mirror that hung in the hallway between family portraits. She had developed too soon for her mother's liking. Phyllis was budding rapidly and receiving too much attention from boys sometimes five years her senior. She loved every minute of the attention and her blooming body. However, as she stood in her mother's doorway, she appeared like a whining child who was trying to get her mother's attention. Jonetta was ignoring her on purpose. She was too engrossed in the letter her sister had written to her years ago about her extraordinary life, married to a white man.

According to the letter, Georgia had moved several times over the years, but this particular letter was postmarked in New York. Although the letter was dated seven years ago, Jonetta made a mental to somehow track her sister down starting with this address. Georgia apparently made good for herself by becoming a crafty seamstress. She had learned this skill, no less, from their mother and continued to perfect it by designing her own dresses. Georgia had caught the eye of a wealthy, Jewish executive, Frederick Steinberg, who inclined her to broaden her talents by tailoring men's clothing as well. He fronted her money that she needed to open her own boutique which she did not mention the name of it in her letter. Jonetta thought she left it out intentionally. Apparently, they secretly married, and did not have children at time the letter was written. *Married a Jewish man? Times certainly have changed,* Jonetta thought.

Although Georgia had light skin and fine, dark hair with a deep wave pattern, the nose was a dead giveaway that she had Negro blood in her lineage somewhere. There was no way she was passing for white so this man must have really loved her, Jonetta concluded. It was probably best that they did not have children just in case one of them turned out peanut butter colored or darker like some of their siblings did. Jonetta could not believe how much she had missed these past few years being stuck in Chicago with two aging aunts.

A tinge of jealousy shot through her as she thought about the life she probably could have had if she had not gotten pregnant so long ago, but decided that she had done well by marrying a light-skinned black man with light brown eyes. As she looked up to see Phyllis standing in her doorway with her hands on her narrow hips, she was pleased with the outcome.

Jonetta sighed, "Well, who is it?" The last thing she was concerned about was a telephone call.

"Some lady named Lorraine," Phyllis replied flippantly. "She sounds weird too."

"In what way?" Jonetta asked rising off the bed with her hands on her narrow hips.

"Like she was crying or whimpering or something," Phyllis shrugged.

Jonetta sighed and pushed Phyllis out of her way, "Dammit! Why didn't you say so?"

Phyllis's mouth flew open as she followed her mother down the hallway, "I tried but you were too busy reading those stupid letters!"

Jonetta stopped in her tracks, turned around and glowered at Phyllis. She did not have to open her mouth because the expression on her face alone signaled to her daughter that if she knew what was good for her, she had better shut up and walk away. Phyllis did just that and disappeared into her room.

"Hello?" Jonetta said finally into the white French style rotary telephone.

"Oh, dear God!" Lorraine sobbed into the phone. "I'm so glad you're home."

After Lorraine finally composed herself long enough to tell Jonetta that Betty Lou had taken a turn for the worse since her last visit a few months ago, she rounded up her children, and called a taxicab service to take them straight to the house.

Lorraine, with swollen eyelids and a runny nose, embraced her on site and briefly greeted the children. She instructed them to sit quietly in the living room while she and Jonetta see about Betty Lou. Phyllis sulked while Dawn played with her toy doll and Colette drew stick people on a sheet of paper that she brought with her. Colette reminded Dawn to keep the noise down, and Phyllis threatened to hit her upside the head the next time she made a peep. Dawn rolled her eyes and shifted in her seat knowing that Phyllis would probably make good on her threats.

When Jonetta entered Betty Lou's room she gasped at what appeared to be a withered, pale, corpse lying in the bed, but it was making gurgling sounds so she was sure that her aunt was still alive. Lorraine squeezed her hand, encouraging her to sit by the bedside.

Jonetta took a deep breath and admitted, "This is worse than I thought."

"I know," Lorraine dabbed a handkerchief at the corners of her swollen eyes.

Jonetta almost felt guilty because she could not show the same emotion. But she did take pity on Betty Lou and her suffering.

"How long has she been this way?" Jonetta furrowed her eyebrows. "Have you called a doctor?"

Lorraine nodded. "There's nothing he can do. She has been like this for about three weeks. I was hoping she would get better, but…" Her voice cracked and trailed off as she shook her head. She was caught up in her grief, as she looked at Betty Lou sorrowfully. "But you spend some time with her now while I go see about your children. I hope they have good appetites. I've been cooking like crazy just to keep my mind off of worrying about when Betty Lou will take her last breath." She left the room closing the door behind her gently.

Lorraine should've called me sooner! Although she was technically the next of kin, Jonetta certainly did not deserve an award for being the best family member. Beside Betty Lou's Queen Victorian style bed was a green silk damask, single Louis XV armchair beckoning Jonetta's warmth in the chilly room. *She always did have good taste*, Jonetta acknowledged as she sat stiffly beside Betty Lou.

"Betty Lou," she whispered. The gurgling continued without acknowledgement of her presence. Jonetta sighed. She reached out to touch her hand but then Betty Lou began coughing before she could make contact. Startled, Jonetta sat back but then offered her some water.

"Who's there?" Betty Lou managed to ask between a few coughs.

"It's me, Jonetta," she replied. "I've come to see about you." Jonetta reached for the glass of water on the nightstand.

Betty Lou opened her weak eyes and focused on her face for a moment. "I'll choke on water like a baby. But I think you would like to see me die anyway." She coughed for a while as Jonetta patted her hand lightly and placed the glass of water back on the silver serving tray. Her hand was cold and her bones were protruding from her transparent skin. It made Jonetta shudder. If this is what death in old age looked like then she did not want any part of it.

"Let's not fight. Lorraine called me and now I'm here to help in any way I can. I brought my children so you could meet them."

Betty Lou showed some delight in her face at that news. "Bring them to me," she said just above a whisper in a raspy voice. She immediately began coughing again as if the words coming out of her mouth were strangling her.

When the children entered the doorway Betty Lou motioned for them to come closer. She wanted to get a real good look at them - with what was left of her sight - to ensure none of them resembled her beloved, Mr. Lucky. Dawn was the first in her reach; she pulled her hand closer to the bed. Betty Lou grunted knowing that she was too young to be Mr. Lucky's child. She motioned to Phyllis and Colette to come closer. They looked at their mother nervously.

Jonetta nodded in the direction of the bed, "Go on girls, she doesn't bite."

They walked together holding hands toward the bed. "You sit

here," Betty Lou insisted of Dawn pointing to the chair. She did and looked to her mother for guidance, but there was none. Colette broke the ice by introducing herself.

Betty Lou nodded approval and pointed at Phyllis with her wrinkled finger.

"Who are you?"

"I'm Phyllis. I'm the oldest," she replied.

That announcement caused Betty Lou to chuckle slightly, but that turned into a coughing spell that even made Lorraine appear in the doorway with worry. "Children, can you go back to the living room while I check on Betty Lou?" Lorraine asked politely. Betty Lou was fine with that too because now she was satisfied that none of them had been Mr. Lucky's children.

"Yes," Jonetta agreed and escorted them out the bedroom. "I'll be back in a few minutes. Mind your manners and just be patient."

They scurried back to the living room as instructed.

"I placed some cookies on the table and I'll get the milk in a few minutes." Lorraine assured the girls with a smile. But as soon as they were down the hall, her expression grew with worry. Jonetta rushed back to Lorraine's aid offering her assistance. Betty Lou shooed them away closing her eyes after she stopped coughing.

"Lorraine, go see to the children," Betty Lou instructed weakly. She wanted time alone with her niece if only for a little while. Lorraine agreed reluctantly, but was comforted by knowing at least Jonetta was there for a while.

"Striking children you have," she managed to say peering at Jonetta. "Fine indeed."

"Thank you," Jonetta smiled genuinely, for she was proud of her daughters.

"Mr. Lucky wasn't that handsome. Your husband must have been a looker," Betty Lou cackled. Even on her deathbed, this old woman still wanted to bring up the past that put a wedge between them all these decades.

Jonetta sighed, "That was a long time ago."

"Lots of memories around here," Betty Lou continued, folding her hands on top of her chest. "Some good. Some not so good. But memories, still."

Jonetta bowed her head thinking of how far she had come since the day she arrived in Chicago with a baby boy in her belly. "Yes, some memories are still very painful for me." Jonetta admitted as her eyes drifted to the window facing the backyard. "I'll have to go in the backyard before I leave. I never had a chance to…"

Betty Lou opened her eyes wide at that news, "For what?"

"You know," Jonetta replied carefully whispering just in case one of the children happened to walk past the door. She figured Betty Lou had forgotten about the burial of her baby in the yard after all these years due to old age. "I never had the chance to pay my respects to my first born child."

"Oh, your son." Betty Lou said closing her eyes. "He's not there." A wry grin came across her face that caused several wrinkles to appear all across her face resembling a road map.

"What do you mean?" Jonetta asked gripping the arms of the chair. "Did you move him to another place?"

Betty Lou let out a deep, wicked laugh that it sent chills down Jonetta's spine.

"Tell me what you did with my son!" Jonetta demanded rising to her feet.

"I threw the bastard in the trash like the piece of garbage that he was," Betty Lou said boldly and glared at Jonetta as she tried to hold back her cough.

"You did *what*?" Jonetta seethed. Her heart was pounding as she stood to her feet.

Betty Lou grinned, and then began to cough again. When she regained her composure, she cackled at the look on Jonetta's face. She had been waiting for the right opportunity to divulge that information to her all these years. Now seemed like the perfect time. She wanted to make sure this announcement stabbed Jonetta in the heart and finally, by the look on her face, the dagger had done its job.

Jonetta felt the blood rush to her face as she glowered at her aunt. Her body trembled with anger. Wasn't it enough that she had been raped, became pregnant, sent away to her aunts in Chicago full of shame, fell down the stairs, broke her body and miscarried her son? As those thoughts raced through her mind, she became enraged. Before Jonetta knew it, she felt bony frail hands clawing at her hands. Several swipes from her thin fingernails tore Jonetta's flesh on her hands, but the only pain she felt was in her heart.

The more Betty Lou clawed at her hands the harder Jonetta pressed the down pillow over her face until she caught a glimpse of someone from the corner of her eye. It was Dawn. Jonetta quickly removed the pillow, wiped the sweat from her brow and regained her composure. Betty Lou began to cough and Jonetta was relieved that she didn't actually kill her although she desperately wanted to finish her off.

"Mommy will be right there. Go back with your sisters," Jonetta told Dawn as softly as she could. Once Dawn disappeared down the hallway, Jonetta turned her attention to her aunt who was still trying to catch her breath. "Not one word of this or I'll be back to finish what I started." Jonetta whispered in her ear. Betty Lou kept her eyes forward as she closed her mouth slowly. For the first time in her life, she was actually afraid of her niece. Jonetta felt the stings in her hands from the clawing and winced at the sight of her flesh being open with specks of blood beginning to rise on the surface. She blotted her hands with her handkerchief cursing at her aunt.

"You would fight until the bitter end," Jonetta scoffed. "Hateful bitch! I hope you burn in hell."

She knew it would only be a matter of time before Lorraine would resurface to check on them so she smoothed the bed covers and quickly shut the door behind her.

Yes. Phyllis knew that name for sure. She actually met Lorraine, but never would've remembered until that now. She turned to look at Bishon. He was so desperate for answers, but Phyllis decided not to mention her memories about Lorraine.

"Please call me if anything changes." Bishon handed Phyllis his business card and walked towards his car, staring at the house.

CHAPTER 16
A Ram in the Bush

Pushing the stroller through the church with one hand and carrying her clipboard with a full list of things to do with the other hand was not on her agenda today, but Georgia was in one of her moods and needed to be alone. Dawn kept doing disappearing acts in Fred's Mercedes, which probably sent Georgia spiraling into a depression. Now that Phyllis was at the house, she agreed to keep the rest of the kids for her. When Colette asked her sister to watch all of them she refused to watch Delilah claiming that her mind was not in a good space to keep a one-year-old baby. Although Colette felt bad that Damien kicked Phyllis out of their house, she was glad for the help. It also gave them an opportunity to talk about what happened that night. If Pastor had not brought to her attention that she provoked Phyllis, she would have never apologized first.

When Phyllis showed up to the house without the girls later that day, Colette knew that something was wrong. Georgia sat them down as sisters in the living room to let them know that she was going to have as much peace as she possibly could under her roof and if they wished to keep up strife that all of them could leave.

"I'm getting too old to play referee with your children and all of you grown women," she had said and left them to talk about their fight.

"You acted like you couldn't wait to hurt me with that news about seeing Damien with *your* husband's pregnant side chick. You put Dawn on the spot, too! That shit ain't cool, Colette. It was a dagger to my heart and you knew it would be." Phyllis explained her hurt calmly.

Dawn nodded in agreement. "It turned out to be nothing, just like I said! But Phyllis was left hurt, confused and so angry that she cut Damien's hair clean off!"

"I didn't chop it *all* off." Phyllis remarked.

Dawn scoffed. "Imagine my surprise when I dropped the girls off and Phyllis has her bags packed looking homeless and Damien standing there looking like the Predator with a new hairstyle!"

Dawn's colorful description gave them all a chuckle.

Colette had to eat humble pie as they continued to tell her how they felt about her actions that night. By the end of their conversation, Colette apologized. They all shed a few tears and gave hugs freely. Dawn went on about her day helping Chena and Phyllis kept herself distracted by playing with her nieces and nephew, occasionally checking her smartphone to see if Damien reached out. He hadn't. A week had passed and he only reached out once to confirm the twins' schedule so he could be home when they got home. Colette could tell that Phyllis was anxious to get back to her own house, but she refused to beg. She was being so helpful with the kids both Georgia and Dawn wanted her to stay as long as she wanted because they were finally getting some peace.

Colette was able to spend more time at the church with Pastor, where she really wanted to be anyway. Although, lately, he wasn't too pleased with her ever since she told him about the fight with Owen. The scar above her brow had not completely healed yet either. She refused to go to the hospital emergency room for stitches because she didn't want to be billed, that's what she told her family, but really she didn't want the questions from the nurses and doctors about how it happened. Instead, she bought some liquid bandage to close her wound and it was taking its sweet time to heal. She used her hair to cover up the scar, but of course, Pastor noticed it since he was always showering her with kisses. Initially, he was angry with Owen and wanted to retaliate, but once again, Colette had laid the first blow so he thought better of it.

"Who is your mother? Didn't she ever teach you to keep your hands to yourself? Tell me now!" Pastor fumed the afternoon she told him. "The last time you fought your sister I showed you exactly how you should be using your hands! God intended them for satisfaction, gratification, and edification for others! Not for fighting!" Pastor rebuked her with his heavy accent. All of his words rushed together so she knew that he was angry with her. Pastor forced her to kneel to pray for forgiveness of misusing her hands. *What's he trying to say? My mother didn't raise me right?*

That time he bound her wrists together with twine that he got out of his locked office closet. Colette tried to see what else he had in there and swore she saw a whip and a thick leather belt, but he closed it quickly and locked it. *Looks like a closet full of torture!*

Colette thought it would be another session of prayer with anointed oil and oral pleasure, but he left her alone in the office on her knees with her hands bound tightly. As she tried to wiggle loose, the twine only dug deeper and it began to burn. She prayed alright! She prayed for clarity on her relationship with Pastor because she wanted to be his woman so badly and she would do anything to please him. Moreover, she also prayed for deliverance from being mistreated by men. *Why do I attract men that need to dominate me? Show me what to do differently, Lord!*

Ever since that last prayer session, Pastor had no sexual desire for her lately. Colette knew exactly how to relieve of a man from stress, relax his mind and put him at ease with his worries, but Pastor wouldn't let her near him. It was strictly all business between them. He even began to suggest that she keep Delilah at home, so they could get through their day faster. Colette tried many ways to become more attractive, more available to him, anything to make him adore her again, but nothing worked.

As the week grew closer to the Pastor Appreciation celebration on Sunday, Pastor grew more anxious and irritable. Regardless of how many times Colette reassured him that she had everything under control with Owen, he seriously doubted it. That doubt transferred right over to her ability to have a successful Pastor Appreciation Day. He questioned everything she suggested and rejected most of her ideas for the event claiming that she had no idea how things were done and what the congregation expected because she was new. Even though everything was finalized, Pastor still had anxious energy and it was getting on her last nerves. She was going to prove to him that she was the best choice for his secretary, event planner and woman.

"Come on, Delilah. We're going to kitchen where it should be nice and quiet!"

Delilah banged her rattle against the tray and Colette had a mind to take it from her, but that would only cause her to cry. *Somebody deserves joy. I guess it's gonna be you today, baby.* When Colette entered the kitchen, she immediately became annoyed. The Sister's Circle seemed to be holding a meeting. These women were supposed to be the elderly, holy example of Christian women living for Christ, but they were the ones who usually started all the gossip around the church. Colette was not their favorite either, but the feeling was mutual.

"Oh, I wasn't aware that anyone was occupying the kitchen." Colette said as she forced a smile on her face. *What are you cows up to now?*

"Actually, we were just meeting about the dinner menu for Pastor Appreciation Day." Sister Kimball replied. "We have a few suggestions for dinner and desserts."

"I already created a menu and discussed it with Pastor." Colette removed a sheet of paper from her clipboard and handed to her. "And... he approved it."

Sister Kimball glanced over it and handed it to another elderly woman to look over. Before she knew it, they were passing it around the table and making comments in hushed tones amongst themselves. Colette was not in the mood for their suggestions. She had already been down that path with Pastor. The menu was final and she was not making adjustments.

"Usually Pastor doesn't get involved with the planning details..." One of the women began, but didn't stand a chance against Colette this afternoon.

"Yes, well, apparently the food choices at the previous Pastor Appreciations always gave him heartburn and digestion issues. He wasn't pleased with it at all. Sooooo, this year we are using a caterer of Pastor's choice. I guess there's no reason for this meeting after all." Colette straightened her posture as she patiently waited for them to gather their belongings and leave the kitchen.

"What about the desserts? I always bake my carrot cake with cream cheese icing and Pastor loves it! He told me so himself." Sister Kimball replied. She was almost beside herself and suddenly Colette felt sorry for her.

Well, if means that much to you! "All desserts are welcome, Sister Kimball. Feel free to bake until your fingers fall off! Have a blessed day, ladies."

Once they cleared out of the kitchen and their voices trailed off, Colette sat at the long, wooden table, bowed her head and exhaled. "Okay, Delilah, let mommy check your pamper. It might be time to change you." She lifted her baby from the stroller to smell her, then squeezed her pamper to determine if she needed changing. Colette frowned when she felt the mushiness of it. "You're a little too wet, babycakes!" Colette planted kisses on her chubby cheeks and placed her back in the stroller. She tugged on one of her curly ponytails and it bounced right back into place. All of her children had hair just like Owen, black, silky and curly. Her children were so beautiful, everyone said it everywhere they went, but she always saw his face in them. Only Lydia had a few features that resembled Colette, but still through her children, Owen was a constant reminder on a daily basis. It was a curse and a blessing.

Colette grabbed the diaper bag and noticed that her smartphone was blinking. She had forgotten that she put it on vibrate mode while she was in the office with Pastor. She did not want to be disturbed while Pastor gave her a list of things to do. As she checked text messages and Facebook notifications, she was puzzled by why she had so many notifications and inbox messages, but then her phone rang.

"Mama! I'm so glad you called!" Colette yelled into the phone with a sigh of relief.

"Hi, Colette." Jonetta replied dryly. "I wanted to know when you'll be home later."

"Mama, I'm so overwhelmed with planning the Appreciation Day for Pastor. There's so much to do before tomorrow and such little time to do it. I have Delilah with me and she's slowing me down. Then these old hags around here tried to take over and then have the nerve to get mad when I do not allow them to walk all over me! They make a preacher wanna cuss! I swear, Mama! They challenge my every word. I get everything approved by Pastor and still they just have to challenge me! I'm sick of it! And don't get me started on Pastor! He's been acting funky towards me since I told him about the fight with Owen. I don't know if he's jealous or angry that I didn't get the divorce papers signed or what. Mama, to answer your question, I have no idea when I'll be home. What's going on?" Colette rubbed her forehead and sighed.

"Colette, we should find some time to talk…"

"Mama, did you hear me?" Colette asked exasperated. "Pastor has been running me ragged with all of his demands! Thankfully, he finally left for the day. But I have to get things done around here. Looks like I will be doing it alone since the Mothers of the church are all in their feelings! I cannot wait until Alyssa has her baby…"

"Colette, take a deep breath and just listen to me…"

"I don't know where to even start. The food is being catered, but I still need to decorate, print the bulletins with a special insert, make the punch, and set up the dining hall tables. I just need some help, Mama." Colette whined as she pushed the stroller back and forth with her foot. Delilah was busy munching on a teething biscuit.

Jonetta grew silent.

"Hello?" Colette darted her eyes around the room and shook her head. *Is she even listening?*

"You're absolutely right." Jonetta finally responded. "You just need some help. Did you say the Pastor left for the day?"

"Yes, he needs his rest for tomorrow."

"I'll tell you what, why don't I come down to the church to help you cook, decorate, or even watch Delilah. How does that sound?"

Colette gasped, surprised by her mother's generosity. "That sounds like music to my ears! I think the angels of heaven just sang HALLELUJAH!"

CHAPTER 17

Sippin' Tea

"Well, did you tell her?" Norman kept nagging her about breaking the news to Colette, but when Jonetta tried, she didn't want to listen. However, Jonetta knew that she needed an escape, just like when she needed one from Mr. Lucky. Of all things, Colette did not possess a heart of a survivor nor the street smarts, but Jonetta knew exactly what to do. It worked then and certainly, it was going to work now. Like Colette said, she needed help, and one day she would thank her mother for solving her ongoing problems with the men in her life. Jonetta was sure of it.

"I'm headed to the church in a few minutes." Jonetta announced when she ended the call with Colette.

"So you didn't tell her?" Norman huffed, stuffing his hands in khaki pants pockets.

"Not yet, Norman. I'm headed to meet her at the church!" Jonetta barked at him.

"And you think telling her at the church while that man is there is the best thing to do, huh?"

"Norman, don't worry about it!" Jonetta waved him off as she grabbed her gardening hat from the hallway closet. "I know how to fix this!"

"Netta, please don't do anything crazy!" Norman pleaded as he followed her to the patio.

"I'm a survivor, Norman!" Jonetta reminded him quickly, putting on her wide brimmed sun hat. "I'm the damn driver on the crazy train." She headed to her garden with a huge smile on her face, her head held high and adrenalin pumping. The basil leaves beamed under the sunlight, void of any brown spots. A healthy bushel of cilantro was planted beside the basil on purpose. It was hiding her secret weapon. Jonetta had hoped that she never had to use it again, but sometimes people just asked for the clever devil in her to be unleashed. Jonetta leaned down and inhaled the aromas of her fresh vegetable garden. The bell peppers and green onions seemed to be in competition releasing their strongest aromas. She carefully separated the basil leaves and cilantro, pleased with her handiwork, she couldn't resist a smile. The baneberries, shiny, red and ripe looked delicious enough to eat. It's no wonder why the poisonous berries were ingested by those who were none-the-wiser. They were very tempting and appealing to the naked eye, but she was ready to put them to use in another way.

When Jonetta secretly planted three roots in Georgia's yard two years ago, she never imagined that she would actually need to use them. However, Norman had become ill right after the New Year with his colon and he worked her last nerves with his constant complaining. She decided to dig up one stalk by the root and plant it in her new garden at his house. *If he gets too sickly, I'll just put him out of his misery sooner than later.* She dried out 12 berries, crushed them and put the powdery substance in an empty pill bottle that she hid in the back of her lingerie drawer. It was her intention to empty his pill capsules and replace the contents with the baneberry; however, Norman bounced back like a cat with nine lives. Jonetta had not thought of the potent baneberry since. Until now.

They had multiplied nicely, thanks to the new fertilizer she bought in the spring. She plucked a few where dozens of berries flowered beautifully, and even plucked a few withered berries. *These will be perfect for boiling.* She reached inside of her shirt pocket for tissue, wrapped them carefully and placed them back in her shirt pocket. As Jonetta turned to head back to the house, she noticed Norman was peering out of the kitchen window to see what she was doing. She quickly gathered some basil leaves, cilantro and one bell pepper so he wouldn't be suspicious. *He is so damned nosey!* She took her hat off, placed the herbs and bell pepper inside and held it almost underneath her chin so she could hide the bulge in her shirt pocket.

Norman slid the patio door open for her when she approached the house. "You cooking tonight or something?"

Jonetta raised her hands to show him the goods from the garden. "Yes, at the church with Colette. You know that girl isn't the best in the kitchen. She needs my help."

"I see," Norman mumbled as she glided past him.

Jonetta placed the hat on the kitchen counter, and headed upstairs before he could ask any more questions. She needed to get that pill bottle and change clothes. Jonetta yelled from the stairs, "I'll be back later. Don't wait up."

□ □ □ □ □

"Mama, I really appreciate your help tonight." Colette beamed, planting a kiss on her cheek. She couldn't believe how Jonetta came through for her at the last minute. She was not the type of mother to drop everything for her daughters. Usually, she let them figure it out their own mess until it was necessary to step in and tell them what to do.

"It's my pleasure," Jonetta kept her eyes glued on the pot as she stirred. It was almost hypnotizing watching the hot liquid swirl around in the pot knowing the result. She knew by boiling it would make it more potent, but Pastor didn't get the nickname "Big Louie" for no reason. It would probably take a larger dose of the baneberries for it to work on his whale of an ass. The special tea gave off a bitter aroma causing the women in the kitchen to ask questions.

One woman was holding Delilah as she slept, spoiling her, but Jonetta didn't mind because she wasn't there to babysit tonight. The other woman sat at the table helping Colette stuff the bulletin with a flyer that had a photo of Pastor Louis Paul on it detailing his service as the Lord's servant. *Yeah, right! Nothing but a pimp!*

"Mama, what kind of tea are you making?" Colette frowned.

Jonetta glanced around the kitchen and noticed that the other women were also waiting to hear her answer. "It's an herbal tea and…it's only for your Pastor," she replied loud enough for everyone in earshot to hear. *Don't blame me if your greedy asses drink this man's special poisonous tea!* "A man of God should always have his own drink, in a sterling silver pitcher or at least a stainless steel one. Please tell me that you all have one for your Pastor." She skillfully changed the subject.

"Yes, of course, Mama." Colette replied. "But his is gold."

"Here it is," one of the women pulled it from the kitchen cabinet, placing it next to Jonetta.

Jonetta grunted. *His arrogant ass would have a gold one!* "Good, once I add the honey to it I'll let it cool down to room temperature and then pour Pastor's special tea into the pitcher." Jonetta replied casually. "Do you all have any plastic wrap?"

Colette pulled it from the drawer, walked towards Jonetta and peered over her shoulder. She couldn't recall her mother ever making a homemade tea. "Wow! It's so red, like blood red. I never you could brew your own tea, Mama."

If she doesn't get the hell off my back! I swear! "Well, there's lots of things you have yet to uncover about me, missy. But the reason it's so red is because I added hibiscus and mint leaves, and dried cranberries. It's a special tea that I hope your Pastor will enjoy." Jonetta responded and turned her attention back to the pot. She turned the fire off to let it cool off a bit before she added the honey.

"If you put some fresh cranberries on top, it'll be so pretty when he pours it into his glass," Colette suggested, raising her eyebrows. She desperately wanted to make Pastor happy.

"Good idea, Colette," Jonetta responded smiling as she locked her eyes back on her handy work. *I can use the other baneberries with the cranberries as garnishment. If he eats the berries and drink the tea...* She stirred slowly and smiled wickedly at the thought of him falling his fat ass out of his seat right there at the banquet in front of the whole congregation. The table they decorated specifically for the Pastor was elaborately fit for a king. His table had a black tablecloth with a gold rope stitched around the hem, a gold scepter laid across the table next to an enormous bible, gold plates, and a gold chalice were all prepared for this bastard. *They worship him like he's God!* Even the large, burgundy velour chair displayed a black sash with gold letters that read: PASTOR PAUL WE LOVE YOU!

His table was set apart from the congregation's tables, high up on a platform. *I hope he chokes and gags right in front of the whole congregation!* Jonetta let out a chuckle and cleared her throat, trying to play it off. Yes, she wanted him to suffer, and maybe she even wanted him dead. So what? Compared to what he did to her years ago, as far as she was concerned, he deserved to be tortured and killed. *Now he wanted my daughter, too? Oh, hell no!*

Big Louie had inserted himself in her life long enough. If Jonetta had known that Colette was attending his church sooner, she would've persuaded her to find another church, but she was none-the-wiser. Colette seemed like she was in love with this bastard. Colette would have either invite them all to a church function to meet him or bring him to their house for an introduction; it was only a matter of time. *Norman would shoot him dead for sure!* All these months he had been around her grandchildren, too. Jonetta stopped stirring. She stood paralyzed for a moment wondering if Big Louie, their beloved Pastor, had inappropriately touched one of her grandchildren. That was an unbearable thought. She reached in her shirt pocket for two more baneberries and dropped them in pot. *Just for good measure because his nasty ass is probably abusing somebody, somewhere. It's up to me to put a stop this man!* She nodded her head. *No turning back.* She came to accomplish getting rid of Big Louie from her life once and for all!

CHICAGO, IL
1972

For a few weeks, Jonetta decided not to have any contact with Norman, not physical nor verbal. She needed Mr. Lucky to believe that she was done sneaking around with another man. She made love to him regularly, cooked for him and it pleased him. Her twenty-sixth birthday was approaching and Mr. Lucky decided to have the greatest party for her at the house. While Mr. Lucky was making plans for the party, she was making her own plans for her freedom.

The night of the party was festive with disco music on the record player and plenty of people. There were so many people in the house that neither Jonetta nor Mr. Lucky knew, but they were there to celebrate Jonetta's birthday just the same. The party scene was actually perfect considering the plans she had. Mr. Lucky would not know what hit him or who did it because it was so many people there to blame. Although Jonetta grew up poor, her mother had taught her about planting an herb garden. "You never know when it may come in handy," her mother had told her with a wink. Most of the herbs were for cooking and others for poison.

She could not seem to get her hands on the one she wanted living up in the north, but the very one that would do the trick was growing right in Mr. Lucky's backyard, red baneberry. Jonetta had collected the baneberries and allowed them to wither in order for them to lose some of its potency. She wanted to poison Mr. Lucky just slightly enough for him just to be hospitalized for a few days then she would make her escape. However, as her anxiety heightened that night she began to crush more and more berries. *Just to be sure it will work*, she had told herself.

She made a makeshift paper envelope, swept the powdery substance inside and kept it close to her breast. As the night progressed, Mr. Lucky became more intoxicated and finally sat down. Jonetta dumped all the powder in the bottom of his glass and poured his last glass of whiskey. He caught her by the wrist as she served him accidentally spilling some of the whiskey on himself. Jonetta sucked her teeth and silently cursed to herself.

His words slurred, and his eyes did not make contact with hers. He was drunk for sure, but Jonetta worried that he was too drunk taste the special drink that she made for him. Before that doubt could consume her, Mr. Lucky eventually stood after struggling a few times, and when he finally stopped stumbling, he made a toast to his one true love, Johnnie. When all glasses were raised, Mr. Lucky was the first to take a long deep swallow of the poison and slumped back down in his plush chair. Jonetta exhaled. *Down the hatchet!*

By the time the guests departed Mr. Lucky was still slumped over in the chair, drooling on himself. A few guests became concerned, but Jonetta assured them that he was fine and she would take care of him. She decided to leave him right where he was until morning. She checked on him by mid-morning only to find vomit soiled in his clothes and on the side of the chair. An awful stench in the living room filled the air. Jonetta called to him repeatedly to no avail. She walked over to him, lifted his chin and saw foam in the corners of his mouth. She released his chin and his head dropped down heavily. She panicked as she checked his pulse. It was barely there. She gasped covering her mouth. Fear struck through her body, and then panic set her into action. She grabbed the glass from which he drank the poison and rushed to rinse it out in the kitchen. *Why am I cleaning it? I should break it!* She threw it in the trash and proceeded to hit it until it shattered. She rushed to phone Norman because she was going to need help. Through her sobs and whispers explaining what she did, Norman advised her to call an ambulance. Norman was always doing the right and sensible thing.

After an hour at the hospital, Mr. Lucky was pronounced dead. He was only 55-years-old. The doctor claimed that he suffered a heart attack, which probably contributed to the alcohol poisoning. Jonetta knew different, she knew the side effects of the baneberry could result in a heart attack, but never mentioned it to a soul other than Norman. She never meant to kill Mr. Lucky. Nevertheless, she wanted out of that relationship so she could be with Norman, her future.

One of the sisters suddenly broke out into song and snapped Jonetta from her memories.

"Soon and very soon. We are going to see the King!" The elderly woman sang with conviction.

That's such an appropriate song, Jonetta thought.

CHAPTER 18

On the Way

She couldn't get enough of this man. No complaints. No strings attached. Their history bound their hearts together, but their lifestyles kept them apart for years. Now that Raffi needed Dawn, she felt that life had come full circle except there were no titles, no expectations, and no demands. The arrangement worked well for all of them. Chena had the help, compassion and friendship that she needed to get through this difficult time. Raffi enjoyed her presence, cooking and especially her sex. It was pure erotic sex between two lovers, who could ask for more? Raffi had her right where he wanted, usually spread naked across the full-sized bed in the guest room right after dinner three nights a week. Whenever Raffi told Dawn that he wanted his "dessert" after dinner, Shiloh thought that he was getting some too. He finally explained to his son that his special dessert wasn't for kids.

But today she woke up alone. No dessert last night after dinner because Dawn made up a lie about it being her time of the month to ward off Raffi because she needed to see Bishon later. He was feeling a little neglected since their last encounter at his office. He thought it had something to do with her mother, but that wasn't the case at all. The time she spent between Georgia's house and caring for Chena didn't leave much dating time with Bishon. Besides, she was enjoying the best sex she had in a long time with Raffi and she didn't even have to leave the house for it. Although, it came with a hefty price of constant guilt, she continued sexing her best friend's husband. Dawn often avoided making eye contact with Chena because she probably knew. Dawn made sure that she was heavily medicated at night so they could moan as loud as they wanted.

Although she felt guilty, it was Chena's idea. Right? Dawn told herself repeatedly that she was actually doing Chena a favor. She was granting her last wishes. That's what best friends do. Right?

"I'm taking Shiloh shopping for school clothes today," Dawn told Chena, placing a saucer of toast next to her. "It's going to be special spending time with Shiloh. Raffi registered him for school and now the fun part, shopping for new school clothes!"

"See? I told you that we would grow on you," Chena replied, smiling at Dawn. "I can't believe my baby is going to the eighth grade in two weeks. Time certainly flies."

"Yeah, he's such a big boy and so handsome, too!"

"How are you and Raffi getting along?" Chena asked as she applied petroleum jelly on her lips. Just like a baby, she choked on water lately and her skin had been drying out terribly. Her lips cracked and bled sometimes as well because she was so dehydrated. She was withering away right before their eyes. Dawn cleared her throat and walked to the window to open the curtains.

"We're okay." Dawn responded trying her best to sound as casual as possible.

"Good. He certainly seems happier and more relaxed since you've been around to help."

"Shiloh will probably need to go shopping again in about six months because he's growing so tall. It seems like overnight he became a giant!" Dawn said, chuckling. She tried her best to change the subject back to Shiloh, but Chena was persistent.

Chena nodded. "Raffi can get mean sometimes, especially when he can't have his way or he's stressed out. I want to keep him happy, Dawn. Okay? The way I'm feeling these days, I don't know if I'll even be at Shiloh's eighth grade graduation or if I'll even be alive in two months. I just want my boys to be happy in this life."

"You're here now, my friend. That's all that matters to us. Get some rest, girl," Dawn said. She walked over to Chena to kiss her forehead and quickly closed the door behind her and exhaled. *That was so fucking awkward!* She told Shiloh to get in the car so they could head out to the mall.

Walking around the mall had begun to wear Dawn out and she was getting hungry. Shiloh quietly sifted through clothes indecisively in every store and he was getting on Dawn's last nerve. *This was supposed to be fun.* Finally, he decided on some jerseys, jeans and the new Jordan's.

"These are expensive, Shiloh." Dawn frowned looking at the sticker price.

"My Dad told me he gave you his credit card and that I could have whatever I wanted," he replied like a spoiled little rich kid. "I want the new Jordan's, Aunty Dawn."

Dawn shook her head in disgust. *Raffi is creating a monster. They should've had more kids.* Once he tried them on and was satisfied, she paid for them and looked for the Food Court.

"What's the matter, Shiloh? You've been awfully quiet today." Dawn took a long slurp of her chocolate shake, waiting for his answer. *I'm gonna get brain freeze waiting for this boy to talk!*

Shiloh shifted in his seat, leaned back and folded his arms across his chest. He exhaled and rolled his eyes. *Damn! That's a lot of attitude for a twelve-year-old boy!* He certainly had Dawn's attention now. She pushed her shake and steak fries to the side of the table, and patiently waited for him to speak his mind.

"You can talk to me, Shiloh. Even if you need to say curse words," Dawn said, laughing. "I'm cool with that, too. So speak your mind, sweetie."

"I saw you and my Dad," Shiloh said through tight lips, looking Dawn square in the eyes.

Dawn saw hurt mixed with anger brewing in his eyes. *Shit! I thought we were being careful!* Her face flushed with embarrassment as she thought about what to say next. "You saw us doing what?"

"Really, Aunty Dawn?" Shiloh leaned forward, reached for his soda and continued, "I'm not a baby. I saw you! How could you kiss him? I thought you were supposed to be my mom's best friend."

Oh, thank God! He only saw us kiss. "Yes, she is still my best friend," Dawn replied, clearing her throat. She reached across the table to touch his hand gently. "We will always be best friends. Your mom is like my sister. I love her a whole lot, Shiloh."

"Then why are you screwing around with my Dad?" Shiloh snatched his hand away quickly.

"Hey! Watch it, Shiloh!" Dawn warned him pointing her finger in his face. *I should've never told this boy that he can speak his mind!* "Listen, there are some things you just don't understand. Okay? Your mom is sick and she wants me to take care of you both. She asked me to love you both like my own… Look, I think we should discuss it with your Dad."

"Nah, I'm cool," Shiloh replied, shaking his head. "My Dad says men will be creatures of habit. We're hunters by nature and the need to hunt doesn't change just because you get married. So he's not doing anything wrong by being a man, but you are."

"Oh, really? That's what he's teaching you, huh?" *That chauvinistic, arrogant asshole is gonna ruin this kid!* "Like I said, Shiloh, let's talk about this with your Dad later. Grab your shit and let's go."

After Dawn dropped off Shiloh at home, she didn't bother to go inside mainly because she was embarrassed. *I'm not in the mood for this shit.* She pulled off from the curb, screeching the tires and blasting music. Of course, five minutes later her phone chimed with alerts for text messages. She ignored it. She knew it was Raffi asking whereabouts, but it was none of his business today.

"Fuck off, Raffi!" Dawn frowned her face and rolled her eyes. She was so upset how Shiloh confronted her, in public no less, as if she was the one in the wrong. *Hell, I'm the single one between the three of us! How am I wrong?* Dawn sat at a red light too long thinking about her lifestyle lately. Nothing seemed to be going right ever since she decided to stay in Chicago. She couldn't find a gig to save her life. Now she felt like the family babysitter, housekeeper, caretaker and chauffer every single day. She knew that she signed up to be the substitute wife and mother and that nobody forced her, well, at least that is what she told herself. The sex was amazing, sneaking around with Raffi and Bishon was fun; however, she never considered the consequences like actually becoming a mother herself. The interruption of her thoughts came courtesy of a blaring car horn. "Alright, alright! Impatient asshole!"

A phone call came through her phone and her mother's number flashed across the touchscreen. Dawn decided to answer because she needed to talk.

"Hey, Mama."

"Dawn, I just spoke to Georgia and she's not happy one bit with you always driving Fred's car. You know how she feels about it."

"Why couldn't she just call me herself?"

"How the hell would I know?"

Dawn sighed loud enough for her mother to hear on purpose. *Aunt Georgia is trippin'!*

"Mama, I feel awful."

"Well, you should because you've definitely upset your Aunt Georgia!"

"Not about that…"

"Oh, what's wrong with you?"

"A couple of things…" Dawn sighed. "Shiloh just told me that he saw me and Raffi together."

"I don't want to hear this!" Jonetta yelled into phone and her voice vibrated over the speakers in the car. "I told your ass it was a terrible idea going to play house over there. Didn't I?"

Dawn sighed again. "I know, Mama, but Shiloh just doesn't understand that it was his mom's idea. I tried to explain that his mom is sick and how she wanted us to be a family because she's not going to be around. Shiloh just doesn't get it."

"Nobody does but you, Raffi and Chena! Anybody with common sense can see what a disastrous situation you got yourself into, Dawn! It is such a damn tangled web that all of you weaved together and you'll be the one suffering from it in the end! I don't wanna hear about it, Dawn!" Jonetta shouted through the phone again. "What else do you feel so awful about?"

Dawn turned the volume down on the steering wheel and sighed, "Well, I don't know if you want to hear this either, but…"

"Just spit it out already, dammit!"

"Mama, I'm pregnant." Dawn grimaced, waiting for her to scream again through the speakers.

Jonetta grew silent.

"Mama?" Dawn turned the volume up again. "You there, Mama?"

"Dawn… you're getting my blood pressure up! I swear you girls are going to be the death of me! You're trying to kill me, aren't you?"

Dawn pulled the car into a grocery store parking lot and put the car in park. She couldn't continue driving to Bishon's house with this load of stress on her. "No, Mama, I'm not trying to kill you. I knew you wouldn't be happy about it, but I just don't know what to do."

"Aren't you still seeing Shon?"

"Yes."

"So who's baby is it, Dawn?"

"I have no clue."

"Oh, my God! You *are* trying to kill me!"

"What should I do, Mama?"

"Dawn, this is a mess! Where are my cigarettes? What the hell are you doing with your life right now? You are being completely irresponsible!"

Dawn could hear her mother flicking her lighter repeatedly. *I guess she found her pack of cigarettes.*

"Mama...please don't lecture me..."

"Just shut the hell up and let me think!" Jonetta hissed. Dawn could hear her pulling another drag on her cigarette. She blew out smoke and continued, "You have two options. One is the obvious and hopefully your first choice! However, if you're foolish enough to have the baby you should just tell Bishon it's his. He's more stable and successful anyway. You and your child will have a secure future if he's the father instead of that Rasta loser Chena married. You'll finally be free to get out of that house of death over there!"

"And it'll be just my luck that the baby is born with a head full of locs looking just like Raffi!"

"Well, you can cross that bridge when you get to it!" Jonetta snapped.

"I won't be added to the list of your daughters who had abortions, Mama!" Dawn seethed.

"What the hell is that supposed to mean? I am so tired of everyone accusing me of forcing my daughters to have abortions! That's simply not true. The decision was theirs just like it is yours, Dawn."

"Whatever, Mama," Dawn replied shaking her head. "I have to tell Bishon and Raffi. There's no other way around this shit!"

184

"No, you don't!" Jonetta barked into the phone. "Don't make a move until we figure this out, Dawn."

"Please don't tell my sisters that I'm pregnant, Mama. I'm still trying to let it sink in for now."

"That should be the least of your worries, Dawn." Jonetta retorted. "First of all, how far along are you?"

"I just missed my period last week."

"When the hell were you going to say something?"

"I'm telling you now, Mama." Dawn rubbed her forehead. "I didn't notice that I missed a period at first. I've been busy between three houses lately and stressed the hell out. I thought it was just stress related, you know?"

"But, if you get too far along, they won't give you an abortion, Dawn!"

Dawn softly banged her head on the steering wheel.

"Mama, yes they will. This ain't the eighties. Regardless of allllll that... Mama, I want to keep my baby, *your* grandchild. I just need to figure out who be dis baby Daddy!" Dawn said, laughing. She tried to lighten the mood just a tad bit.

"It's not funny, Dawn!" Jonetta scolded her. "You're playing with fire, girl! You're messing up people's lives with news like this and you want to make light of it? What you should be doing is breaking out a calendar and try to do the math, and then you'll know who the father is! Unless, you were screwing them at the same time. Please don't tell me that you were out here being a little slut bucket!"

"Mama, I'm going to see Bishon tonight and I'm going to tell him."

"Don't you dare say a thing to..."

"This is my mess and I'm going to fix it!" Dawn ended the call abruptly. She was pissed off at her mother for suggesting that her first option should be an abortion. *I'm not having an abortion! She's always encouraging us to get a damn abortion! What the fuck?*

Dawn had to figure out a way to break the news to Bishon later when she saw him. They made plans to have dinner later and spend the night together. She had not seen him in two weeks and he was missing her terribly. She shifted the gear into drive and continued her journey to the South Loop.

□□□□□

When she stepped off the elevator, Bishon was waiting there with a single red rose and huge smile across his face. "I missed you, little lady." Bishon handed her the rose and planted a kiss on her lips. "Follow me." He led her to his condo, opened the door and watched the expression on her face change.

Dawn gasped. "Wow! You did all of this for me?" She walked inside, covered her mouth and hugged Bishon. There were lit candles, all sizes strategically placed around the living room, dining room and kitchen. A flavorful aroma filled the air that led her to the dining room where their plates of chicken parmesan and a medley of vegetables were waiting on them with a bottle of Gewürztraminer.

"I told you that I missed you, girl." Bishon pulled out her chair and gestured for her to take a seat.

Dawn gobbled her food as she tried to fill in Bishon on what she had been doing lately for Chena, Shiloh and Colette. Of course, she never mentioned Raffi's name once. Bishon stared at her in awe as she rattled on and on. He probably didn't hear a word she said, he was just happy that Dawn was finally in his presence.

"I have some news to share with you," Bishon said, raising his eyebrows.

"I'm listening."

"I think that I'm getting really close to finding my birth mother."

"Seriously?" Dawn smiled. "That's good news! Well, at least I hope it'll be good news."

Bishon exhaled. "Yeah, me too. I've been driving around this city visiting every single location that used to be a brothel. There's this one house in particular in Beverly that might be it."

"Beverly? That's my neighborhood."

"Yeah, you told me. I spoke to an older woman living in the house and come to find out her aunts used to run the brothel. When I mentioned it to my Dad, he got really quiet. I think he knows more than he's letting on. I had no idea that Chicago had so many brothels back in the day! Did you?"

Dawn yawned, not purposely, but she was completely drained after walking the mall for hours. "I'm sorry. You're not boring me, I'm just extremely tired."

"Well, I'm glad that you're tired because the next thing I have planned only an exhausted person will enjoy." Bishon cleared the table. "You didn't touch your wine. Drink up. I need your muscles relaxed."

Dawn smiled and reached for her wine glass. *It won't hurt you, I promise baby.* She sipped the wine, allowed it to linger on her tongue, and then gulped the rest down. Goosebumps raced down her arms as the wine rushed through her body. Over the past week, she stopped indulging in liquor with Raffi the moment she realized that she was pregnant. They always had a shot or a cocktail before they escaped into her bedroom for the evening. She sat at the table and thought about that for a moment. *Why do I get tipsy just to have sex with Raffi?* She didn't have long to wonder about it as she felt Bishon touch her shoulder.

"Follow me." Bishon took her hand and led her to his bedroom. There were more candles lined up on the dresser. Spread across the bed were two towels, and massage oil was waiting on the nightstand. He stroked the side of her face, pulled her in for a kiss and began to undress her.

My pregnancy news will just have to wait. "Ohhhh, Doctor Franklyn, are you about to rub me down?" Dawn cooed, running her hands up and down his chest.

"All that and more." Bishon promised.

CHAPTER 19

Come Home but Come Clean

Damien left early as usual on Saturday to play basketball with his longtime friends at the gym. This time he dropped the twins off with Phyllis along the way. She was happy to see her husband after a week without him. His sandy brown locs were now unraveled into a curly afro Mohawk with his sides shaved low took her by surprise. It was sexy on him, but she couldn't tell him that. Not now anyway. He was still pissed that she chopped off his locs. She almost didn't care because he looked so handsome with his new hairstyle. She was tempted to run her fingers through his natural hair texture because she had never seen it before because when they met, he had just started to lock his hair. *It looks so soft, like the twins' hair when they were babies.*

Phyllis knew that he was dropping off the twins early so she made sure to let her hair down, keep on her mint green robe only wearing panties. Damien stared at her for a moment. He was wearing basketball gear, sported sunglasses and Phyllis could smell his fragrance from eight feet away. The twins were almost carbon copies of Damien, but they were her babies. Phyllis was so happy to see her daughters she hugged them until they squirmed away from her arms. They ran inside to join their cousins who Phyllis volunteered to keep for the day.

"They're waiting on you!" Phyllis smiled as she watched the twins dash into the house.

"I'll be back in two hours to get the twins." Damien said finally.

"Don't worry about it. I'm keeping Colette's kids today so they can stay to play with their cousins. I'll just drop them off later.

Besides, I'm sure you need a break by now." Phyllis leaned against the doorframe, folded her arms across her chest, revealing major cleavage and smiled seductively.

Damien grunted and jiggled his keys in his hand as if he were contemplating on whether or not to take up the offer. "Alright, cool," he agreed. "I'll see you later, then."

"Have a good day, babe." Phyllis smirked, closing the door behind her. She knew that would catch him off guard. *You're still my man!* She watched him out of the living room window until he drove off.

"You seem happy." Georgia said softly.

Phyllis jumped, fully closed her robe and pulled the sash tighter. She didn't know that she was being watched. "Good morning, Aunt Georgia. You startled me."

"It's been a week, that's long enough for cooler heads to prevail. If you let this go on too long, you leave too much room for opportunity."

"What opportunity?"

Georgia shot her a look and headed to the kitchen. Phyllis followed curiously.

"Coffee?"

Phyllis nodded. She watched her aunt carefully as she moved about the kitchen. *She is so mysterious sometimes.* She took a seat at the table and waited for Georgia to answer her question.

"Temptation. It's always lurking." Georgia replied. "Don't allow it to creep in due to pride."

"You think Damien is being tempted?"

Georgia grabbed the coffee canister from the pantry and shook her head. "Phyllis, everyone has arguments and fall outs," Georgia replied as she poured water into the coffee pot. "The key is to know when to cease fire and invite love and understanding back into the situation."

"We aren't arguing."

"Only because he kicked you out."

Well damn! Phyllis jerked her neck. "Ouch!"

"But now that things have cooled off," Georgia continued casually. "Damien has a new hairstyle, and it looks good on him…"

"You were watching us?"

Georgia measured the coffee grains, sprinkled them strategically inside the brew basket, ignored Phyllis and continued. "He was able to look at you in the eyes this morning. Phyllis, your husband is not angry with you anymore. If I were you, I'd pack my things today and go back home."

Phyllis nodded and pondered her aunt's suggestion for a moment. She had not considered going back home until Damien invited her back. "But he's the one who kicked me out. Shouldn't he be the one to right this wrong by inviting me back home?"

"When love is involved and you're trying to resolve a problem the next move is on both people to come to a solution… if they truly love one another." Georgia leaned against the counter and stared off into space.

Phyllis got up from the table and planted a kiss on her aunt's cheek. "Thank you, Aunt Georgia. I'll go pack now."

"Oh, Phyllis, before I forget… You know that young man who stopped by here the other day?"

Phyllis looked confused. "Who?"

"The one you were outside talking to for a while."

Damn! She sees everything.

"Anyway, he came back more convinced than ever that his birth mother lived in this house way back when. He had so much paperwork supporting his suspicions. And something about his father knowing the woman who dropped him off at the church."

Phyllis raised her eyebrows. "Okay?" *Would you hurry the hell up so I can go pack?*

"Well, I don't think he's wrong. He actually might be on to something." Georgia paused for a moment. "I told him about our aunts who lived here and around the time I think the brothel was closed."

"You didn't tell him about my mother being a prostitute, did you?"

"Heavens no! But I have been meaning to tell your mother that he came by, but it's a lot going on around here with you, Colette, Dawn and keeping up with the children. Just in case I forget again, can you make sure that you mention it to your mother?"

Not a chance in hell! "Sure! I'm gonna pack my things now, Aunt Georgia. Thanks again!"

□□□□□

As promised, later in the afternoon, Phyllis took the girls at home along with her packed duffle bag. Damien's SUV wasn't in the driveway when she pulled up and she sat for a moment contemplating whether to call him or just going inside the house. *This is still my house! What am I thinking?* She eagerly exited the car with the girls, unlocked the front door and exhaled a sigh of relief when she felt a rush of cool air greet her.

"Did Daddy get the air fixed, girls?"

"I think so because a man was here with a white van." Serena volunteered the information.

Thank you God! "Good job, Daddy!" Phyllis dropped her duffle bag by the stairs and nodded her head with approval.

"Mommy, where's Daddy?" Serena asked.

"I'm not sure, babycakes." Phyllis replied as she inspected the house carefully.

"Can you call him?" Sabrina asked.

"Why?" Phyllis turned around to see both of them staring at her wide-eyed. "What's going on girls?"

"Daddy promised to take us to the movies today," Sabrina replied.

"Yeah, can you call him, mommy?" Serena asked, whining.

"Girls, let me get settled in first. I just got home. Didn't you miss me?"

"Yessss…" they replied together, looking like innocent angels.

Phyllis opened her arms and they rushed to embrace her. "Before you girls go anywhere in public I have to do your hair. Just give me a few more minutes and then I'll call your Daddy. Go on upstairs to play." *I'm not calling him any time soon.*

Once the girls were upstairs in their own world, Phyllis continued her inspection of the house making sure no signs of a temptress was around. Everything seemed to be the same on the first floor. There weren't any unfamiliar smells lingering in the air, and the kitchen utensils, spices and cutlery were all still in their rightful place. She tip-toed upstairs softly so the girls wouldn't hear her and headed to her bedroom. When she saw the bed unmade on one side of the bed a smile spread across her face. *Doesn't look like temptation creeped in here at all! Better not had either!*

Phyllis checked her phone for the time. It was almost three o'clock, the girls would be hungry soon and Damien should be home in a while. She decided to start dinner so as soon as he walked in he would smell a delicious aroma greeting him. The well-stocked refrigerator had fresh vegetables, meats and other new items. *I guess the man's gotta eat and feed my girls! Good job, baby.* Finally, after sifting through the refrigerator, she decided on Smothered Garlic Chicken with spinach, tomatoes, mozzarella cheese and bacon sprinkled on top. Since she had been gone, it didn't occur to her that she had not recorded on Facebook Live since her sisters came by that night she had a fight with Colette. She decided to fix that.

"Hey there, Friday Food Fanatics! I know it's Saturday afternoon and you haven't seen my face in a while. Well, guess what? I missed you too! Today, I'm going to make some mouthwatering smothered garlic chicken, but not like your Mama used to make. Nope. This recipe can be done right here on the stovetop with lots of mozzarella cheese, bacon, and spinach. Sounds interesting doesn't it? Good! So, let's get started!"

Phyllis held up each recipe item to the camera that she was going to use for the chicken. Once the minced garlic was in the pan sizzling with the olive oil, the aroma filled the air and she smiled. "Y'all smell that? I know you do!" she laughed to herself. "Is anybody out there cooking with me today? Go on and click the Love button if you're with me so far!" Only a few hearts danced across her screen, but she was still happy with that. *Thank goodness! Somebody is cooking with me!* The girls made their way downstairs eventually, wanting to be on camera. "Something smells good, mommy!" Serena said, hugging her around the waist.

"Hey, everybody as you can see I have company! Wave to the viewers girls."

Sabrina began jumping up and down waving frantically. "Hi everybody!"

"Okay, alright, calm down and let mommy finish cooking." Phyllis scooted them out the kitchen. "Yes, I have twin girls. They certainly have lots of energy and keep me super busy! But anyway, so now what you want to do is let this simmer for a minute. Your chicken should look like this." Phyllis place the camera phone over the pot on the stove, then back up to her face again. "Send me some likes if yours is looking like mine." She waited and saw several blue thumbs up slide across the screen. "Good! I see you Ms. Verna. I can always count on you to tune in! I'm not going to take up too much of your Saturday afternoon because it's fairly quick and easy. However, I did want to mention if you wanted to throw in a few more veggies feel free. Just make sure you sauté them separately since this pot is already full then sprinkle them in later. Okay, let's check the inside of the chicken now. You cannot eat raw chicken or you will die. Trust me!" Phyllis laughed and suddenly stopped as she heard Damien come through the front door.

"Hubby's home!" Phyllis whispered to her viewers. "Hold tight. I want to show you all a real quick and easy summer dessert, too! I'll be right back!"

Phyllis turned down the fire and left the kitchen to greet Damien at the door. Her heart raced just a little because she didn't know what to expect. It's not like he invited her back home, but she was there now and she wasn't going to leave.

"Hey," Damien said softly. "Smells good in here."

Phyllis exhaled. "Thanks. I was just getting dinner started."

"Good, because I'm starving and thirsty." He placed his gym bag in the corner and stared at Phyllis for a moment. "I decided to stay at the gym longer and play ball with some other teams since you said that you were going to bring the girls home. I see you decided to come home, too."

"Yeah, I did." Phyllis shrugged. "Home is where the heart is and I miss my family. I'm really sorry about everything, Damien."

Damien nodded, walked closer to her, and stroked the side of her face tenderly. "Well, don't burn nothing, girl."

"Oh, right!" Phyllis dashed back into the kitchen, checked on the chicken and sighed. "Whew! Okay, I'm back y'all. You still there?" She checked the number of viewers, it dropped by 30 people. *Whatever. My man is home now.* She opened the refrigerator to grab some fresh fruit, whip cream, lemon juice and honey from the cabinet when she heard Damien yell her name. She sucked her teeth and rolled her eyes, but put a smile on her face before she turned to face the camera. "Like I said, my hubby is home. I'm signing off for now, but I'll be back later to show you this delicious summer time dessert!" Phyllis hit the Finish button and went to see why Damien called her name like that.

"Phyllis! What the hell is this?" Damien asked with his chest heaving. In his hand was the water jug that she stashed in the basement door.

Phyllis' eyes widened, her mouth dropped open, but no words were able to form.

"I get a jug of water from the basement, start gulping only to taste that you have vodka in here?" His face twisted with anger and frustration. "What the fuck, Phyllis?"

"Damien… I'm sorry… I really meant to…"

"I swear! It's one thing after the next with you! Things go from sugar to shit with you so fast I can't keep up! First, you cut my hair off because you think I'm cheating! Now this shit?!" Damien shoved the jug of alcohol in her face. "I thought you were on the wagon since after Christmas?"

Phyllis slumped her shoulders, shook her head and began crying. "I've been trying. I really have, but…"

She stopped midsentence when she heard the twins coming down the stairs.

"Go back upstairs, girls." Damien told the twins.

"Daddy, are we still going to the movies?" Serena asked.

"Did you hear me? Go back upstairs and in your room now!" The girls turned around and headed back into their room quickly. Once their bedroom door closed, Damien continued. "Phyllis, I am really trying to work with you and be understanding and patient…Follow me."

They walked to the kitchen out of earshot of the twins.

"I'm sorry, babe. I haven't been drinking like you think," Phyllis explained, walking into the kitchen. "I promise it's only sometimes that I need it. I am doing much better than I was last year. I swear."

"Phyllis, what if our daughters found this jug, thinking it was water like I did? Huh? Did you ever think what could've happened to them? If adults die from alcohol poison just imagine what could've happened to our girls! I would never be able to forgive you!"

Phyllis shook her head, covered her face with her hands and cried. "I'm so sorry. I was hiding it in there so you wouldn't know that I still had a drink once in a while."

"We need to go to counseling or something," Damien said, pouring the alcohol down the sink with tears in his eyes. "I love you, Phyllis. I love you all enough to stop gambling because I didn't want to lose my family. Do you know how difficult it was for me to stop gambling? I did it because I love my family. But when you cut my hair off, I questioned your love for me. Now this?"

Chimes on her phone started going off rapidly distracting her from the conversation. She grabbed it off the shelf to put it on silent and gasped. "It was still recording?"

CHAPTER 20

Bitter Truth

"You poisoned Pastor Paul?" Colette conveyed so much contempt in her voice towards her mother over the phone in a hushed tone because she was at the hospital visiting Pastor. The rage she felt at that moment had her wanting to claw Jonetta's eyes out of her head.

"You're damn right I did!" Jonetta snapped. "I knew if I told you who he really was that you wouldn't listen to me because you call yourself being in love! We all know how stupidity runs rapid through your brain when you think you're in love, Colette!"

"Here I was thinking Mama is really being helpful and kind in her old age! Ha! You only offered to help so you could poison him!"

"Colette, that man raped your mother! You cannot side with him. There are no sides to take here!" Norman tried to reason with her over the speakerphone, but he knew that nothing was getting through to her. "Why are you still at the hospital with that man?"

"She's still there because Colette chooses to stay in prison when the gate is wide open!" Jonetta remarked. "My only regret is that I didn't use enough poison to kill his ass!"

"Mama! I cannot believe you just said that! What type of devil worshipper are you? I should report you to the police!"

"Nobody's calling the police!" Norman shouted into the phone.

"Pastor had a heart attack, Daddy! He could have died right there during the banquet!"

"Colette, a heart only needs blood flowing through it to survive. There's really no room for anything else." Jonetta replied flippantly. "It was my full intent to make sure that no more blood

196

would ever flow through his cold heart again. Unfortunately, I failed!"

"There's a special place in hell for you, Mama. I swear!"

"Oh, we're all going to hell for our sins, Colette. The only difference is…I'll make it there before you do. But don't worry, sweetie, I'll save some room for you."

"You are a piece of work, Mama!" Colette shouted, looking into her phone. She grew angrier when she realized that her mother hung up on her. In a minute, she was going to need to see a doctor because her blood pressure was rising by the second.

Frustrated and confused, Colette sat in the waiting room area to collect her thoughts. Pastor Louis Paul was the one who had helped her gain confidence, employed her, prayed for her and showed compassion while she tried to move on with her life without Owen. She was sure that Pastor Paul loved her and that's why he had the divorce papers drawn. Maybe he was ruthless back in the day, but he had changed. He was a Pastor now. If Colette didn't know anything else, she knew for sure that God can change people.

"Dear God, I love this man. Please help me make the right choice. I want to be happy for once, but my mother tried to destroy that. Am I wrong for being angry with her, Lord?" Colette prayed fighting back tears. The vibration of her phone interrupted her prayers. It was her father calling back.

"Daddy, I don't want to talk right now."

"You chose a rapist over your own family? How could you do this to your mother, Colette?"

"She's always acting so perfect! I've only ever been with one man in my whole life. Finally, I meet a good man and she tried to take that away, too!" Colette sobbed. "Mama is always ridiculing me about my life choices and she's out here committing crimes!"

"That man you're protecting has caused your mother so much grief. You were sitting right there during Thanksgiving when she told us how he came to take the house from her! Now we know that he also RAPED your mother years ago! Your loyalty is to this family, not a stranger, Colette!"

"There's no such thing as raping a whore!"

"You need to watch your mouth, little girl! How dare you disrespect your mother?" Norman fumed.

"Why don't you check on your other daughter, Phyllis? By the looks of things on Facebook, she's the one who needs a lecture! Good-bye, Daddy." Colette disconnected the call, headed towards the ICU to sit by Pastor's bedside and wiped away her tears. *Loyal to my family? Nobody but Aunt Georgia offered me and the kids a place to stay after the fire. Where was their loyalty then? To hell with this family!*

Colette rounded the corridor leading to the ICU and spotted a familiar face.

"Alyssa?" Colette called down the hallway.

She turned around slowly to see who called her name. "Hi, Colette."

"I almost didn't recognize you!" Colette wiped her nose and eyes with the back of her hand as she walked closer. "How are you?"

"I just had the baby yesterday." Alyssa said, cracking a smile. "A little girl weighing eight pounds and three ounces."

"Congratulations!" Colette gave her a light hug, but Alyssa still clung to the walker. "And you're up walking around?"

"They're making me walk around. What are you doing here?"

"Pastor got sick at the Appreciate Day dinner," Colette replied, shaking her head. "He's here in ICU. I was just checking on him."

"Oh," Alyssa replied dryly.

"I think he'll pull through. The doctors say it looks like food poisoning or something, but he had a mild heart attack too." Colette explained more than Alyssa cared to hear. She stared at Alyssa for a moment, but there was no reaction, no concern in her eyes for Pastor. *She's acting like she doesn't even care!* "Well, I have missed you terribly at the church. I can't wait until you come back, girl."

"I won't be back, Colette."

Colette raised her eyebrows at that news. "Oh, I thought you were coming back after..."

"There's nothing like some pain to change your whole life." Alyssa sighed. She kept her eyes forward and continued, "I can't bear to look at him."

"You have nothing to be ashamed of, Alyssa." Colette said, touching her shoulder. "Pastor was pretty upset about your pregnancy, but I told him that we all sin and he shouldn't judge you so harshly."

"Can you tell him something else when he wakes up?"

"Sure!"

"Tell Pastor that I expect him to take care of his child!" Alyssa said with contempt. She turned to continue her slow walk down the hallway, leaving Colette standing there with her mouth wide open.

CHAPTER 21

Hang Yourself

Jonetta leaned back in the chair, propped her feet up on the ottoman and lit a cigarette. She looked up towards the sky and shook her head in disbelief. Her daughters had single-handedly caused her blood pressure to rise in one weekend with their reckless behaviors, stupidity and lifestyle choices. She couldn't help them this time. No. The pieces would have to just land where they may. She was done trying to help them. The only way she would intervene now would be on the behalf of her grandchildren.

"Phyllis is still a drunk and now the whole world knows thanks to Facebook. Colette wants to be with a rapist, pimp disguised as a Pastor. Dawn has cornered the market on free prostitution and got pregnant doing it! What an idiot! They are all a bunch of simpletons!" Jonetta pulled a drag and released the cloud of smoke to sky.

"Netta, that's pretty harsh." Norman retorted. "They made some mistakes."

"A mistake is putting on mismatched socks, Norman!" Jonetta seethed, flicking ashes on the patio. "I'm really pissed at Dawn. Sleeping around with different men at the same time without getting paid is just plain foolish!"

"So you would rather her prostitute herself?"

"No! I would rather her be more responsible instead of having us wait nine whole months to find out which family we'll be tied to for the rest of our lives!"

"How is this about you, Netta?" Norman snapped. "Just imagine how Dawn feels for once!"

Jonetta waved him off. "I need to help Georgia with the kids since Colette's dumb ass is still at the hospital with that piece of shit!" She rose from the chair, huffing. "I don't need to be lectured by you, Norman! I know what I'm talking about. Your precious daughters have fallen from grace and I will not be around to pick up their pieces! I'm getting too old for this shit!"

□ □ □ □ □

"Can you pour your old aunt a glass of that special tea your mommy brought home?" Georgia asked Cornell. He shuffled to the kitchen and returned with a tall glass of tea. She gulped half the glass down and frowned. "Your grandma needs to work on her brewing skills. This is kind of bitter. But don't tell her that I said that. I'll just fix it up later with some sugar."

Cornell chuckled. "Okay, I won't tell her. Is she on her way?"

"Yes. But your grandma isn't in a good mood at all." Georgia warned him. "You and the girls keep the noise to a minimum."

"We will," Cornell said. "You want me to bring Delilah in here?"

"You might as well," Georgia replied. "Bring her walker, too." She enjoyed holding Delilah, but she was enjoying her freedom as she learned how to walk. She stared out the window, looking for Jonetta to pull up any minute and mindlessly finished the remainder of the tea.

An hour later when Jonetta arrived, her mood changed instantly when she saw the children behaving themselves. *Good, I don't have to yell at anybody.* Cornell was the first one to say that they were hungry. She had not even seen Georgia yet and her grandchildren already had her in the kitchen. Delilah came around the corner, bumping into the walls, babbling. Jonetta picked her up and placed her in the high chair. She pinched her chubby cheeks and finished making lunch for them.

"Eat your sandwiches and chips." Jonetta told the kids as she wrapped a bib around Delilah's neck and searched the refrigerator for her food.

"Grandma, can I have juice, too?" Lydia asked.

"I want some, too!" Ruthie said, pouting.

"Alright, alright. I'll put juice on the table for everyone. Just give me a min…" Jonetta locked eyes on a pitcher in the refrigerator. She reached for it, pulled the plastic wrap off and looked inside. When she saw the baneberries and cranberries bobbing on top her heart sunk. *Oh, my God! How did this get here?* "Did anybody drink this tea?" Jonetta asked worried.

The children grew silent as they looked at one another.

"Nobody is in trouble. Grandma just wants to know if any of you drank this tea. Please tell me now." Jonetta bit her bottom lip to keep it from quivering. *Please God, don't let these babies die.* Her eyes darted back and forth between the children who were shaking their heads no.

"No, grandma, we didn't. But…" Cornell replied, fidgeting with his t-shirt.

"But what?" Jonetta asked anxiously. She bent down to look Cornell in the eye. He was only eight-years-old and did not want to scare him from saying whatever he needed to say, but she needed to know right away.

"Aunt Georgia asked me to pour her some earlier."

"Did she drink it?"

Cornell nodded. "She said it was bitter and you needed to learn how to make sweeter tea."

Oh, my God! Jonetta dumped the tea in the sink, rinsed out the pitcher and dowsed it with dish liquid soap. She stood frozen watching the suds form in the pitcher. "How long ago did she have a glass?"

"Ummm… it was a while ago, grandma. Before you got here." Cornell replied. "Am I in trouble?"

Jonetta turned around slowly, forced a smile on her face and replied, "No, sweetie. Can you feed Delilah while I go check on my sister?"

Jonetta began to head upstairs when Cornell let her know that Georgia was napping in the living room. Her knees weakened as she entered the living room. Georgia looked peaceful resting in her favorite chair. Jonetta walked closer, hoping to see her chest rising and falling or at least her eyes moving in her sleep. She held her breath; tears welled up in her eyes instantly when she didn't see any movement from her sister.

"Georgia." Jonetta called her name softly. She extended her trembling hand to touch her sister's hand and quickly snatched it back. Georgia was cold.

CHAPTER 22

Breathe No Air

"You've always been the best listener. I love you."

"I'm here for you, Chena." Dawn patted her frail hand. Her best friend was withering away right before her eyes. The advanced drugs to shrink the cancer cells didn't work like they hoped. The doctors admitted that there was no need for chemo treatments anymore and advised just to keep her comfortable at home. Her bedroom wreaked of death. She looked like death. It was getting difficult to even look at her anymore. One thing Chena always committed to was her looks, especially having her eyebrows perfectly arched and now she didn't have any at all.

"I had a talk with Shiloh. He was pretty upset, but I explained to him that I asked you to keep Raffi happy…"

"Oh, my God." Dawn covered her face with her hands. "I'm so sorry, Chena."

"Don't be, Dawn." She patted her knee. "They need you and your love. Just continue to love on them for me, okay?"

Dawn sobbed softly and nodded her head.

"Look at my friend, Dawn. So beautiful, so successful, always had the boys going nuts over you. Everything always came so easy to you. Nobody can hold a match to you, Dawn. My God, you've lived the life that I always saw for myself…being flown all over the world, being desired by men. Living your dreams in reality. You've lived, girl! I've always been so jealous of those go-get-em qualities in you. The day I asked you to take on these responsibilities was the day I found out that I only had a few more months to live."

Dawn groaned. "Girl, why didn't you tell me?"

Chena shrugged her bony shoulders as tears welled in her eyes. She grabbed Dawn's hand with all the strength she could muster and replied, "I'm sorry that I interrupted your lifestyle, but I need you."

"We don't have to talk about it, girl." Dawn squeezed her hand lightly. "I'm here for you."

Dawn exhaled as she left Chena's room. *I cannot tell her that I'm pregnant. It would kill her for sure.* Her heart was heavy with everything going on with her family lately. Harboring her pregnancy secret was not easy either. When her father called to beg her to move into his house, she knew that her mother told him that she was pregnant. But Dawn knew exactly what her mother was capable of and she refused to allow her mother to poison her, push her down some stairs or kill her for not getting rid of her baby. Soon enough Dawn would have to make a decision on where to live but it certainly wasn't going to be with her mother.

"I'm heading out." Dawn announced as she came down the stairs. "Chena is sleeping. You should check on her in an hour or so, she doesn't feel well."

"Did you dope her up?" Raffi asked casually.

Dawn shot him a look. *What an asshole!* "I gave her what was prescribed by her doctor, yes." She grabbed her purse and searched it frantically for her lip gloss. "Don't forget, Shiloh will be home in like twenty minutes with his friend, Carl."

Raffi grunted as he gave Dawn a once over. She had on a bodycon black dress, black closed-toe stilettos, and her hair pulled back in a sleek ponytail. "You look nice." He said walking towards her.

"Thanks." Dawn replied dryly as she applied her lip gloss in the hallway mirror.

"You getting thick, girl! You've been eating real good around here lately, huh?" Raffi teased patting her belly and cupping her ass. "You puttin' on weight, Queen. It looks good though." He kissed her neck.

Dawn shrugged him off. "Go do something with yourself, Raffi! Goodness! I'm trying to get out the door."

"Why have you been so moody lately? You know I got something to fix that." Raffi pulled a joint from his pants pocket. "You wanna hit before you go?"

Dawn was tempted. She definitely needed something to help the knot in her stomach and calm the thoughts racing through her head. However, she thought better of it. *This wasn't the time to show up high.* "Nah, maybe when I get back from the funeral."

Raffi pulled her close to him. "I was only teasing about your fat belly. You still fine as hell, my bronze Queen. What's wrong with you?"

You really wanna know what's wrong with me? "I'm pregnant." Dawn blurted out and pulled away from him.

"What? Seriously?" Raffi asked, pulling her closer to him again and lifting her chin.

"Raffi, I wouldn't joke about that!" She jerked away from him.

He took a step back, rubbed his chin thoughtfully, and then a wide smile spread across his face. He grabbed her by the hand and led her to kitchen out of earshot of the bedrooms upstairs. Dawn followed his lead reluctantly. Now she regretted telling him because she had to get going to the funeral. *Mama will have a fit if I'm late.*

Raffi rested on the island in the kitchen, nodded his head and smiled at her. "Honestly, Dawn, I've always wanted more than one child. This is a good thing that you're carrying my seed." He leaned in to hug Dawn.

"No, this isn't good, Raffi." Dawn pushed him away. "It only complicates things."

"How?" Raffi asked confused. "Chena already knows about us. She damn sure can't give me anymore kids. We argued so much about that until we found out she had ovarian cancer. But, this is what *she* wanted… for us to carry on like a family after she's gone. So adding another child to the mix shouldn't be a problem at all. It's a blessing from Jah! Look, just let me handle telling Chena. I'll talk to her in a way she'll understand."

Dawn exhaled, wringing her hands together nervously. *Just tell him and get it over with already.* "But… Raffi, it may not be yours."

"What the fuck?" Raffi stood up straight, twisted his face and stepped towards Dawn. "Whose baby could it be other than mine, Dawn?"

"That's not important, Raffi."

"Like hell it ain't!"

Dawn shrugged. "I'm just being honest about the situation. I don't know if I'm even going to keep the baby. It's just too complicated."

"Honest? How about you could've let me know you were letting some other dude hit raw at the same time I was! That would've been honest! Now that your ass is caught up, you wanna be honest? Miss me with that bullshit, Dawn!" Raffi spewed venom as his nostrils flared. He pointed his finger in Dawn's face and continued, "And if that's my baby, you're keeping it! Real talk!"

"Would you lower your damn voice before you wake up your wife? I don't owe you any explanations, Raffi!" Dawn smacked his hand from in front of her face. "You are *not* my man! I'm not the one in a marriage! I'm single and I will do what the fuck I wanna do!"

"We have an arrangement, Dawn!" Raffi yelled angrily. "I can't believe as much as we fuck you were still fuckin' somebody else!"

"So part of this live-in arrangement was for me to be faithful to you?" Dawn folded her arms across her chest. "Oh, sorry, I must've missed the memo."

Raffi lunged forward, grabbed her by the throat and pushed her against the wall. "Yes! That's right! All of this is mine!" Raffi roughly grabbed between her legs with his other hand. "You had no right to give it away! Who is this muthafucka? I'm gonna kill his ass!"

Dawn couldn't breathe and Raffi knew it, but he didn't release his grip from her neck. She began to push him off her but the more she pushed the more he held on tight. Her vision blurred from the tears welling in her eyes, but she could not mumble one word because the palm of his hand pressed hard on her neck.

"I will fuckin' kill you before I let you kill my baby!" Raffi whispered in her ear. "You hear me, bitch?"

In that moment, she remembered the stories Chena used to tell her about how controlling he was and how he used to jump in her face when they argued. Now she realized the part that Chena left out was he was physically abusive, too. All of those conversations about his behavior were flooding back to her memory now that he held her life in his hands…literally.

"You fuckin' whore! I thought you were a Queen! I worshipped you, Dawn! I thought what we had was good enough for you! Your ass never was satisfied with nothing! Always wanted more!" Raffi growled, squeezing her neck with more pressure. "I could fuckin' kill you right now!"

Dawn shook her head slowly, eyes pleading with him not to kill her. A single tear slid down her face as she felt the blood building in her face, the rest of her body felt cold. *Please don't kill me, Raffi! Let me go!* She clawed at his thick hand that he often wrapped around her neck, passionately, when they made love. He wouldn't let go. She tried to claw at his face, but he extended his arm, creating distance between them and added more pressure. She felt her legs give way and she began sinking to the floor. The room began to darken and disappear as she grew lightheaded. Dawn finally closed her eyes. *I can't breathe. I can't breathe. Somebody help me!*

CHAPTER 23
Take Me Now

The day of the funeral was grey and humid. It was threatening to rain all morning and Jonetta wished the sky would open up to pour down on them. Her spirit was broken and she wanted to walk barefoot in the woods while it rained as she used to do back in Pennsylvania. She did not utter a word to anyone about what she knew. The truth was too unbearable. Unthinkable. Instead, her piercing eyes were locked on the casket. *My sister. I'm so sorry.*

The doctor's voice rang in her ears repeatedly, "Her heart simply gave out. It happens to elderly people all the time." However, Jonetta knew better. Other than grief over her beloved Fred, Georgia was healthy and nowhere near death. All the drama that her daughters had brewing lately didn't amount to much since Georgia died.

For just a moment, they all pushed their petty issues aside to come together as a family. Phyllis sobered up quickly once her secret was aired on social media. The news of their only aunt in Chicago dying made her grow closer to Damien. Instead of turning up the bottle, she turned to him for comfort and in return, he welcomed this tender, vulnerable side of her. They sat inside the funeral home with the twins holding one another. Damien softly kissed her forehead as she placed her head on his shoulder.

Colette finally broke from her cloud of delusion and apologized to her mother once she learned that Georgia died. She packed her things at the church in silence as the women asked her questions about Pastor's condition and her reasons for leaving, but she remained silent. *You'll find out soon enough!* Now that she had the house to herself with her children, she quickly realized how much of a help Georgia had been to her ever since she moved in after the fire. Since her relationship with her mother was strained, she couldn't look to her for help. Regardless of her anger towards

Pastor, she was still going to use his attorney to finalize her divorce with Owen. She needed to get those papers signed and filed while Pastor was still in the hospital. Moving forward was her mission at this point and nobody was going to stop her.

Jonetta inhaled deeply, closed her eyes and allowed a single tear to trickle down her face. She once believed that her daughters were going to give her a heart attack, but as grief took over these past few days she was convinced that sadness and regret could do the job even better. A tight knot formed in her throat as turmoil erupted in the pit of her stomach. She covered her mouth to keep from making any sound that resembled a gag.

Phyllis grabbed her mother's hand and whispered, "Are you alright?"

Jonetta nodded and squeezed her daughter's hand in return. Phyllis was a sweetheart when she wanted to be one.

"Has anybody seen Dawn?" Jonetta asked.

"Not yet, Mama," Colette replied, leaning forward. "You know she's always running behind unless it's for one of her gigs."

"I sent her a text, but she hasn't responded yet." Phyllis said.

"Where did she sleep last night? At Chena's house or Shon's?"

"Who is Shon?" Phyllis asked.

"Her new guy, my old boss, Doctor Bishon Franklyn." Jonetta responded looking at Phyllis puzzled. "You don't know about him?"

Phyllis cocked her head to the side as she recalled that odd name. *That's the guy who stopped by the house that day.* "Wait a minute...the dentist? Dawn is dating him?"

Jonetta sighed and nodded. *Unfortunately.*

"Mama, I totally forgot, but Aunt Georgia wanted me to tell you something..."

"I have to use the bathroom, mommy!" Serena announced.

"Shhh..." Phyllis put her finger up to her mouth. "Just a minute."

"Take her to the restroom, Phyllis." Jonetta said softly. "We'll talk later."

The funeral services began and ended so quickly you would think Georgia did not have a full life, but she did. Georgia had been their angel in disguise. She offered herself willingly, selflessly to make sure that her daughters had a place to go for

210

peace. Lately, she had been more of a mother to them than Jonetta. Her heart was pure, free from anger, bitterness and malice. Jonetta never did understand how her sister was so quick to forgive people. She shook her head in awe. The repast was at Norman's house in a few hours, but she was not in the mood for people. Jonetta sat for a moment in silence as the room cleared out. She looked down at her aging hands, clasped them together, and prayed for forgiveness.

"Owen is here," Norman alerted Colette in the foyer. "But please don't cause a scene today. Your mother is too fragile right now for any drama, Colette."

Colette nodded. "I just want a divorce, Daddy. Not a fight."

"Divorce isn't that simple," Norman admitted. "I should know...I've gone through it twice."

"Twice?"

"Yeah, I was married before I met your mother."

"That's news to me!"

Norman shrugged and shook his head. "There's so much that you girls just don't know."

"Can we continue this conversation later, Daddy? I really need to talk to Owen."

"Sure, and I need to find your mother."

〇〇〇〇〇

Jonetta headed to the car to smoke a cigarette. Her nerves were bad and the guilt consumed her. *My hatred for Big Louie killed my own sister! God, what have I done?* She sniffed, flicked a tear away, and stopped in her tracks when she heard a familiar voice.

"Mrs. Miller!" Bishon called from the parking lot. He maneuvered between cars until he reached her.

"Bishon? What are you doing here?" Jonetta asked, confused. "You didn't have to come to the funeral..."

Bishon bowed his head, and slowly looked up to meet her eyes. She could tell that he had been crying, but found it very odd. He didn't even know Georgia.

"Where's Dawn?" Jonetta asked. "Did she ride with you here?"

"No, I haven't seen Dawn."

That's odd. Where the hell is Dawn? "Well, what's wrong, Bishon?"

"I finally found my mother," he said just above a whisper.

"That's good news!" Jonetta replied, touching his shoulder. "I needed to hear some good news today. How did you find her?"

"Turns out that my Dad knew more than he wanted to admit. He finally told me that he knew the woman who dropped me off at the church, but she wasn't the mother. It was her niece's baby. She had told my Dad that her niece was too young to raise a baby and… they had a business to run… so…she told her that the baby died."

"That's terrible. Is your mother still alive?"

"Very much so," he replied nodding his head.

"Oh, good! Who is she? Where is she?" Jonetta asked anxiously.

"My birth mother lived in brothel ran by her two aunts in Beverly. She was a prostitute...back then. My mother thought her baby was stillborn."

Bishon stared at Jonetta without uttering another word. His eyes welled with tears that were threatening to stream down his face. Jonetta raised her eyebrows as she realized what he had just explained. Suddenly, her expression drastically changed from expecting an answer to knowing the answer. Her mouth slowly dropped open as she clutched her necklace taking deep quick breaths. Jonetta tried to form a sentence as her bottom lip quivered, but only more quickened breaths escaped. *Oh, my God!*

All these years Jonetta had believed that her aunt Betty Lou had tossed her stillborn son in the trash, like she admitted on her deathbed. Jonetta hated her aunt for it, almost smothered her to death over it! Jonetta inhaled sharply as her whole body trembled as she realized what this meant to her and her daughters. *I have a son? My girls have a brother!* Her eyes widened as she thought about the news Dawn had recently shared with her. *Dawn is pregnant by...*

"Oh, my God! Dawn!"

Bishon nodded and sobbed. "I didn't know that she was my sister…"

Jonetta clutched her chest, then reached for Bishon's shoulder but missed making contact by inches. Bishon tried to catch her, but it was too late.

Editor's Edition Alternate Ending…

CHAPTER 22

Breathe No Air

"You've always been the best listener. I love you."

"I'm here for you, Chena." Dawn patted her frail hand. Her best friend was withering away right before her eyes. The advanced drugs to shrink the cancer cells didn't work like they hoped. The doctors admitted that there was no need for chemo treatments anymore and advised just to keep her comfortable at home. Her bedroom wreaked of death. She looked like death. It was getting difficult to even look at her anymore. One thing Chena always committed to was her looks, especially having her eyebrows perfectly arched and now she didn't have any at all.

"I had a talk with Shiloh. He was pretty upset, but I explained to him that I asked you to keep Raffi happy…"

"Oh, my God." Dawn covered her face with her hands. "I'm so sorry, Chena."

"Don't be, Dawn." She patted her knee. "They need you and your love. Just continue to love on them for me, okay?"

Dawn sobbed softly and nodded her head.

"Look at my friend, Dawn. So beautiful, so successful, always had the boys going nuts over you. Everything always came so easy to you. Nobody can hold a match to you, Dawn. My God, you've lived the life that I always saw for myself…being flown all over the world, being desired by men. Living your dreams in reality. You've lived, girl! I've always been so jealous of those go-get-em qualities in you. The day I asked you to take on these responsibilities was the day I found out that I only had a few more months to live."

Dawn groaned. "Girl, why didn't you tell me?"

Chena shrugged her bony shoulders as tears welled in her eyes. She grabbed Dawn's hand with all the strength she could muster and replied, "I'm sorry that I interrupted your lifestyle, but I need you."

"We don't have to talk about it, girl." Dawn squeezed her hand lightly. "I'm here for you."

Dawn exhaled as she left Chena's room. *I cannot tell her that I'm pregnant. It would kill her for sure.* Her heart was heavy with everything going on with her family lately. Harboring her pregnancy secret was not easy either. When her father called to beg her to move into his house, she knew that her mother told him that she was pregnant. But Dawn knew exactly what her mother was capable of and she refused to allow her mother to poison her, push her down some stairs or kill her for not getting rid of her baby. Soon enough Dawn would have to make a decision on where to live but it certainly wasn't going to be with her mother.

"I'm heading out." Dawn announced as she came down the stairs. "Chena is sleeping. You should check on her in an hour or so, she doesn't feel well."

"Did you dope her up?" Raffi asked casually.

Dawn shot him a look. *What an asshole!* "I gave her what was prescribed by her doctor, yes." She grabbed her purse and searched it frantically for her lip gloss. "Don't forget, Shiloh will be home in like twenty minutes with his friend, Carl."

Raffi grunted as he gave Dawn a once over. She had on a bodycon black dress, black closed-toe stilettos, and her hair pulled back in a sleek ponytail. "You look nice." He said walking towards her.

"Thanks." Dawn replied dryly as she applied her lip gloss in the hallway mirror.

"You getting thick, girl! You've been eating real good around here lately, huh?" Raffi teased patting her belly and cupping her ass.

"You puttin' on weight, Queen. It looks good though." He kissed her neck.

Dawn shrugged him off. "Go do something with yourself, Raffi! Goodness! I'm trying to get out the door."

"Why have you been so moody lately? You know I got something to fix that." Raffi pulled a joint from his pants pocket. "You wanna hit before you go?"

Dawn was tempted. She definitely needed something to help the knot in her stomach and calm the thoughts racing through her head. However, she thought better of it. *This wasn't the time to show up high.* "Nah, maybe when I get back from the funeral."

Raffi pulled her close to him. "I was only teasing about your fat belly. You still fine as hell, my bronze Queen. What's wrong with you?"

You really wanna know what's wrong with me? "I'm pregnant." Dawn blurted out and pulled away from him.

"What? Seriously?" Raffi asked, pulling her closer to him again and lifting her chin.

"Raffi, I wouldn't joke about that!" She jerked away from him.

He took a step back, rubbed his chin thoughtfully, and then a wide smile spread across his face. He grabbed her by the hand and led her to kitchen out of earshot of the bedrooms upstairs. Dawn followed his lead reluctantly. Now she regretted telling him because she had to get going to the funeral. *Mama will have a fit if I'm late.*

Raffi rested on the island in the kitchen, nodded his head and smiled at her. "Honestly, Dawn, I've always wanted more than one child. This is a good thing that you're carrying my seed." He leaned in to hug Dawn.

"No, this isn't good, Raffi." Dawn pushed him away. "It only complicates things."

"How?" Raffi asked confused. "Chena already knows about us. She damn sure can't give me anymore kids. We argued so much about that until we found out she had ovarian cancer. But, this is what *she* wanted… for us to carry on like a family after she's gone. So adding another child to the mix shouldn't be a problem at all. It's a blessing from Jah! Look, just let me handle telling Chena. I'll talk to her in a way she'll understand."

Dawn exhaled, wringing her hands together nervously. *Just tell him and get it over with already.* "But… Raffi, it may not be yours."

"What the fuck?" Raffi stood up straight, twisted his face and stepped towards Dawn. "Whose baby could it be other than mine, Dawn?"

"That's not important, Raffi."

"Like hell it ain't!"

Dawn shrugged. "I'm just being honest about the situation. I don't know if I'm even going to keep the baby. It's just too complicated."

"Honest? How about you could've let me know you were letting some other dude hit raw at the same time I was! That would've been honest! Now that your ass is caught up, you wanna be honest? Miss me with that bullshit, Dawn!" Raffi spewed venom as his nostrils flared. He pointed his finger in Dawn's face and continued, "And if that's my baby, you're keeping it! Real talk!"

"Would you lower your damn voice before you wake up your wife? I don't owe you any explanations, Raffi!" Dawn smacked his hand from in front of her face. "You are *not* my man! I'm not the one in a marriage! I'm single and I will do what the fuck I wanna do!"

"We have an arrangement, Dawn!" Raffi yelled angrily. "I can't believe as much as we fuck you were still fuckin' somebody else!"

"So part of this live-in arrangement was for me to be faithful to you?" Dawn folded her arms across her chest. "Oh, sorry, I must've missed the memo."

Raffi lunged forward, grabbed her by the throat and pushed her against the wall. "Yes! That's right! All of this is mine!" Raffi roughly grabbed between her legs with his other hand. "You had no right to give it away! Who is this muthafucka? I'm gonna kill his ass!"

Dawn couldn't breathe and Raffi knew it, but he didn't release his grip from her neck. She began to push him off her but the more she pushed the more he held on tight. Her vision blurred from the tears welling in her eyes, but she could not mumble one word because the palm of his hand pressed hard on her neck.

"I will fuckin' kill you before I let you kill my baby!" Raffi whispered in her ear. "You hear me, bitch?"

In that moment, she remembered the stories Chena used to tell her about how controlling he was and how he used to jump in her face when they argued. Now she realized the part that Chena left out was he was physically abusive, too. All of those conversations about his behavior were flooding back to her memory now that he held her life in his hands…literally.

"You fuckin' whore! I thought you were a Queen! I worshipped you, Dawn! I thought what we had was good enough for you! Your ass never was satisfied with nothing! Always wanted more!" Raffi growled, squeezing her neck with more pressure. "I could fuckin' kill you right now!"

"Dad! Let her go!" Shiloh shouted, entering the kitchen.

Raffi released his grip and Dawn coughed trying to catch her breath. Raffi stumbled backwards with his eyes wild and chest heaving. "Get out of here, Shiloh!"

"What are you doing to Aunty Dawn?" Shiloh rushed to her aid, patting her on the back. "Are you okay?"

"Should I call the police?" Carl asked holding his phone.

"No!" Raffi yelled. "Y'all get out of here!"

"What's going on?" Shiloh yelled at his father. Tears rolled down his face waiting for his father to explain.

Dawn leaned over the table, still coughing unable to explain what just happened. Raffi profusely apologized to her as he pulled out a chair for her. "Sit down, Dawn. Please. I'm so sorry."

Dawn finally opened her eyes and they were bloodshot. Shiloh gasped and looked at his Dad with such contempt.

"Y'all go upstairs now and let me handle this." Raffi said, turning his back towards them. He was suddenly ashamed and couldn't look his son in the eyes. Shiloh was hesitant at first but he obeyed his father and went upstairs with his friend.

Raffi sat next to her at the table and whispered to her. "I'm sorry, Dawn. I'm so sorry." He hugged her and kissed her forehead.

"Get away from me!" Dawn tried to yell, but her voice was strained. She pushed him away, jumped up from the table and slapped him in the face with all of her strength. "You tried to kill me you fucking bastard!"

CHAPTER 23
Take Me Now

The day of the funeral was grey and humid. It was threatening to rain all morning and Jonetta wished the sky would open up to pour down on them. Her spirit was broken and she wanted to walk barefoot in the woods while it rained just as she used to do back in Pennsylvania. She did not utter a word to anyone about what she knew. The truth was too unbearable. Unthinkable. Instead, her piercing eyes were locked on the casket. *My sister. I'm so sorry.*

The doctor's voice rang in her ears repeatedly, "Her heart simply gave out. It happens to elderly people all the time." However, Jonetta knew better. Other than grief over her beloved Fred, Georgia was healthy and nowhere near death. All the drama that her daughters had brewing lately didn't amount to much since Georgia died.

For just a moment, they all pushed their petty issues aside to come together as a family. Phyllis sobered up quickly once her secret was aired on social media. The news of their only aunt in Chicago dying made her grow closer to Damien. Instead of turning up the bottle, she turned to him for comfort and in return, he welcomed this tender, vulnerable side of her. They sat inside the funeral home with the twins holding one another. Damien softly kissed her forehead as she placed her head on his shoulder.

Colette finally broke from her cloud of delusion and apologized to her mother once she learned that Georgia died. She packed her things at the church in silence as the women asked her questions about Pastor's condition and her reasons for leaving, but she remained silent. *You'll find out soon enough!* Now that she had the house to herself with her children, she quickly realized how much of a help Georgia had been to her ever since she moved in after the fire. Since her relationship with her mother was strained, she couldn't look to her for help. Regardless of her anger towards

Pastor, she was still going to use his attorney to finalize her divorce with Owen. She needed to get those papers signed and filed while Pastor was still in the hospital. Moving forward was her mission at this point and nobody was going to stop her.

Jonetta inhaled deeply, closed her eyes and allowed a single tear to trickle down her face. She once believed that her daughters were going to give her a heart attack, but as grief took over these past few days, she was convinced that sadness and regret could do the job even better. A tight knot formed in her throat as turmoil erupted in the pit of her stomach. She covered her mouth to keep from making any sound that resembled a gag.

Phyllis grabbed her mother's hand and whispered, "Are you alright?"

Jonetta nodded and squeezed her daughter's hand in return. She was a sweetheart when she wanted to be one.

"Has anybody seen Dawn?" Jonetta asked.

"Not yet, Mama," Colette replied, leaning forward. "You know she's always running behind unless it's for one of her gigs."

"I sent her a text, but she hasn't responded yet." Phyllis said.

"Where did she sleep last night? At Chena's house or Shon's?"

"Who is Shon?" Phyllis asked.

"Her new guy, my old boss, Doctor Bishon Franklyn." Jonetta responded looking at Phyllis puzzled. "You don't know about him?"

Phyllis cocked her head to the side as she recalled that odd name. *That's the guy who stopped by the house that day.* "Wait a minute…the dentist? Dawn is dating him?"

Jonetta sighed and nodded. *Unfortunately.*

"Mama, I totally forgot, but Aunt Georgia wanted me to tell you something…"

"I have to use the bathroom, mommy!" Serena announced, interrupting Phyllis.

"Shhh…" Phyllis put her finger up to her mouth. "Just a minute."

"Take her to the restroom, Phyllis." Jonetta said softly. "We'll talk later."

The funeral services began and ended so quickly you would think Georgia did not have a full life, but she did. Georgia had been their angel in disguise. She offered herself willingly, selflessly to make sure that her daughters had a place to go for peace. Lately, she had been more of a mother to them than Jonetta. Her heart was pure, free from anger, bitterness and malice. Jonetta never did understand how her sister was so quick to forgive people. She shook her head in awe. *Georgia was something else.* The repast was at Norman's house in a few hours, but she was not in the mood for people. Jonetta sat for a moment in silence as the room cleared out. She looked down at her aging hands, clasped them together, and prayed for forgiveness.

"Owen is here," Norman alerted Colette in the foyer. "But please don't cause a scene today. Your mother is too fragile right now for any drama, Colette."

Colette nodded. "I just want a divorce, Daddy. Not a fight."

"Divorce isn't that simple," Norman admitted. "I should know...I've gone through it twice."

"Twice?"

"Yeah, I was married before I met your mother."

"That's news to me!"

Norman shrugged and shook his head. "There's so much that you girls just don't know."

"Can we continue this conversation later, Daddy? I really need to talk to Owen."

"Sure, and I need to find your mother."

Jonetta headed to the car to smoke a cigarette. Her nerves were bad and the guilt consumed her. *My hatred for Big Louie killed my own sister! God, what have I done?* She sniffed, flicked a tear away, and stopped in her tracks when she heard a familiar voice.

"Mrs. Miller!" Bishon called from the parking lot. He maneuvered between cars until he reached her.

"Bishon? What are you doing here?" Jonetta asked, confused. "You didn't have to come to the funeral..."

Bishon bowed his head, and slowly looked up to meet her eyes. She could tell that he had been crying and found it very odd. *He didn't even know Georgia.*

"Where's Dawn?" Jonetta asked. "Did she ride with you here?"

"No, I haven't seen Dawn."

That's odd. Where the hell is Dawn? "Well, what's wrong, Bishon?"

"I finally found my mother," he said just above a whisper.

"That's good news!" Jonetta replied, touching his shoulder. "I needed to hear some good news today. How did you find her?"

"Turns out that my Dad knew more than he wanted to admit. He finally told me that he knew the woman who dropped me off at the church, but she wasn't the mother. It was her niece's baby. She had told my Dad that her niece was too young to raise a baby and… they had a business to run… so…she told her that the baby died."

Dawn sat in the car as she nervously watched Bishon and her mother talking. "Mama, what are you doing? Please don't tell him I'm pregnant." She glanced in the rear view mirror to check her eyes. They were still red. *Shit! I hope that Mama will just think I've been crying so I wont' have to tell her that I was almost choked to death!* She placed her dark sunglasses on and fixed the scarf around her neck before she exited the car.

"That's terrible. Is your mother still alive?" Jonetta asked.

"Very much so," he replied nodding his head.

"Oh, good! Who is she? Where is she?" Jonetta asked anxiously.

"My birth mother lived in a brothel ran by her two aunts in Beverly. She was a prostitute...back then. My mother thought her baby was stillborn."

Bishon stared at Jonetta without uttering another word. His eyes welled with tears that were threatening to stream down his face. Jonetta raised her eyebrows as she realized what he had just explained. Suddenly, her expression drastically changed from expecting an answer to knowing the answer. Her mouth slowly dropped open as she clutched her necklace taking deep quick breaths. Jonetta tried to form a sentence as her bottom lip quivered, but only more quickened breaths escaped. *Oh, my God!*

All these years Jonetta had believed that her aunt Betty Lou had tossed her stillborn son in the trash, like she admitted on her deathbed. Jonetta hated her aunt for it, almost smothered her to death over it! Jonetta inhaled sharply as her whole body trembled as she realized what this meant to her and her daughters. *I have a son? My girls have a brother?* Her eyes widened as she thought about the news Dawn had recently shared with her. *Dawn is pregnant by...*

"Oh, my God! Dawn!"

Bishon nodded and sobbed. "I didn't know that she was my sister..."

Jonetta clutched her chest, then reached for Bishon's shoulder but missed making contact by inches. Bishon caught her before she hit the ground.

"Mama!" Dawn screamed, rushing towards them. "Somebody call an ambulance!"

REBEKAH S. COLE

Special Note to Readers...

Thank you for your patience. I hope you see why I waited to release this sequel to *Women's Voices*. I owed it to my readers to deliver a novel worth the read. I wanted this sequel to blow your minds and I hope that I accomplished some draw dropping moments for you.

When I first began writing this novel, it was going down a completely different path. Then life began throwing blow after blow my way and it really made me rethink writing ever again. However, thanks to some positive people on my team, I mustered the courage to finish this novel. That's right, I needed the courage to sit down to create again. The characters began talking to me again and the words rushed out of me. Sometimes you have to go through some pain to make serious changes in your life. I have no regrets because I'm pleased with the results.

I especially want to acknowledge my rock and shelter during my personal storm, Dortanian Franklyn. Your words of wisdom and encouragement comforted me when I felt like giving up. God knew that I needed you all along and you were there lifting me up the whole time. Thank you for supporting and loving me. I love you, King Dot. To my daughters who have seen me tirelessly pump out chapters, and completely tune out sometimes, thank you for understanding. Reaching goals require lots of sacrifice, but always remember that mommy loves you!

Don't hesitate to tell me what you think about the Miller family. I'm sure they remind you of people that you know or have encountered along the way. Keep riding this journey with me because I have a lot more coming your way.

It's always love,

Rebekah S. Cole
Email: beckywrites2@gmail.com
Facebook: www.facebook.com/rebekahscole
Instagram: www.instagram.com/rebekahscole
Twitter: @rebekahScole

#JonettasDeath by #RebekahSCole

Book Club Questions

1. Mother and daughter relationships can be so beautiful, yet so fragile. Do you think the Miller women will ever create a lasting bond or is it too late?

2. If your best friend asked you to take on her role with her family, would you do what Dawn did? Or would you reject the whole idea?

3. Do you think that Colette can be easily manipulated or just suffering from low self-esteem? Is there a difference or a direct correlation?

4. How do you think Phyllis should've reacted when Dawn and Colette broke the news to her about Damien? Should she have given him the opportunity to explain?

5. Both Georgia and Jonetta expressed their concerns for the daughters. Which one do you think Phyllis, Dawn and Colette listened to the most? Why?

6. Jonetta could have a quick, sharp tongue at times. Were you surprised to see a softer side of her with Norman? Do you think all she needs is love from a man to change her views?

7. Have you ever had a Raffi or Dawn in your life? Someone you were always curious about. If given the green light to satisfy your curiosity, would you?

8. Was Phyllis right or wrong to withhold pertinent information from her mother about Dr. Bishon Franklyn showing up to the house? Do you think it would've made a difference if she said something?

9. Do you think Georgia offered too much of her time to Jonetta's daughters? Or did she find being motherly to her nieces comforting since she did not have any children?

10. Now that Dr. Bishon Franklyn is caught in the Miller web of deceit, what do you think he will want Dawn to do? What do you think is the right decision?

11. What is your definition of a mother's love? Did Jonetta go

too far to prevent Colette from making a huge mistake? Or was she being a protective mother?

12. What is your definition of loyalty to your family? Is there a thin line when it comes to siding with family or is it a line that should never be crossed?

About The Author

Rebekah S. Cole is a fresh literary pearl from Chicago, IL. In March 2016, her debut novel, Women's Voices was published and received rave reviews. Thanks to the feedback from readers she decided to create a sequel, Jonetta's Death. Rebekah continues to write realistic, fluid novels that showcases relatable characters with human issues. Follow her on social media for more updates.

REBEKAH S. COLE

Synopsis

JONETTA'S DEATH

JONETTA, matriarch of the Miller family, put most of her secrets on the table. A fresh start was hers for the taking, but she soon learns that she wasn't the only one harboring secrets all these years. New discoveries from her past changes everything.

PHYLLIS finds purpose as a housewife by streaming her own cooking show live, but things go awry with her husband Damien when she allows her suspicions of his infidelity to get the best of her.

DAWN enjoys her freedom but her best friend, Chena, has a dying wish that will test their friendship and sanity as Dawn tries to balance a new relationship with Dr. Bishon Franklyn and two households.

COLETTE finds life after Owen by working at her church as the new secretary. She has her sights set on the pastor not realizing his past and connection to her mother.

This time revenge and secrecy have gone too far as The Miller Family returns in this sequel to ***Women's Voices***. For a family bound together by deceit, their truths will come at a devastating price.

Made in the USA
Monee, IL
20 July 2023

39328168R00146